SOFT

IN THE

MIDDLE

PHILIP WATSON

For Lynn

My wife, without whose continuous encouragement and support this book would not have been possible.

CHAPTER ONE

Nick Charles Howard had no difficulty in recognising the middle-aged woman – how she would love that description – who had walked into his office without even a perfunctory knock. She was of average height and build (for her age), her hair was a dark(ish) brown and what he would have called short and tidy. (She'd have said "layered", or "styled", or "sculpted" or God-knows-what.) Her hazel eyes were cold, a look he remembered well, but they were tinged with a hint of uncertainty that he didn't recall. She stood in front of his desk awaiting a response to her arrival.

What could his ex-wife want? Nick felt defensive, half expecting a verbal mugging, even though they hadn't seen each other for six months, and all of the divorce issues were long since done and dusted. He didn't move and tried to look relaxed as he struggled to find a smart way to open up a conversation. He found one.

'Hello,' said Nick, and braced himself.

'Hello,' replied Ruth. 'I see business is brisk,' raising an eyebrow in the direction of Nick's feet. Only then did he realise they were still on his desk. He sat up sharply, almost slipping off his chair as it shot backwards clattering into the wall behind.

He pulled himself back to his desk and replied, 'I *am* busy actually... I... I have several cases on the go. I... was in the middle of prioritising them in my mind actually.'

1

'I'm sure you were... *actually*.'

Ruth clearly hadn't changed, but he knew better than to react to her sarcastic tone, especially when, far from prioritising cases, he had *actually* been wondering how soon he could claim unemployment benefit. The only reason he was in the office on a Saturday morning was to clear the place. Technically there was still a week left on the rent, but he intended to give himself a "hard earned" week off before he registered as officially unemployed. It would feel more like a holiday if he still had an office to be on holiday from. All he needed today, the day when he was giving up on his dream, was for his ex-wife to come and gloat about his failing business and tell him how she'd been right about him all along.

'So what do you want?' asked Nick. It came out a bit harsher than he'd intended but he couldn't bring himself to say 'How can I help you?' At least not and make it sound sincere.

'Is that how you address all your prospective clients?' replied Ruth, 'No wonder the place is like a morgue. Although a morgue would probably smell better.'

'A client? You!' She had to be joking!

'Well you are still a Private *DICK* aren't you?'

'I am still a Private *Investigator*, yes.'

'Good. Well in that case I have a job for you - if you're not too busy.'

'Oh! Right. Well, if you sit down and give me the details,' said Nick guardedly, 'I'll let you know if I think I can help.'

'You mean you'll prioritise it with the other cases in your mind?'

'Yes, if it falls within my area of expertise.'

Ruth couldn't resist a sneer, 'Your area of expertise! What on earth's that? Playing with yourself on your games machine?'

'You mean playing *by* myself.'

Ruth raised the other eyebrow; she was just showing off now. 'I know what I mean.'

'Do you want my help or not?' replied Nick, 'Like I said, I am busy. I don't come to work on a Saturday morning for the sheer hell of it.'

Nick was pleased with this response. It reminded both of them that Ruth was asking for *his* help and, he thought, reinforced the idea that he really was busy. She sat down and looked around the office at the bare, grubby, once white walls. She smiled condescendingly at the degree and chartered engineer certificates hanging up behind Nick, but only tutted and shook her head at the first aid certificate, dated 1996, and a certificate for completing a Half Marathon in 1986 hanging on a side wall. Eventually she turned to Nick and looked him in the eye for a moment or two, as if gathering her thoughts or perhaps even her courage.

'Look Nick, no offense or anything...' a sure sign that she was about to offend him, 'but are you any good at your job?'

He'd not expected that question – at least not put in such an honestly enquiring way - and he didn't really know how to answer. He knew what he should say to a prospective client, but her tone almost demanded an honest answer and he honestly didn't really know if he *was* any good as a Private Investigator. He'd had very few cases, and they'd all involved gathering evidence for messy divorces. All he'd had to do was follow people, make notes, and take photographs. He'd never had anything a bit meatier like a missing person's case, and had often admitted to himself that he probably wouldn't know where to start.

He decided to be totally honest with her.

'Well, I've had my successes. Never failed a client yet. What sort of work do you have in mind?'

'A missing person.'

3

'Ah,' said Nick.

Apart from his total lack of experience, something else bothered him. He could think of only one person whom Ruth would want to find, and if he were missing, then as far as Nick was concerned, he could stay missing.

'What's the matter? Don't you do missing persons work?'

'No... I mean yes, of course I do. It's just that... I mean, who's missing?'

'John,' replied Ruth. She was clearly upset; as if just mentioning his name reminded her how much she missed him.

Nick was right, and he couldn't hide *his* feelings.

'Oh, him. I thought it would be.'

'What do mean? Are you trying to say you expected him to leave me? Or that I deserve it after leaving you? Or ...?'

'Whoa...whoa. I wasn't trying to say anything. I just thought he'd be the only person that you would *want* to find again if he went missing.'

'You mean I don't care about anyone else!'

'Do you?' asked Nick calmly.

Ruth paused, and let out an exaggerated sigh.

'Look Nick, I'm sorry. I over-reacted. Will you help me find John? I'll pay you of course – whatever the going rate is.'

Nick thought for a few moments. He remembered all of the things she'd said to him as she'd left the house. All the reasons she'd given for leaving him. All the ways she was going to make him pay for being such a loser; such a let-down to her. And now here she was, asking for his help. He examined his options. He could:

a)   Tell her to sod off. That would probably make him feel better for at least a couple of minutes and it would get her out of his life again immediately, or...

b)   He could listen to what she had to say and take the job, (or not) based entirely on whether he thought he could help her, or...

c)   He could tell her he'd have to think about it, and then lock up his office as soon as she'd gone and hide out somewhere until he thought it was safe, (his personal favourite) or...

d)   He could take the job because he needed the money, even though he had no experience and probably couldn't help – not exactly the ethical option....

Looking down at his desk, he said, 'OK, I'll take the job.'

Ruth smiled. 'Good. I've been thinking...'

'Just hang on a minute Ruth. We've got "history", as they say. Quite a lot of it. So there are a few things we have to get straight right from the off. Ground rules I suppose you could call them.'

'Such as?'

'Well, obviously I'll be totally professional. Treat you like any other client. Forget about our past; that you left me for the man you *now* want me to find. Forget about all the things you said when you kicked me out of *our* life.' He looked up at Ruth. She was seething and just about to explode, when he added, 'Of course you'll have to forget the past as well. Forget what you *thought* of as my little shortcomings...'

'What I *thought* of as your little shortcomings!!' Ruth erupted.

'Exactly. I'm glad you agree.'

It had occurred to Nick whilst considering his options, that there must be some reason why she had come to him, and not sought out a more experienced investigator. Had she even been to the Police? Under normal circumstances there was no way Ruth would approach him for help, not even if he were the last intelligent (not a term she'd use) life-form in the known universe. There had to be some fairly compelling reason for her to come to him. He hadn't a clue what it was, but she hadn't stormed out so there had to be something, and that was a little worrying – what could it be? Still, at least he could get paid while he tried to work out what it was, or until she realised that he wasn't helping her at all. After all Ruth owed him. And who knows? He might have some fun.

'So John's missing then...' he stated, barely concealing a smirk.

Ruth glared back at him.

'Yes.'

'Right I'd better get some details.' Nick looked around his desk, found a pen, and then continued looking until he saw a used envelope. He turned it over, smiled, and said, 'This'll do. Right, name?'

'Whose? You know mine, and John's.'

'Ha! That's quite true, but are you still using your married name?'

'Yes.'

'Good. I mean "good" because I know it: not "good" because you're still using my surname. You can call yourself whatever you want, it's nothing to do with me... obviously. Although I am too.'

'You are too what?' Ruth asked, clearly puzzling over whether her response made any sense.

'Using my married name!' said Nick smiling. He was quite enjoying this. He was playing it bright and breezy with a hint of incompetence. The "bright and breezy" was put on. The hint of incompetence came a little more naturally.

'Right,' he said again, as he began to write on the back of the envelope, 'Client: Ruth Howard, Subject: John Anderson. Address... *He* moved in with *you* didn't he? So I know that address as well, since it used to be mine.'

He looked up and smiled again. Ruth stared back.

'So when did you last see John?'

'On Wednesday, at work.' replied Ruth.

'At work? How is everyone back at the ranch by the way?'

'They're not missing you, that's for certain.'

'That's fine with me. I'm not missing them either.'

Up until he'd left to set up his detective agency Nick had spent five, (or was it six? – it felt like longer), unsatisfactory years working for Regional Water Services PLC (RWS) the local Water Company. Ruth was still there as she had been for the vast majority of her working life. John Anderson had joined about a year after Nick, although their paths had really not crossed – until John started seeing Ruth and not much even then, since Nick and Ruth had already split up.

'You didn't see him on Wednesday evening then? I thought he lived with you. Has he gone away?'

'He went out for a drink with some friends and stayed at his place.'

'His place?'

'Yes. He still has his own house. He said he'd stay there, so he didn't disturb me coming in late.'

'Considerate. Didn't he turn up at work on Thursday?'

'No. I rang him and he said he was just hung-over. He rang me later to say that he was still feeling too rough to come round that evening.'

'What about Friday? Yesterday, in fact.' asked Nick.

'He didn't turn up at work and his mobile was switched off. And he didn't answer his house phone.'

'I see. These friends he went out with on Wednesday; who were they?'

'I don't know. I've never met them. People he knows from where he used to work.'

'Where was that?'

'I don't know,' replied Ruth.

7

'So you don't know where he went, or who he went with on Wednesday night, and you've not seen him since. That a fair summary?'

'Yes, I suppose so.'

'Plenty to go on then,' said Nick, and then added, 'I don't suppose he rang in sick on Friday?'

'Of course not, I'd have mentioned it if he had.'

'Well, I suppose we could do with knowing who he was with on Wednesday night. Might there be something at his house?'

Ruth brightened at that suggestion, and it sounded like a good idea to Nick too, who felt distinctly pleased with himself - not to mention surprised. Perhaps he would be good at this missing-person stuff after all.

'Yes, there might be,' said Ruth. 'Shall we go and look?'

'Well yes, *I'll* go and look. We don't know what we'll find and besides, you're *paying* me remember? So I should do the work. Which reminds me, I've not told you my fee yet. You may not be able to afford me.'

'So how much is it going to cost?'

Two hundred pounds per day,' replied Nick.

'*How much?*' exclaimed Ruth.

'Two hundred pounds per day...Plus expenses,' said Nick, 'and that's mate's rates. I have to make a living.'

'If that's what you charge your friends...' said Ruth.

'Mate's rates I said,' replied Nick, 'I didn't say "friends". I'm not sure we were ever "friends", but we were mates. That is to say,' smirked Nick, 'we did mate, quite often at one time I recall.'

Nick was clearly quite pleased with himself. That was clever.

Ruth obviously didn't agree.

'OK,' she said, 'Two hundred pounds per day plus expenses it is, but I *am* coming with you to John's house. If

I'm paying that much I want to make sure I'm getting my money's worth. Let's go.'

'Whoa! Slow down will you? I have a few things to do here before I can go dashing off. *On my other cases*. I do have some, remember? I presume you want me on this full time?'

'Damned right I do at two hundred pounds-a-day.'

'Well, I'll have to sort a few things out first. How about if I meet you there at about two o'clock? What's the address?'

'35 The Avenue,' replied Ruth.

'Nice,' said Nick, 'I'll see you there. Don't go in without me. Remember, *I'm* the expert.'

Ruth seemed to accept this surprisingly affably.

'All right,' she said as she stood up. 'Don't be late.'

'I still have some more things to ask you now,' said Nick.

''You can ask me later,' she replied, turning and walking to the door.

As she put her hand on the handle, Nick asked, 'Ruth, if I'd gone missing would you have spent two hundred pounds-a-day to find me?'

Ruth smiled sweetly, 'What do *you* think?' she replied, before closing the door behind her.

'I think not,' muttered Nick, as he put his feet back up on his desk, 'but then again, would I have wanted to be found? But then yet again,' he pondered, 'does John?'

9

CHAPTER TWO

Having sorted things out on his 'other cases', (sent an e-mail to his landlord extending his rental of the office for another month, switched off his computer, and spent a couple of minutes trying to raise *one* eyebrow without having to push it up with his finger), Nick drove to his appointment with his new client. He parked a hundred yards down the road from the drive of number 35 The Avenue at precisely two pm. He had no idea why he parked a hundred yards away, other than he'd seen it done in the movies. He had meant to arrive early, for exactly the same reason, but he'd had to go and get a new tyre fitted to his Fiat Punto and there'd been a queue. He got out of his car and locked it. He paused to admire his new tyre. He didn't mind spending the money on the tyre when the car was in such good condition. He could remember when he used to joke repeatedly that Fiats seemed to be soluble in water. Not anymore: there was not a spot of rust on his ten year old Punto, and he was proud of it.

Nick crossed the road to walk up to John's house. He presumed Ruth had parked on the drive and was already inside, despite what he'd said about not going in without him. As he walked along the avenue, he was bordered on his left by mature chestnut trees along the kerb whilst on his right, tall, well trimmed hedges hid the large detached houses from view. As he approached number 35 he could hear an alarm sounding. He turned on to the drive to see Ruth standing near the open front door. A man in a police uniform, the jacket hanging open as though he was either just putting it on or taking it off, was coming out of the house next door. Nick realised that it was John's house alarm that was sounding.

'You all right Ruth?' asked the neighbourly policeman.

'Oh, thank God. Yes Alan, I'm OK. I'd just come round to get a couple of things from John's when I found the alarm going off and this man coming out of the front door in a hurry.'

'Right you. Come here,' ordered the policeman.

Nick decided not to 'come here' and, having vaguely assessed that the man doing the ordering looked like a rather mature policeman probably restricted to desk work, decided to leg it instead. He sprinted off as quickly as he could, but soon discovered that he was not as 'naturally fit' as he thought. He was not making much ground on the 'mature' policeman. He turned left, then right, then left again, and soon didn't know where he was. He had by now, increased his lead a little but knew he could run no further. He would have to hide or give himself up. He turned a sharp left and ran into a green 'wheelie' bin. It fell over easily. It was empty. Without thinking, he picked it up, hopped on to a low garden wall, clambered into the bin and closed the lid. He waited, but heard nothing. Then he began to be aware of an unpleasant smell. More of a stench really - like rotting vegetables. This was a green bin, and that meant it was for garden and food waste. The stench *was* rotting vegetables mixed with a bit of rotting garden waste. He was also now aware that the sticky, smelly mess was all over his shoes. The good news was that he seemed to have outrun the policeman.

'*No wonder the crime rate is so high,*' he thought, '*with unfit coppers like that on the job. Now to get out.*'

He was just about to push the lid open a crack and have a look round when he felt the wheelie bin suddenly jerk and a man shout, 'Bloody Hell. I thought this had been emptied.'

The lid flew open, a man in a t-shirt that couldn't quite cover his huge belly, and with what Nick hoped was a tomato sauce stain and not blood on it, looked inside and said, ''Ere! What you doing in my bin?'

'Er...I was just...' Nick thought rapidly. Could he be inspecting wheelie bins on behalf of the council? No, that was ridiculous. 'I... I'm from the "Benefits" department. We believe that someone over the road there is fraudulently claiming benefits, and I was keeping an eye on them!'

'Spying you mean? Snooping on my neighbours?'

'Well they might be claiming benefits that they shouldn't have. Taking money that should be going to someone else who deserves it. Look, I've not seen anything anyway. Can you help me out of here? I don't think I can get out on my own.'

'Course I can mate,' came the reply. And with that, the man with the bare belly kicked the side of the wheelie bin so that it toppled over. Nick hit the deck hard, but he managed to crawl out. As he stood up he muttered a 'Thank you,' in as un-provoking a tone as he could manage, and received a 'Bugger off, before I put you back in there headfirst! Bloody snoop!'

Nick needed no further encouragement and staggered off. His shoes were full of whatever had been in the bottom of the bin and the bottom half of his trousers were covered in it. He could smell it despite the strong breeze blowing. His mobile phone rang. He searched all of his pockets, eventually pulling it out of the pocket that he'd checked first.

'Hello,' he sighed.

'Where the Hell are you?' demanded Ruth. 'I've been waiting here ages for you to come back.'

'I don't know really. I lost track when I was running. What about the policeman?'

12

'Alan? Oh, he's gone to work. I told him I'd be OK. Said I could get the window fixed.'

'Window fixed?' said Nick.

'Yes, while you and him were doing your Paula Radcliffe impressions, I thought I'd better make it look as though you'd really broken in. So I broke a window round the back. Even thought to break it from the outside. Clever eh? Anyway, get back here, you've got work to do. I'm not paying two hundred pounds a day for you to go out jogging!'

'I told you,' replied Nick. 'I don't know where I am. I don't know how to get back.'

'Walk to the end of the road, where there'll be a road sign, and then ring for a taxi to pick you up and bring you back here. Honestly, it's not rocket science!' said Ruth before hanging up abruptly.

Nick had to acknowledge to himself that it was a good idea, so he trudged to the end of the road, and gave his location to the taxi firm whose number he had on his mobile.

Five minutes later he was jumping into the back of the taxi and giving the driver John's address. The taxi driver pulled out of the junction, drove twenty-five yards, turned right, drove another twenty-five yards, pulled up and said, 'There you are mate. That'll be twenty-five quid.'

Nick looked out of the window. He was outside number 35 The Avenue all right. He'd only been about fifty yards away! 'Twenty-five quid! You must be joking,' he exclaimed. 'You've only driven me about fifty yards!'

'Five quid minimum charge and twenty quid to clean up the taxi. You stink mate!'

Nick had to agree. He did stink, but he protested nevertheless, 'Twenty quid to clean the car? There's only a bit of,' he looked at his feet. 'A bit of something or other on the carpet down here.'

13

'Whatever it is, it stinks. You can either pay up or I'll drive straight round to the local nick, and you can explain it all there.'

Nick had to give up. He took out his wallet and handed over twenty-five pounds.

'No tip?' asked the driver.

'Yes,' said Nick as he got out, 'find a cheaper car valeting service.'

He trudged up the drive and rang the doorbell.

Ruth opened the door, 'Come in quickly before anyone sees you,' she said.

Nick stepped inside, 'What the Hell were you doing: setting PC Dibble on me?'

'Sorry,' she replied. 'I found where John keeps his spare key easily and opened the front door, but the alarm went off and I didn't know what to do. Then Alan came out from next door just as you turned up at the bottom of the drive. I panicked. I didn't want Alan thinking I'd broken in, so I blamed you. Why were you gone so long anyway? Alan got back ages ago. He said you must be some sort of athlete to be able to outrun him. I don't know who he thinks he is. You'd hardly have to be Usain Bolt to outrun *him*!'

'I didn't think I *was* going to outrun him so I hid in a wheelie bin...'

'You did what?' Ruth noticed Nick's shoes for the first time. 'Right, you can get those off. You're not traipsing that mess all over the house.'

Nick opened his mouth to argue but thought better of it, and leant against the wall while he undid his laces and took his shoes off.

'You owe me twenty-five quid by the way,' he said.

'What?'

'Expenses – the taxi. You told me to get one.'

'Twenty-five quid? How far did you run for goodness sake? A bloody marathon? Come on let's start looking round,' said Ruth as she headed off into the lounge.

The room ran from the front to the back of the house with a large window at the front and a patio door leading out to the garden at the back. Nick stood in the doorway and looked round. It was a large room, almost twice the size of the lounge he and Ruth had had. The paint on the walls, he thought, was probably magnolia, but it could easily have been 'antique Moroccan buttermilk mist' or 'meadow fresh promiscuous hessian' or just plain old cream. The carpet was a light-ish brown that complemented the walls, as were the curtains. Everything was tidy, neutral, not going to offend anyone. Nick had a thought.

'Does John own this place?'

'No, he rents it, replied Ruth.

'Thought so. Everything's so neutral.'

'Nice to see your detective abilities are well honed. What else do you see Sherlock?'

'You tell me, he replied. 'Do you see anything different in this room? Is it always this tidy?'

'Yes it is. It's easy to keep a place tidy when you live on your own.'

'It is?' said Nick. 'Made even easier when you spend most of your time at your girlfriend's, I suppose.'

Ruth ignored the comment and headed upstairs. Nick followed, poking his head round each of the four bedroom doors, eventually joining Ruth in what was obviously the 'master'.

'Notice anything?' he asked. Ruth shook her head pensively.

Nick looked at two oak wardrobes standing against another magnolia painted wall opposite him. 'Try the wardrobes,' he suggested.

15

Ruth checked the contents of both of the oak wardrobes, and then the drawers in the chest next to them. 'Yes,' she said. 'There are clothes missing, trousers shirts, jackets, underwear. And he keeps a suitcase in the bottom of there,' pointing at the larger of the two wardrobes, 'and that's gone as well.'

'Where does he keep his passport? Do you know?'

'His passport? Why on earth would he want that?'

'*I* don't know, Ruth. You've asked me to look for him remember? So you think he's disappeared. And if you're right, he could be anywhere in the world, unless you know something you're not telling me. But if we can find his passport then there's a fair chance he's still in this country.'

'Of course he's still in this country, said Ruth.

'Is he? Why'd you say that? What are you not telling me? How much looking have you already done?'

'What do you mean?'

'Well I would have asked you in my office, but you ended the meeting rather abruptly,' said Nick. 'For instance have you rung round the hospitals? He may have had an accident.'

'Wishful thinking?' suggested Ruth.

'Not at all,' replied Nick, only half lying. 'It's an obvious possibility that's all. Probably even the right place to start.'

'I'm sure I'd have heard if he'd had an accident. My name's in his mobile, as are people at work. *Someone* would have heard by now.'

'Possibly,' agreed Nick. 'But I'll still try the hospitals just to make sure. Now what about his passport?'

'I don't know where he kept it. We'll just have to look around and see if we can find it.'

'OK,' said Nick, quite liking the idea of justifiably rummaging through someone's belongings. You never know what you might find.

Half an hour later they both knew what they'd found. Nothing! No passport. No clues at all about where John might have gone. There was no computer in the house to check. Apparently John had a laptop, which he took everywhere with him. When Ruth and he were out together he kept it locked in the boot of his car. It had 'confidential' company stuff on it, and he didn't want to leave it in the house.

'What if the car had been stolen?' asked Nick.

'He said the stuff on it was encrypted so it was safe,' replied Ruth.

'So why couldn't he leave it at the house?'

'I don't know!' shouted Ruth, obviously beginning to think something didn't quite hang together.

There was nothing more to be gained from searching the house. It was almost sterile - hardly lived in. This wasn't where John Anderson really lived. That had been at Ruth's; perhaps there'd be something there.

'Right,' said Nick. 'Let's go and look around your place.'

'I beg your pardon?' said an indignant Ruth.

'I said "let's..."'

'I know what you said, but if you think you're sniffing round mine and John's things you've got another thing coming.'

'Ruth, I just want to see if John's left any...'

'Clues! I know. But I can look for them. I'll know if there's anything missing. You won't. You can go and ring round the hospitals, since you seem to think that's necessary.'

Without waiting for a reply she led the way downstairs. Leaning against the wall in the hall and pulling a disgusted face as he slipped his feet back into his wet and sticky shoes, Nick saw a pile of post on a table next to him. Ruth noticed and said, 'I found that lot on the floor inside the door.'

17

'Anything interesting?' said Nick as he picked up the pile and leafed through it. There wasn't - it was just the usual utility bills, bank statements and junk mail. Ruth didn't notice his frowning at some of the envelopes before he put them back on the table.

Then he asked, 'How did you stop the house alarm going off by the way?'

'I guessed the right number to disarm it of course.'

'You *guessed?*'

'It was his birthday.'

'Original. I wish you'd thought of that sooner. Then I wouldn't have been chased half way round town.'

'Stop moaning, you obviously needed the exercise,' said Ruth as she shepherded Nick out of the front door. He stopped in the porch to check that the neighbourly Policeman had not returned before saying, 'I'll ring you later,' and jogging off back to his car, his feet squelching in his shoes.

He was soon back at the flat he rented on the second floor of a fifteen storey block on the southern outskirts of the city. He took off his dirty clothes and put them in the washing machine with the rest of the week's washing, before jumping into the shower. He soon regretted his eagerness to put the washing machine on, as the shower ran alternately very cold and very hot as the machine drew in water. His customary singing was heavily punctuated with curses and girly screams. After dressing in the last of his clean clothes, he settled down with a 'nice cup of tea' and the telephone directory, and rang the surrounding hospitals to check that John had not turned up at any of them.

Nick was surprised at how easy it was to find out if a patient by the name of John Anderson had been admitted to hospital. All he had to do was claim to be John's brother and they were all happy to check their admissions before confirming that, 'No. No one by that name has been

18

admitted in the last couple of days.' He wondered if they'd have been as equally forthcoming about John's condition if he had actually been admitted and if patient confidentiality would have then kicked in. Somehow he doubted that.

Nick then realised that he had been working for most of the day, and that it was Saturday. He couldn't remember the last time he'd worked on a Saturday. His job at RWS, developing operating standards and procedures, had not required that, but he also realised that if it had, he would have been paid at a premium rate. He would mention that to Ruth when he rang her the following day, especially as that would be Sunday when double pay was the norm! Anyway, he'd done a hard day's work and he deserved a relaxing evening, but he was too tired to go out with any of his mates. Actually all of his friends were married and not allowed out with him, so he put a pizza in the oven and vegetated in front of the television for the rest of the evening.

CHAPTER THREE

At ten o'clock the following morning Nick became dimly aware that someone was shouting that he ain't seen nothing yet. It took him a moment or two to realise that it was Bachman Turner Overdrive, (BTO) - the new ring tone on his mobile - and he muttered a curse as he snaked his arm out from under the duvet to drag the offending phone from the bedside table.

Who the hell could be ringing him at this time on a Sunday morning? What time was it anyway? And why hadn't he remembered to switch his phone off when he went to bed? Because nobody ever rang him –that's why. So who was it?

'Hello,' he groaned into the phone, as he lay on his back, his eyes still closed.

'Hello? Is that you?' came the reply.

'No it isn't. It's some other bugger. *I* don't wake up at this time on a Sunday.'

'Stop pissing about Nick, I haven't got the time,' said Ruth.

'Or the inclination, if memory serves. What do you want for God's sake? Ringing at this time – its' still dark!'

'It is not still dark as you well know. Your curtains are closed that's all. It wasn't funny when you said it every weekend we were married and it's not funny now. I am ringing to ask you what you intend to do today, as I am paying you an exorbitant daily fee.'

A light bulb went on in the dark recesses of Nick's brain, 'I was going to mention that,' he said. 'It's Sunday today and people normally get paid double-time for working on a Sunday.'

'The operative word being "working"' replied Ruth. 'I repeat; what are you intending to do today? I have to go to my mother's, so you're on your own and I want to know what I'll be paying for.'

'Ah well, firstly. I can confirm that John has not been admitted to any of the hospitals within fifty miles...'

'Obviously, or you'd have rung me last night.'

'Oh, right, yes I would. You want to know what I intend to do today then?'

'Yes, I still want to know.'

'Well I was hoping to talk to you about John. Get some more background that sort of thing. And then... perhaps, er... go back and have another look at his house. By the way did you find anything when you looked around your house?'

'Did I ring you?'

'No you didn't.'

'Then I didn't find anything. And why do you want to go to John's house again?' demanded Ruth.

'Er... well, I felt a bit rushed and flustered yesterday after the chase. I don't think I was giving it my full attention, and it occurred to me last night that we didn't check the loft.'

'The loft?'

'Yes I presume the house has one. Like I said I must have been a bit flustered not to think of it while we were there.'

'And what do you expect to find in the loft?' asked Ruth.

'I don't know,' Nick replied. 'Something useful hopefully, His passport perhaps?'

'Why would he keep his passport in the loft for goodness sake?'

21

Nick didn't answer but Ruth relented. She felt happier letting Nick look round on his own, now that she'd been there and seen that there was nothing embarrassing to be found. 'OK. You have another look round John's house. The key's under the plant pot in the porch and the alarm number is 8270. I'll ring you when I get back from Mother's. You can report to me then, and ask me some more background questions if you must.'

She put the phone down without saying good bye. '*Charming,*' thought Nick. '*Love you too... Oh no I don't. Not anymore. I was forgetting. Now, what was that alarm number?*'

He recalled the number without difficulty and put it into his mobile phone just in case. Then he stretched, sighed and said out loud, 'Well I won't get back to sleep now, so I may as well get up', which he did.

After breakfasting on a bowl of bran flakes and a cup of tea, showering, taking his washing out of the machine and draping it all over his flat in an attempt to dry it, he left the house at almost eleven o'clock precisely.

As he drove to number 35 The Avenue, Nick noticed the thin, wispy, cirrus clouds moving slowly across the otherwise clear blue sky. As a young boy he'd known the names of all of the different cloud formations: clouds and dinosaurs, those had been his areas of expertise. He wondered what his areas of expertise were now. He felt depressed, as he could think of none. Again, as a matter of good practice he parked a hundred yards away from the entrance to the drive of number 35, feeling more depressed, as he decided his area of expertise was now Saturday evening television.

He mooched along through the shadows cast by the chestnut trees lining The Avenue, keeping his head down in case anyone saw him and remembered him, particularly as he passed number 37, the home of 'Officer Dibble'. It was all clear so he jogged up the drive to the cover of the porch and quickly retrieved the key from underneath the flowerpot. Then he cursed himself for not finding the alarm number in his mobile before he arrived in the porch. He felt exposed even under the cover of the porch but he soon found the alarm number, opened the door, stepped inside, and disabled the alarm.

Now what?

'How about a nice cup of tea?' he thought. Then he remembered that there'd be no fresh milk, and that reminded him about the letters on the table next to him. He picked them up and examined the postmarks again. They were as he remembered; some of them were three weeks old. John hadn't been home for at least three weeks and he was supposed to have stayed there last Wednesday night. Ruth had spoken to him on Thursday, so where had he been then? Nick made a mental note to ask her if she'd asked him.

He wandered through the house again, taking more time to rummage in drawers and cupboards without the sense of Ruth keeping an eye on him. He was struck again by how neat and tidy the place was - how little sign there was of anyone doing any real living in the place. There were no newspapers left lying around, no cup on the draining board and only a few tins of food in the kitchen cupboards. If John did spend any time here, then he always tidied up before he left: a little unusual for a man living alone, if his own experience was anything to go by. Once again he found nothing so he went in search of the loft access and found it in the landing ceiling. He was in luck. It had an 'eye' attached to it, and the hook to pull it down with was in the airing cupboard.

He opened the loft cover and pulled down the spring loaded ladder. At the top of the ladder he yanked at a light cord and the roof space lit up. Again the area was very tidy, with half a dozen cardboard boxes neatly lined up on the

23

boarding. He climbed into the loft and knelt down to examine the boxes. He grimaced as his right knee cracked. Opening the first box, Nick was surprised to find files bearing a very familiar company logo – Regional Water Services. He moved the boxes around so that he could remove the lids. All six boxes were full of RWS files. John was certainly very conscientious; Nick had never brought so much work home with him. Although if he had he wouldn't have kept it in his loft. There were files containing details of the Company's capital investment programme, details of individual projects covering budgets and spend profiles, of operational performance, reports made to the water industry regulators, customer services, IT support, just about everything the Company was involved in. Nick sat back for a moment. There was a lot of detailed information in these boxes – information about how RWS conducted its business - going back a long time. Why on earth would John have all that in his loft? How long had he been with the company? Five years at most. John worked in 'Audit', that was true, but there was no way he would need to refer to all of this in the normal run of his work. One thing was for certain, Nick would have to get this lot down from the loft and take it home to look at it properly.

He carried the boxes down from the loft one at a time and piled them up in the hall downstairs. He couldn't risk carrying the boxes out to his car one at a time - someone might think he was robbing the place, which technically he was, since he didn't have the owner's permission. However, he knew that the door in the wall opposite him was a personnel door that led into the empty garage. So if he could open the garage door from the inside without a key, then he would be able to drive in and load the car up, hopefully without being seen. He unlocked the personnel door with the key that lay on the shelf next to it and switched on the light in the garage. Examining the garage door he found that he could unlock it by pulling down on a cable that controlled the latch at the top. The door swung open, and Nick checked that all was clear before jogging back to his car. Fifteen minutes later he had filled his boot and back seat with the boxes, locked the house up, and was on his way home with his booty, feeling rather pleased with himself.

It was one-thirty pm by the time he'd arrived home, and unpacked the car. Ten minutes later he was in his 'local,' 'The Royal Oak' with a pint of bitter in front of him watching the United/Chelsea game. He'd almost forgotten about it in the excitement of actually finding some clues. He fully intended to make a thorough examination of the boxes after the match, and give Ruth a detailed report later that evening.

Unfortunately, after several pints on top of only two packets of dry roasted peanuts, Nick was in no state to go home and start looking through some boring RWS files; he'd had enough of that when he'd worked for them. He needed food, so he called at a kebab shop on the way home. After polishing off his 'Döner and chips' he stretched out on the sofa and dozed off watching 'Songs of Praise'.

He was woken by Bachman Turner Overdrive's thunderous stuttering double negative and it took him a moment or two to get his bearings and pick his mobile up off the carpet. 'Hello?' he croaked.

'Hello? Is that you Nick? It's Ruth.'

'Yes, it's me,' he sighed. 'Who else is going to answer my phone? My secretary doesn't work on Sundays – not even for double time.' His words were slightly slurred and probably sounded more so, as he was lying down, talking with his chin buried in his chest.

'Have you been drinking?'

'It's Sunday. United beat Chelsea 2-1: of course I've been drinking! My world doesn't revolve around you, you know. Not anymore! That's John's job – if he hasn't resigned his post that is, and run off.'

There was a stony silence for a few moments before Ruth answered in a very deliberate tone, 'You know, I was hoping that you might have grown up - having to look after yourself, run your own business and all that, but I can see that I was wrong. You are still a complete MORON!'

'I think you're confusing me with the Osmonds,' replied Nick.

'They were Mormons not morons you idiot!'

'You obviously don't remember "Crazy Horses"!' said Nick before singing the title – the only two words of the song that he could remember - at her.

The phone went dead. Nick shrugged, dropped the phone on the floor and closed his eyes.

He awoke a few hours later with a stiff neck, took a couple of paracetemol and went to bed. After a night's sleep, broken only by the usual couple of trips to the bathroom, he woke relatively early, feeling he thought, surprisingly chipper. He put this down to United beating Chelsea and to his having had the common sense to have a decent meal on his way home from the pub. Who said kebabs weren't good for you?

Whilst he was in the shower, he reflected on his conversation with Ruth; probably not the way to talk to one's client. He resolved to get to work on the boxes he'd retrieved from John's loft as soon as he'd had breakfast. Then he'd have some progress to report to Ruth when she rang to berate him about his behaviour. Since she was employing him, he supposed that she had some right to do this, and he was expecting a call at any minute. However, by nine o'clock there had still been no call and Nick was beginning to wonder if she'd sacked him when they'd spoken last night. Perhaps it had simply not registered with him due to his relaxed state at the time. He decided that he

26

would ring her and give her the news about the boxes to demonstrate that he really was 'on the case'.

He rang Ruth's mobile number, waited interminably for it to start ringing and then an equally long time for Ruth to answer. When she eventually 'picked up', Nick heard Ruth say, 'Sorry, I think I should take this. Do you mind?' There was then a pause as Ruth presumably walked a little away from whomever she was with. Then she said, 'Well, what have you got to say for yourself?'

'What do you mean?' asked Nick entirely innocently.

'You know very well what I mean,' replied Ruth through gritted teeth. 'But never mind that now. I'm with Jane Edwards and Richard Seaton. They'd like to meet with you.'

'They would? Why? When?'

'As soon as possible, and you'll find out when you get here. So get here as quickly as you can. I presume you *are* up and dressed.'

'Of course I'm up and dressed – I'm working on your case!'

'I'm glad to hear it. But stop whatever it is you're doing, and get here now.'

'You're the boss,' sighed Nick as if he were having to drag himself away from something really important. 'See you later.'

Two of the directors wanted to see him! Why was that? They never wanted to see him when he worked there.

Only one way to find out. Best not keep them waiting!

CHAPTER FOUR

As he drove the thirty-five minutes or so into RWS's headquarters, Nick mulled over what he knew about the case so far. What could he tell the Managing Director and the Audit Director? That was presuming that it was this case they wanted to speak to him about. Who knows? Ruth may have been so impressed with him so far, that she had recommended him to Jane and Richard for an entirely different case. He laughed out loud at the very idea, and thought, '*Yeah, right!*' But why were they interested? Why was Ruth talking to them? Had it got something to do with the boxes he'd found in John's loft? Ruth knew nothing of those. At least he thought she didn't. He decided that he would say nothing about the boxes to anyone yet, and just listen. After all it's harder to look stupid if you say nothing - a maxim he'd lived by for much of his working life.

Arriving at the site gate he decided that, just for the hell of it, he would try to get all the way to Ruth's desk without being announced. So as the security guard emerged from the gatehouse Nick raised his hand in recognition and received a wave back. Nick had never seen this particular security guard before, but he'd found during the years he'd worked on the site that if he waved confidently, before the guard had chance to look to see if there was a site-pass on the windscreen, then he'd been able to drive straight in without stopping. He was pleased to see that it still worked. Now he just had to get into the building. He had to park a hundred yards or so away from the door and make his way across the almost full car park. He regretted not bringing a brief case with him, just to look a little more businesslike.

But he was pleased to see someone that he recognised from his own time at the company walking towards the same door. He speeded up his walk so that he arrived at the entrance at the same time, and then made a show of delving into his pockets to retrieve his non-existent pass. Inevitably he was beaten to it by his 'co-employee', who duly swiped his access card and then held the door open for Nick to walk through first. '*Easy peasy*,' thought Nick.

Fortunately, the reorganisation which had seen Nick leave the company had not necessitated Ruth moving from her old desk and he presented himself before her with a smirk on his face, 'Good morning again,' he said. 'Not that you had the manners to say "Good morning" the first time we spoke this morning.'

Ruth looked up with a surprised expression and said, 'How did you get in here without an access card?'

'I'm a detective,' he replied smugly. 'It's part of the job to be able to get into places without anyone knowing. And I see that you've still not said "Good morning".'

Ruth ignored his last remark. 'Well now you're here, we'd better go and see Jane and Richard straight away. I'll just ring Jane's secretary.' She picked up her desk phone.

Nick noticed that Ruth seemed a little jumpy. He wasn't sure if this was due to the fact that John was missing or that she was having to deal with the Managing Director.

'Hang on a minute,' he said. 'What do they want to see me about?'

'About John missing of course. Richard asked me again this morning if I'd seen John.'

'Again?'

'Yes, he asked me on Friday, remember? I told you.'

'No you didn't. In fact that reminds me; we need to have a chat. I need a lot more background information if I'm going to able to look for John. I don't even know where his parents live. In fact I don't even know if he *has* any parents!'

29

'Never mind that for now. We can talk later. Jane wants to talk to you about John. It's as simple as that. They know he's missing and they want to know if there's anything they can do to help. That's all.'

She picked up the phone again and spoke to the MD's secretary. Nick watched as Ruth looked puzzled and even a little hurt, as she said, 'Oh, OK then. I'll send him along... Oh, thank you.' She put the phone down.

Nick looked at her and raised his eyebrows as if to say, 'Well?'

'That was Jane. You're to go to her office on your own. They don't need to speak to me again,' said Ruth frowning, before going on. 'I suppose that's fair enough really. I can't tell them anything else. They just want to talk to you in your *professional* capacity. And she said I can go home if I want - if I'm too upset to work.'

'Very understanding of her,' said Nick without a trace of sympathy. 'Is her office in the same place?'

Ruth nodded, 'I'll wait here for you. Then we can go have that meeting you want. *And* you can tell me what they say.'

Nick found his way to Jane's office easily. He saw plenty of new faces sitting at desks in the open plan offices he walked through, but also plenty of puzzled old faces to whom he said a bright and breezy, 'Hello.'

Jane, dressed as Nick remembered her, in a dark business suit with a white, open-neck blouse, welcomed him into her office with a handshake and a 'Good to see you again' followed by a 'Please sit down,' and a 'You know Richard, of course'.

Nick replied with a 'You too,' a 'Thanks,' and a 'By sight only really, but nice to meet you,' as he shook Richard's hand.

Richard, also dressed in a dark suit and a white, open-necked shirt, completed the formalities with a 'Nice to meet you.'

There followed a slight lull in the proceedings, as Jane and Nick each seemed to wait for the other to start. Nick had barely known Jane Edwards when he'd worked at RWS, but what little he had known, largely through the 'motivating' presentations she'd given, he hadn't liked. He hadn't liked the way she had seemed to fill the room with words without actually saying anything. He hadn't liked the way she had reduced staff numbers to take advantage of new IT systems; systems which then did not work and had to be scrapped. He hadn't liked the way she used her catch phrases, 'Doing nothing is not an option' and 'If you keep doing things the same way how can you achieve better results?' to imply that the staff had to work harder or to justify reorganisations which simply reduced staff numbers rather than changed processes. And he hadn't liked the way she always claimed she was being 'open and honest' using the phrase 'to be honest' ad nauseam. Nick realised that he was having a mental rant, and he ended it just as Jane spoke.

'I think you know why we asked you here today,' she said, sounding to Nick like she was a head-teacher talking to the parents of some errant child. He looked Jane in the eye before responding. According to the 'Communications Skills Course' to which RWS had subjected him, maintaining eye contact was supposed to mean you're honest, with nothing to hide, and confident in your own abilities – both essential qualities in his line of work.

'Presumably something to do with the apparently missing John Anderson?'

God, her eyes seemed to be drilling right into him, looking deep into his soul, finding every morsel of self doubt, (and there were plenty). But he mustn't weaken. He must not look away first.

'Apparently? Don't you believe he's missing?

'Well, I believe he's been missing from Ruth's life for the past couple of days. Whether he's missing from anywhere else at the moment I couldn't say. I was hoping *you'd* tell *me*.'

'Well I can confirm that he's missing from work as well.'

'For how long?'

'He's not been in since last Wednesday.'

'That means this is only the third day that he's missed work. It's a bit early to panic isn't it? To call for the cavalry.'

He was doing remarkably well maintaining eye contact but his eyes were beginning to water. *'Blink you fool! You're not trying to stare her out!'*

'There's no panic, Nick,' interjected Richard.

Now Nick switched the eye contact to him.

'Ruth asked me on Friday if I knew where John was; if he was away on business. I told her that as far as I knew, he wasn't. Today she expressed her concern to me again. I mentioned that to Jane and she, as a concerned employer, brought Ruth in for a chat. It was then that Ruth told us that she'd employed you to find John. She suggested that if we shared her concerns, we might like to talk to you.'

Although he'd never met Richard before, the condescending tone reminded Nick that he hadn't liked what he'd heard about him when he'd worked at RWS. *And* Richard had dropped his eyes as soon as Nick had looked at him.

'And are you? Liking talking to me I mean?'

Jane jumped in before Richard could respond. 'The thing is Nick, to be honest, you could say we've had our eye on John for a while.'

Talking of eyes: back to Jane.

32

'In what way? Was he on "the lift off" scheme?' asked Nick referring to a fast track development and promotion scheme for those identified as having particularly high potential. (Nick had referred to it as 'the crash landing' scheme, as more often than not, the candidates turned out to be a total disaster in their elevated roles and were moved sideways, downwards or even out of the company after a matter of months.)

'No,' said Jane flatly. 'Not in that way at all, to be honest. We suspected that he may have been involved in some... how shall I put it? Dishonesty.' She looked down momentarily. She broke eye contact first.

'*One Nil! Back of the net!*'

Nick shook his head to bring himself back to the conversation and stop his mental lap of honour.

'Interesting. What sort of dishonesty? More than a little pilfering of the odd stapler or hole-punch I presume.'

'Before I can answer that Nick, I think we need to consider putting our... relationship on a more *professional* footing.'

'You mean you want to employ me?'

'I mean that we are considering it. I presume that should we become your client, then you would have no objection to signing a confidentiality agreement, ensuring that anything we discuss becomes a matter strictly between the three of us in this room, and would not be divulged to anyone else – including Ruth?'

'There's no need for such a document. If you become my client I will automatically treat everything we discuss as strictly confidential.'

'I'm sure you would. But we'd have to have the piece of paper to cover ourselves nevertheless.'

'No problem.'

'Right. Well I'll have the necessary paperwork drawn up by this afternoon. Can you come back at say, four p.m.?'

'Yeah, sure. You haven't told me what the job is yet by the way. If you want me to find John, I'm already being paid for that by Ruth. You could save yourself a lot of money. Well, some money.'

'That's only part of it Nick. To be honest, there's a lot more to it, which I can only go into *after* you've signed the confidentiality agreement.' Jane stood up to indicate the meeting was over.

Nick stood up as well to indicate he agreed.

'I'll see you at four,' he said shaking her hand. 'And can I just make an observation?' he added, not waiting for a reply. 'Every time you say "to be honest," it makes me wonder if when you don't say it, you're *not* being honest. Something I picked up on a "Communications Skills Course". Just a little constructive feedback. I know how keen RWS directors are on that.'

'Thank you, it's just a figure of speech I can assure you, but I'll bear it in mind,' said Jane smiling.

Richard held the door open for Nick and shook his hand as he left.

Nick smiled to himself as he walked back to Ruth's desk. The phrase 'to be honest' had always been a pet hate of his for some reason, and he'd always wanted to put someone right on it. Why he'd picked the managing director of a FTSE 100 company and a potential client to boot, to be the butt of his critique he had no idea. But he'd enjoyed it, and he was still smiling when he arrived back at Ruth's desk.

'What are you looking so pleased with yourself about?' she asked.

'Nothing really. I was just thinking that Clients are like buses: you don't have any for ages and then two come along in three days. Come on, let's take advantage of your MD's kind offer and take you home for our meeting.'

'No... I mean yes. Let's go, but let's go to a pub or a coffee shop or somewhere to have a chat. Taking me home might... well it might stir things up. After all you used to live there and...well...'

'You mean it might remind me how *you* left *me*, but I was the one who had to move out, and I am the one who ended up living in a rented flat on the edge of the biggest council estate in Europe?'

'You've just proven my point, so we'll meet on neutral ground.' Ruth stood up picked up her handbag and said, 'You follow me. I'll decide where we're going on the way.'

'Anything you say - after all you're paying.'

Ruth led the way to the car park. There was no further conversation until they'd parked in front of a parade of shops and were entering a coffee shop.

'I'll have a cappuccino,' said Nick. 'I presume you're paying. I mean I can pay, but then I'll only have to put it on my expenses, with the customary management fee of course.'

Ruth gave an exasperated sigh, 'Look', she said. 'Can you cut all this crap about me paying? It sounds so childish and unprofessional. I *know* I'm paying and I know *why* I'm paying. And every time you mention it, it reminds me that I'm having to pay because I'm looking for John... because he's missing.'

She sounded genuinely upset and Nick somewhat regretted his teasing, but before he could find the right way of responding without actually apologising, Ruth said, 'You go and sit down, I'll bring them over.'

'OK,' said Nick. 'But I just need to go for a "Nelson" first.'

His using the term 'Nelson' (Nelson Riddle – Piddle), was something that had always annoyed Ruth. Mind you she preferred it to his saying he was going for a 'Sir Arthur',

(Sir Arthur Bliss). Perhaps he'd use that one next time he had to go.

When he returned, Ruth was already sitting down. 'Sorry,' he said. 'I've reached that age when I can't pass up the opportunity of using the facilities.'

Ruth smiled thinly, 'You make it sound like a fetish.'

'No, I meant I always seem to have to...'

Ruth interrupted. 'I know what you meant. Can we get on please? You said you needed some more background or something.'

'Well, first of all when did you and John start erm... seeing each other?'

Ruth sighed again. Nick noticed he seemed to be having this effect on her – unless she had some sort of breathing problem.

'Look, it was after we'd...split up, if that's what you're getting at.'

Nick realised that Ruth didn't have a breathing problem and that it was his question that had caused the sigh. She simply thought that he was trying to find out if she'd been unfaithful to him with John.

'Sorry,' he said. 'I know that. What I should have asked was, how did you get together? I know it was after we split up.'

'So why do you need to know?'

'I don't know if I do, but I won't know that until you answer me.'

There was that sigh again.

'John came into the department one day. He said that he'd been asked to re-examine an audit that had been done the previous year. It was confidential so I wasn't to mention it to anyone - not even to Richard himself, as John wasn't even supposed to have told me.'

'So Richard had asked him to do it without anyone knowing?'

36

'Yes. But as he said at the time: how was he supposed to do an audit in Finance without me knowing about it? Typical of directors that is, never think about *how* things are supposed to get done. They only come up with the grand ideas and then let someone else work out *how* to do it.'

'Careful, Ruth. You're beginning to sound like I did when I worked at RWS.'

'Heaven forbid that I ever get that cynical.'

'I preferred to think of it as "battle hardened",' said Nick.

Ruth went on. 'Anyway, we ended up spending a lot of time together, as I had to provide him with the files and explain things to him. And we hit it off I suppose. We were soon going out and well...'

'One thing led to another. I know.'

Ruth was about to respond, when Nick added, 'So did he find anything in the files? Anything untoward with the previous audit I mean?'

'No, I don't think so. He didn't say so. In fact, come to think of it, he did tell me that everything seemed to be OK. Nothing to worry about. Although that didn't seem to satisfy Richard, because he had him do similar checks in other departments.'

'Which departments?'

'Most of them really. Capital delivery, Procurement, Customer Services, even Operations.'

'That explains the files in the loft' thought Nick, *'although not why he'd put them up there.'*

'And did he find anything wrong in any of the other departments?'

'No, he said it was all a total waste of time.'

'He must have got a bit pissed off with it all then.'

'I suppose so, but he just got on with it.'

'Did he take work home with him?'

'Yes he did. He said he wanted to get through it all as quickly as he could, so that he could get back on to proper work.'

'That must have made the evenings fun for you; him working all evening and you having to stay out of his way.'

'Oh, he always made time for me, but he didn't work at my house,' explained Ruth. 'He said he didn't want to impose his work on me. So a couple of evenings a week he'd stay at his place and do the work there. He said he could get more done – without me to distract him.'

Nick tried not to think about how his ex-wife might have been a distraction, instead he just said, 'Considerate.'

They both took a sip of their coffees and then Nick asked, 'So was John still spending a couple of nights at his place? I mean right up until recently?'

'Oh yes,' said Ruth. 'As he got closer to the end of it all he couldn't wait to get it finished, so that we could spend *every* evening and weekend together.'

'Weekends?'

'Yes, he often had to work weekends. Richard didn't want his normal work to suffer, or for people to know what he was working on. Apparently it could have been bad for morale or something; if they'd know that John was checking old audits – as though someone thought they'd been covering things up.'

'He could have had a point there. Unusual for a director to be so considerate of staff feelings. So you didn't see John much at weekends?'

'No, hardly ever. What with the audit work, a couple of courses he was sent on, and then he had to go and visit his mother once as well. She wasn't well.'

'Blimey, did you ever see him at weekends?'

'Oh yes,' said Ruth unable to suppress a smirk. 'We had some very memorable weekends.

'I don't want to know,' said Nick.

'Don't worry I have no intention of telling you. Is there anything else you *do* want to know?'

'Not that I can think of at the moment. Oh yes. John's mother. You said he went to see her. Do you have an address or a phone number? She might have heard from him.'

'Good idea,' said Ruth. 'I'll give her a ring. You know you might actually be good at this job. That's your second good idea since we started.'

'I meant *I'd* contact John's Mum. That's what you're paying me for.'

'That's all right, I don't mind. I probably have more chance of doing it without worrying her. I'll tell her we've had a huge argument or something. Of course I'll have to say it was all my fault – if she's anything like your mother.'

'What do you mean?'

'Never mind. Are you going to tell me how you got on with Jane and Richard?'

'Nothing much to say really. It looks like they're going to employ me as well. They want me back later to sign a confidentiality agreement.'

'A confidentiality agreement? Whatever for?'

'Standard practice.'

'Does that mean you'll be getting paid twice for doing the same job?'

'It might. But I don't know for certain if that's what they want me to do...find John I mean.'

'What else could it be?'

'I don't know. But I don't think big companies normally get a private investigator in to look for an employee who's only been missing a couple of days. Not unless there's something else going on'

Ruth drained her cup and put it down. 'Well let me know what they say.' She stood up to leave.

'I won't be able to, replied Nick, also standing.

Ruth looked puzzled.

'Client confidentiality,' he said smiling, before adding. 'I'll speak to you later. I need to go for another "Nelson". That coffee's gone straight through me.'

Ruth left the coffee shop feeling that Nick had acquitted himself quite well so far as an investigator, but she still felt dissatisfied.

'Ah well, that's not the first time he's left me feeling dissatisfied,' she reflected as she set off home for the remainder of her day's compassionate leave.

CHAPTER FIVE

Back at his flat Nick checked his watch; he had a couple of hours before he had to go back to RWS to meet Jane Edwards. That was enough time to make a little headway looking through the files he'd taken from John's house.

Regional Water Services PLC, (wholly owned by an American environmental conglomerate with ambitions of running all of the UK's water companies), was the local regional water company providing drinking water and disposing of sewage for over five million customers. This entailed operating and maintaining in excess of two hundred Water Treatment Works, (WTW), and over six hundred Wastewater (sewage) Treatment Works, (WwTW), as well as over thirty thousand kilometres of both water distribution pipes and sewers. This network of treatment facilities, pipelines and sewers had to be maintained and improved constantly to meet the existing and increasingly stringent regulations governing water supply and wastewater disposal standards. This meant spending hundreds of millions of pounds every year on major maintenance programmes, and on the installation of brand new treatment equipment, distribution pipe work and sewers. This was known as the 'Capital Investment Programme'. The actual money spent was 'Capital Expenditure' or 'CAPEX'.

This was where Nick started. He opened the first file labelled 'Capital Projects', and the first one he came across was the Company's flagship project, 'The Sludge Treatment and Combined Cycle Power Generation Plant.' He read through the brief but impressive description. Wastewater sludge, it explained, was a by-product of the sewage treatment process. The Company currently had three methods of disposal of this odorous by-product; application to agricultural land as a fertilizer, incineration (using old technology) and landfill - the most expensive option. This new project would use a combination of 'cutting edge' technologies; drying, gasification, and heat recovery via gas and steam turbines to provide a 'highly efficient and elegant solution to maximise the beneficial use of an otherwise unpleasant waste product'.

The budget for the total project was a hundred and fifty million pounds. The figure was underlined in red ink. *'Impressive project with an impressive budget,'* thought Nick. He knew the project had run into some problems. All major projects did. He also knew that despite the problems the plant was now fully operational. Why had the budget figure been underlined? (Presumably by John.)

He turned to the next project in the file. This was entitled 'Regional Monitoring and Control Project'. Again he read the impressive description, which described a total upgrading of the Monitoring and Control, (M&C) system that was used to monitor, and sometimes remotely control, the equipment on the Company's two thousand or so water and wastewater treatment works and pumping stations. The project would increase the system availability and reliability, (*'whatever the difference between those is,'* thought Nick) enable faster response times to any alarm conditions and greatly increase the amount of automatic and remote control possible.

The project description explained reviews by the Drinking Water Inspectorate, (DWI), of the Company's operational incidents, (resulting in disruptions to the water supply), had identified the monitoring of, and response to alarms, as a weakness. The proposed improvements to the M&C system would greatly improve the response to alarms and hence the service to customers. It was all way over his head, but whatever it was, there'd been thirty million pounds, (underlined in red ink again), allocated to the project. Written alongside, also in red ink was, 'In 2 AMP submissions and still not started.'

Looking further through the file he found three projects all to do with sludge storage on what seemed to him, a vast scale: 'Operational Sludge Storage Facilities', 'Emergency Sludge Storage Tanks' and 'Strategic Sludge Storage – a Regional Solution'. The projects were all very similar in size and description, comprising of a number of large tanks with reception and exporting facilities. The proposed locations for the projects were vague but the budget for each was in the order of forty million, (underlined in red), pounds.

He found a description of proposed improvements to a large water treatment facility, in fact the largest in the Company. This was based on membrane technology which was apparently also the latest cutting edge technology and would provide drinking water to the highest possible standards to almost one million customers. It would be the largest plant of its kind in the world. There was seventy million pounds budgeted, and that was just for an additional stage of treatment at the site. A scrawled note said, 'Installed – never worked!'

The technical detail in the descriptions was giving Nick a headache and he scanned the remaining files in the box less thoroughly. He noticed more projects with the budgets underlined in red, but no more of the size of the first three.

It was time to go and meet Jane, hopefully his soon to be new client. He put the files back in the box and put the box back in his bedroom. As he reached the door he tutted, turned round and went to the bathroom muttering, 'Bloody coffee.'

As Nick drove back through the site gates at RWS, his increasingly frequent toilet visits intruded on his thoughts.

During one of his few previous cases, whilst he was on what they call a 'stake out' on the television, (he thought of it more like 'stalking'), he'd missed the object of his surveillance leaving a building with her lover because he'd had to go for a 'comfort break'. It was starting to be a problem. *'Should I go to the doctor's?'* he wondered, *'or just try drinking less coffee for a while?'* He decided to drink less coffee, and with that problem solved he parked up and made his way to Jane's office.

He was shown in at four o'clock precisely. The office was light and airy, with a large window overlooking a landscaped area laced with footpaths to enable the staff to get out for some fresh air at lunchtime - and come back refreshed, ready to give their all for their loving employer. Modern oak, (or was it beech?) furniture was supplemented by a comfortable looking dark brown sofa against the wall, with a coffee table positioned in front it. It was exactly as Nick remembered it. *'Why wouldn't it be?'* he thought. *'I was only here five hours ago!'*

Jane's greeting snapped him out of his aimless thoughts.

'Hello, thanks for coming.' She had stood to shake his hand and now sat down behind her large desk with her back to the large window.

'No problem,' replied Nick, sitting down in front of the desk. The window behind Jane faced south and Nick couldn't help thinking that earlier in the day he would have been quite dazzled if the sun had been shining in. He couldn't help wondering if Jane had placed her desk in front of the window for that very reason – to make her visitors feel a little uncomfortable.

'Would you like a coffee?'

Nick paused for only a moment before answering, 'No thanks, I've just put one out.'

Jane acknowledged his pathetic attempt at humour with a pathetic attempt at a smile. 'Right. Well here's the confidentiality agreement. If you'd just like to sign that then we can get down to business.'

Nick dragged it across the desk and scanned it. He hadn't put his glasses on and the print was a little small so he couldn't read it but he pretended anyway. After what he thought was a suitable time to spend reviewing such a document, he said, 'It all looks pretty standard to me,' and he reached across the desk, picked up a pen, and signed the document before pushing it back across to Jane.

Jane held her hand out for the pen, which she took and signed the document herself.

'Nice pen,' said Nick. 'Is it real gold?'

'Only ten carat,' replied Jane, as though everybody had one.

She put the confidentiality agreement away in a drawer.

'Will Richard be joining us?' asked Nick.

'We don't need him for this. He's fully up to speed with what I'm going to say to you.'

'Fair enough,' said Nick.

'You are obviously aware that John Anderson has been missing from work, and, it seems, his home for the last few days. As you said earlier that would ordinarily not be something a company of the size of RWS would react to by bringing in a Private Investigator. But, to be honest...' she paused and looked at Nick who simply raised both of his eyebrows but only because he couldn't raise only one. 'It's not as simple as that,' she went on. 'Maxine Hudson has also gone missing.'

This was news to Nick.

'The new HR director? When?' he asked.

'She's not been seen since last Thursday.'

'And you think the two may be related?'

'It's possible. A hell of a coincidence if they're not.'

It was customary in this sort of situation, thought Nick, to say something along the lines of, 'I don't believe in coincidences.' But he believed that when you analysed any series of events they were inevitably the result of a number of coincidences.

Instead he replied, 'Do you have anything to go on?'

'To be ...' she began, but hesitated and then went on. 'Look I want to be open and honest with you Nick,' that phrase, particularly with the use of his name made her sound even more insincere to Nick, but he said nothing.

'Since Martin's death, you know about that don't you? Absolute tragedy.'

'Yes, I heard. Fell from a great height on a site in the Middle East, on one of your international projects – dodgy scaffolding wasn't it?'

'Yes, unfortunately Health and Safety doesn't have quite the same priority over there. I know people complain about it over here but I'm a great believer in our Health and Safety regulations. As you know it's one of our KPM's'

Nick had the impression that Jane had lost the plot for a moment, and gone on to auto pilot, introducing the Company's Key Performance Measures into the conversation. She was probably upset at mentioning the death of one of her friends - the then Finance & Procurement Director, Martin Worsley.

Jane hesitated again, realising that she was off the subject, 'Anyway,' she continued, 'yes, it was down to shoddy workmanship, the scaffolding gave way and Martin fell a hundred feet from the top of a storage tank. Richard was out there with him. You know the sort of thing - meeting the clients, showing our people out there that we appreciated their efforts, that we hadn't forgotten them. Richard took it very badly of course. He'd known Martin as long as I had. We all started at the same time as graduates, about twenty years ago.'

Nick watched Jane's face while she spoke. She was genuinely upset. Her eyes filled with tears. She had lost a friend.

'When Richard returned, we had to make a decision. Did we replace Martin straight away or did we wait a while? Neither of us could face the prospect of trying to find a replacement for Martin so soon. We'd have been comparing applicants with Martin, not just as a Finance Director but also as a friend. So Richard offered to take on the Finance & Procurement role alongside his role as director of Risk and Audit. We had to give that serious thought because as you may remember, (I think it happened in your time with the Company), we had to split the two roles following an external audit on our procedures. But it's only temporary. We are about to advertise for another Finance & Procurement Director.'

'Can we go back a bit?' asked Nick.

'Certainly.'

'You mentioned that the Finance and Audit Directorates were split following an external audit of procedures. There was more to it than that wasn't there?'

'I'm surprised you don't know the whole story already. I'm sure it must have been all round the Company. We only just managed to keep it out of the Press.'

'I was never sure what was true and what was just wild rumour.'

'No, I suppose it must have seemed pretty unbelievable at the time, if you weren't involved.'

'Go on.'

'Well whatever you heard was probably no more bizarre than the truth. You remember Mike Shaw?'

'Yes, didn't he commit suicide? I heard that his wife had left him and he couldn't take it.'

'That's part of it. He did commit suicide; took an overdose washed down by a bottle of Scotch, and his wife

47

had left him. But she'd left him because he told her that he'd been caught embezzling money from the Company. So he was going to go to prison *and* his wife had left him. That's why he killed himself. In a way he did the Company a favour, since we didn't have to take him to court. But it was a tragic waste. Anyway, the external auditors believed that the combination of audit and finance in the same directorate could lead to a conflict of interest and so they recommended that Audit should be a standalone directorate. We managed to convince all of the relevant regulators that we'd put our house in order and that there was no benefit in going public with it all - with the resulting potential catastrophic effect on the share price and then on our capital investment programme. However, they made it quite clear that they would not stand for any sort of repeat occurrence. And that, before you ask, is why we can't go to the Police'

'So what are you saying? Are you suggesting that John and Maxine were doing something similar? John's not in Finance. He's in Audit. And Maxine's in HR. I don't see how...'

'Neither do I really. It may be that John has unearthed what Mike Shaw was doing, and they were somehow doing the same thing. It may be that they simply unearthed what happened and are planning to sell the story to the highest bidder.'

'Blimey, that's some story. And I thought it was easy being an MD - getting everyone else to do the work. So you want me to find John *and* Maxine?'

'Yes, although I also want to know what, if anything, they were up to. And that may be an easier place to begin. In fact, that *is* where I want you to begin. With Richard concentrating on Finance, John had a free rein more or less. I suppose our "Employee Empowerment" Course must have worked for him. We know he was spending time in a lot of different departments, including Finance.'

'I know. That's where he met Ruth.'

'Of course, I'm sorry,' said Jane, apparently sincerely sorry to be opening up old wounds.

'It's OK Ruth and I had already split up by then, although I was still working here.'

'That must have been quite hard,' said Jane.

Nick appreciated her concern. She really seemed to care about people. He was very pleasantly surprised. Perhaps he'd misjudged her.

'It wasn't too bad. Nobody had the insensitivity to gossip about her in front of me. I just acted as if I didn't care, which I didn't. Not much anyway. So where exactly do you want me to start?'

'With finding out what John had been working on. That will confirm, or not, if he and Maxine are up to anything and may give a clue as to what he's going to do and possibly even where he is.'

'What if they're ready to go public with the story about Mike Shaw?'

'We'll just have to risk that and try to pass it off as water under the bridge. Hopefully we'll get the Regulators' support, although I wouldn't bank on it.'

'So how do I get access to what John was working on?' Nick had decided not to tell Jane about the files he'd found. He'd work on those more tonight. It would give him a flying start. And it would be an opportunity to impress, if he could come up with some quick answers.

'You can start here tomorrow. We'll bring you in as temporary agency staff filling in for John. We'll say he's had to take compassionate leave to go and look after his mother. Can you have a word with Ruth and get her to back us up?'

Nick nodded, 'Sure.'

'We'll say that you're taking on John's work for the time being but that he's not left any notes so you're having to go over all his recent work again.'

'OK, sounds good to me. There's just one more thing...'

'I presume you mean payment?'

'Yes. Sorry to...'

'Not at all. We're employing you. I understand that in your line of work you have to budget for not working fifty-two weeks year. What do you work on? Seventy-five percent of that?'

'*In my dreams!*' thought Nick as he replied, 'Yes, about that.'

'OK, well how about five hundred pounds-a-day?'

'Five hundred pounds-a-day?'

'Plus expenses of course. Although we'll have to be pretty strict on receipts. Especially bearing in mind what you're going to be investigating. Tell you what we'll make it six hundred, plus expenses. Is that OK?'

Nick suppressed his choking reflex and said in as matter-a-fact way as he could, 'Yes, that'll be fine.'

'One more thing,' said Jane. 'I want you to report to me on this, and only me. I know you're working for Ruth looking for John and that's fine. But if you find anything out about his whereabouts, you tell me. OK?'

'Of course.' Six hundred pounds-a-day outranked two hundred pounds-a-day, especially when he wasn't at all sure he'd ever *see* the two hundred pounds-a-day.

'And I mean that you report only to me – not to Richard. He knows what you'll be doing, but you report to me. If he asks, just tell him that we've agreed one point of contact would be best.'

Nick frowned. 'Are you saying that you suspect Richard?'

'I'm not saying anything of the sort. Richard has been a friend and colleague for over twenty years, but technically he's in charge of John, *and* he's Acting Finance & Procurement Director, so whatever's going on, if he's not involved, (and I'm sure he isn't) then we must ask why he doesn't *know* what's going on.'

She paused for a moment, as if saying out loud that her friend may be involved, or at least at fault in some way, had just brought it home to her for the first time.

'Come on,' she said pulling herself back together. 'I'll walk you out. If people see me with you it should give you at least *some* credibility when you start poking around.'

As they walked through the office she said, 'Thanks by the way.'

'What for?' said Nick.

'Pointing out that I say "To be honest with you" a lot. It's something I've slipped into. You're right. If you tell the truth all the time, you don't need to say it.'

'No problem. I hope I didn't seem too rude. I'm afraid I have a bit of a thing about grammar and people being precise in their speech: not using unnecessary words. I don't know why. It's not as though I'm an expert.'

'Well I'll try and remember in future.'

'Try *to* remember. Not "try *and*"' said Nick smiling

'Don't push it. See you tomorrow at nine?' said Jane smiling broadly as they shook hands at the main door. Nick nodded agreement to the meeting time and walked off re-evaluating his opinion of RWS's Managing Director. She may be a driven business woman, and she may wear just a little too much make-up for his taste, (but she was in her late forties and probably had things to cover up), but she did seem honestly concerned and upset by what had happened to her friends and what could happen to the Company. He was prepared to forgive her 'open and honest' speech.

However, he couldn't see how looking through the work that John had been doing would help find him; but if that's what Jane wanted him to do, that's what he'd do.

After all, as he'd considered earlier, 'six hundred pounds-a-day out ranks two hundred pounds-a-day.'

Nick drove home in a good mood. Jane's suspicions had given him a reason for John's disappearance; something which he'd been short of up until now. And he'd got John's files to work on so he could be able to start reporting back to Jane on progress relatively quickly. If he impressed Jane it could lead to more work. He knew they had some petty crime occasionally in the offices at RWS, which they preferred to deal with 'in-house'. And he also knew that the security manager was ill-equipped to deal with it and didn't like investigating. Perhaps he had a chance to establish his business.

Things were looking up.

It could only go downhill from here.

CHAPTER SIX

Nick's good mood continued when he arrived home and he decided to treat himself to his 'signature dish', so he put a steak pie and some frozen chips in the oven and took a can of cheap lager out of the fridge. Then he settled down to look through more of John's files. The box he opened this time was labelled 'AMP SUBMISSIONS' and consisted of extracts taken from the Asset Management Plan, (hence the 'AMP') submissions to the Regulator, which are made every five years. These submissions detail the work each water company proposes to carry out during the next five year period, together with budget costs. It is the total of these costs for capital projects and operating costs, together with an allowance for a reasonable profit that the Water Industry Regulator, (OFWAT) uses to determine how much money the water companies need to run their businesses. This in turn determines how much customers have to pay for the drinking water coming out of their taps and the treatment and disposal of the sewage being taken away from their property. Since each water company holds a monopoly in its own region, it is essential there is an independent body – OFWAT - to control the amount of money a company can charge for its services.

Nick found that the descriptions he'd seen in the first box were all repeated in this box, but each file included a justification for the project. This was inevitably a statutory requirement imposed by the Environment Agency or the EU for higher standards of sewage treatment to protect the environment (the river or the sea into which the treatment works discharged their effluent), or a requirement for even higher drinking water quality imposed by new EU regulations.

Each excerpt from the business plan also included a spend profile showing when the budget would be spent over the next five year period. This was important as it helped the regulator determine how much the bills should go up by for each year. There was a folder for each of three consecutive AMP periods in the box. He found that the titles of some projects in the second and third folders were underlined with the words 'previous AMP?' written alongside. This caused Nick to look back into the first folder. He found that some of the projects seemed to appear in more than one AMP submission. At first glance it seemed that RWS had asked for money for the same projects more than once. Was that because the project had not been completed? Or not done at all? And if so, where had that money gone? Was it right that RWS should effectively get paid more than once for the same project? That was something he could start looking at when he started working in the office.

BTO interrupted his thoughts and he reached for his phone. His neck had stiffened through sitting in one position for so long and he rotated his head to ease it. He hadn't realised that AMP submissions could be so engrossing – not while he worked for RWS anyway.

It was Ruth – a little later than he'd expected.

'How did you get on?' she asked immediately.

'I'm fine thanks,' replied Nick. 'How are you Ruth?'

'Never mind all that. What happened when you met Jane and Richard?'

'Richard wasn't there. Only Jane.'

'Really?' said Ruth sounding a little surprised. 'So what did she want? I presume she has asked you to find John as well.'

'As well as what?'

54

'You damned well know what I mean! As well as me!'

'She might have. I'm not sure I can really divulge...'

'Don't give me any of that "client confidentiality" crap,' said Ruth in an exasperated tone. 'Did she ask you to find John or not?'

'That's part of it,' he admitted.

'Why? What else has she asked you to do?'

'That, I'm afraid, I really can't tell you.'

'*And when I say "afraid",*' he thought. '*I mean "glad".*'

'Oh for goodness sake Nick!'

'No, really,' said Nick. 'I had to sign a confidentiality agreement, remember?'

'All right. I suppose so. But she asked you to find John?'

'Yes.'

'So you can't be expecting me to pay you now. You can't expect to get paid twice for doing one job.'

'I thought that's what you'd say. To be honest, Ruth, ('*Now I'm at it,*'), I would have thought you'd be too worried about finding John to be worried about the possibly of me getting paid by two different people for doing the same job.'

'I am, of course. It's just that I'm not made of money, and with John away...'

'Yeah, yeah,' said Nick without an ounce of sympathy. 'Like I said, Jane is paying me to do other things as well, so not everything she's paying me is for looking for John. And if you want me to report back to you about John, then you really have to pay. Otherwise you'll be relying on hearsay.'

'How can you be like this Nick? We were married for God's sake. For fifteen years.'

'*Don't remind me,*' thought Nick, but he said, 'I'm not made of money either Ruth, in fact I'm made of a lot less than you. So if you want me to carry on working for you and reporting to you, then you'll have to carry on paying.' Obviously, he mentioned nothing about who he would be reporting to first.

'Oh all right then. But I still think you're being unreasonable,' said Ruth.

'Didn't you always?' replied Nick. 'How did you get on with John's mother?'

'His mother?'

'Yes, did you ring her? Has she heard from him?' Nick couldn't help but notice Ruth sounded distracted, perhaps she really couldn't afford to pay him. He'd think about that later – when *Jane* had paid him. Perhaps then he could be generous.

'Oh... no she hasn't. She hasn't a clue where he is. I told her we'd had a big row and that he'd stormed out. She told me not to worry. Said he always used to do that when he didn't get his own way. Said he'd be back.'

'Well, it was worth a shot. I start work, back at RWS tomorrow by the way.'

'You do what?'

'I start work back at...'

'I heard you! What on earth for?'

'Jane suggested it. She thinks it'll help put some background together. From your point of view, I suppose if I can look into what John was working on and ask around, I might find that John mentioned something to someone in passing, accidentally if you like, about his plans.' Nick didn't sound too convincing, even to himself.

'You mean you think he was planning to leave me!'

'Let's not get into all that again, Ruth. It's somewhere to start that's all. Oh, and by the way, the story is that John has taken compassionate leave to look after his sick mother. And he could be gone for some time, so I've been brought in on a temporary basis to pick up his work load.'

'What are you supposed to know about what John did? I mean does,' said Ruth, suddenly realising that she'd spoken about John in the past tense.

'What does *anyone* know about what they do in "Audit"?' replied Nick. 'You can say that I'd fallen on hard times - that my business was failing, (*'Not far off –in fact spot on,'*), and that you've pulled a few strings to get me the job.

'I suppose so. What time are you starting?'

'I report to Jane at nine.'

'Right, I'll see you after that then.'

Ruth ended the call.

Nick went back to the box on the AMP submissions. He found a file dedicated to the methodology adopted for gathering information on the maintenance and operating cost requirements of the sites. Armed with a detailed questionnaire, teams of experts had visited a large number of sites, representative of the different types of treatment works across the company. The file referred to a huge, detailed report providing schedules of work and costs for operating and maintaining the sites. Someone had written on the inside of the folder, 'why wasn't this used?'

Nick's neck was hurting again so he decided he'd had enough for the evening and put the box to one side and stood up. Both knees went 'crack' as he straightened his legs and he grimaced at the sound although there was no pain. He put his hand on the back of his neck and rubbed it as he moved his head around slowly, then he tried to ease his aching back by leaning back as far as he could against his hands and rotating his hips slowly.

'Cracking joints, aching muscles, weeing every five minutes, and arms too short for me to be able to read without glasses. Who says I'm getting old?' he thought to himself. And with that he withdrew to the Royal Oak for a couple of pints of bitter and a game of dominoes.

'Now there's a young man's sport.'

CHAPTER SEVEN

Nick was shown into Jane's office at precisely nine o'clock the following morning. *'Bang on time again. She does run a tight ship.'*

They shook hands again, 'You're wearing a suit and tie today, I see.' She smiled as they sat down; she behind her desk and he in front of it, squinting slightly against the sun shining in behind her. He'd been right about that.

'Old school. I've always worn a suit and tie to work. I never went for the smart casual, open necked shirt look. I think wearing a tie looks more professional.'

'Appearances can be deceptive.'

'That's what I'm hoping.'

Jane gave him a look.

'I want everyone to accept me as my old self, so I'll dress as I always did. I don't want them thinking I've changed. That could put them on their guard. If I'm going to be chatting to people, digging into what John was working on, they have to believe that I'm doing it because it's my new job and for the reasons that I give them. They have to believe that I'm still the same old Nick Howard.'

'And what was the old Nick Howard like?'

'Like most of your employees – the older ones anyway. Came in and did his job. Didn't get involved in office politics. A little world or office weary. Didn't get excited about any of the "new" initiatives that were meant to change things. He'd seen them all before. Never saw one that made a lasting difference. Some might even say he was a bit of a cynical bastard.'

And the "new" Nick Howard?'

'Same as the old one.'

'And you believe most of our employees feel the same?'

'Definitely. That's why I get on with so many of them. Like minds.'

'But we've spent thousands on initiatives to empower people. Getting them to feel more involved, more valued.'

'Yeah, but it's all bollocks really isn't it?

'Is it?'

'Of course: the vast majority of your staff want to come to work, do their job and go home again. They want a decent salary, and if they come up with a good idea then they want someone to listen and do something with it. They don't need go on courses for self development or have initiatives to change their culture so that they know how to behave as decent human beings. If they don't know how to behave properly, no RWS course is going to teach them.'

'Hmmm. I'd like you to report back to me every evening on how you're getting on with your investigation *and* I'd like to talk more about your opinions on our employee initiatives if you don't mind.'

'You may be sorry. Once I get started...'

'We'll see. I've had a word with IT and you should be able to log on to our network by lunchtime. If you can't, let me know and I'll bite someone's head off. You'll be sitting at John's desk. So you'll have access to his files.'

'Can you get me access to John's IT account as well? And Maxine's come to think of it?'

'Maxine's?'

'If you think they might have both been involved in something then there could be something there as well.'

'I'll see what I can do. Shall we meet back here, at say five this evening?'

Nick looked doubtful.

'What's wrong? Have you got a heavy date? We *are* paying you well.'

'It's not that,' replied Nick. 'When I worked here before, I arrived before eight and left at about four. I was intending to keep that routine – same old Nick Howard.'

'I see,' replied Jane. 'But then you weren't an agency employee, being paid by the hour. Now you are, and you need to earn every penny you can before John comes back.'

'That's true. Anyone would think you were well practiced in deceiving your employees,' said Nick. Adding, 'Joke!' as Jane looked genuinely hurt at what he'd implied.

'See you at five then,' he said and went off to restart his career, albeit temporarily, at RWS.

Nick found John's desk easily - it hadn't moved since Nick had worked there. It was one of many in a large open plan office. John was privileged – he had a corner seat, which meant he had both a view out of the window and his back to the wall so no one could catch him unawares. Nick draped his jacket over the back of his swivel chair. He knew that at least three times that day he would push the chair back and catch his jacket under the wheels, but there was no coat stand. Blue fabric-covered partitions to the front and side of the desk were of such a height that if Nick sat up he'd be able to see over them, but if he got down to work he wouldn't be bothered by background office noise or movement. Behind the chair was a grey metal filing cupboard about three feet wide and three feet high. Taped to the doors of the cupboard were two A4 pieces of paper. One said, 'I HAVE NO PROBLEMS: ONLY CHALLENGES'. The other said, 'DO IT. DO IT RIGHT. DO IT RIGHT NOW.' He tore both of them down and dropped them where they belonged - into the bin at the side of his desk.

However pleased Nick might have been with the desk setting, he soon found it difficult to get anything done as word spread and all his old colleagues came to find out if it were true. *Nick Howard was back*. He was fielding questions rather than asking them all morning.

Why was he back? Wasn't he a 'Private Detective now? What happened to that? Did he solve any big cases? Did he *have* any big cases? What was he doing at John Anderson's desk? Where was John? Had John left Ruth? Were he and Ruth back together? (The last two were from women.)

He turned down numerous offers of a cup of coffee in the company's restaurant, promising to catch up with them later. He did, however, arrange to meet Ruth there. He decided it would be better to demonstrate to everyone that he and Ruth were definitely not back together. If anyone started to resent his questioning then they might go to Ruth to moan if they believed that he and Ruth were definitely not at all close. That could give her the opportunity to find out what they were feeling so sensitive about.

As he sat waiting for Ruth, with a cappuccino for each of them in front of him on the coffee-ring stained easy clean table, Nick looked around the restaurant. It hadn't changed. It was clean and bright, (apart from his table), but there were still too many tables for the space provided, meaning that the sitting customers were often in danger of wearing someone else's coffee as they squeezed between the chairs trying to carry two coffees with a file of some description tucked under their arm. The people hadn't changed either, it seemed. He could have sworn the people there now, had been sitting there when he left the building all those months ago. He knew about half of them to talk to and recognised most of the rest of them by sight. There was only one other man wearing a tie, and that was a stupid 'Mickey Mouse' one.

At some of the tables small groups sat discussing the files they had in front of them, whilst sipping at their skinny lattes or coffee Americanos that were too hot to drink. Most of the people there, however, were having a break, either chatting in small groups or sitting alone reading a newspaper. A break paid for by the Company. He also knew that most of them would have spent a good half an hour or more having breakfast after they'd arrived at work. Again in time paid for by the Company. They'd also be back for an afternoon snack. The Company seemed to encourage it. After all they provided the newspapers.

He supposed that HR would say that it was good for 'morale'. He could never understand it. He was old enough to think that you got paid for a full day's work. But he knew that if he challenged them they would say that they 'put the hours in'. That they never left at five o'clock. It was always much later, often after six. But he also knew that they did very little work during that time. They were only engaging in the current fad for 'presenteeism' - it was good for the career to be seen to be 'working late'. Nick had always preferred to arrive early and leave when he'd done his contracted time. Theoretically his contract didn't have set hours – he was to do the hours required to do the job. But he'd found that things were rarely so urgent that they couldn't wait until the next day. On the relatively few occasions when things were so urgent that they had to be finished before he left then he would work until they were finished. But in reality that didn't happen that often to him. He knew it didn't happen to most people, but they were committed to 'presenteeism'.

Nick had left on time because he'd preferred being at home to being in the office. Even when things had not been so good at home, he'd still preferred being there. Perhaps it was a habit or a routine he'd established early on in his marriage when he'd looked forward to going home. Over the years though he'd found that whenever he drove home in a good mood, really looking forward to seeing Ruth, she'd always been in a foul mood for some reason when he'd arrived. Eventually he'd stopped looking forward so enthusiastically to the welcome he'd get from Ruth but still he'd gone home on time. It was important to establish your 'work/life balance'; they'd preached that on some course or other – the product of yet another initiative. Well he'd done that already, and his emphasis was on the 'life' side of the scales.

It occurred to Nick as he continued to wait for Ruth, who was now a couple of minutes late, that since taking on the case, (or cases), he seemed to have become more reflective. Presumably that was because the two major influences in his life, (prior to nine months ago), Ruth and RWS had returned as large as ever. Was that such a bad thing? Neither had been anything to shout about from the rooftops the first time around. But then neither of them had been a total unmitigated disaster either. Nothing to hide away in the dark recesses of his mind lest they turn him into some vengeful serial killer.

Did he regret marrying Ruth? He could hardly claim that his marriage had been an unqualified success. After all they had divorced and they'd been unable to have children; so they couldn't say that at least they had the children to show for their fifteen years together. If he were so inclined, he could say that he had wasted fifteen years of his life married to Ruth. The passion had disappeared very early on and inertia had taken over until, as Carole King had sung, it was 'too late baby'. What would the RWS coaches say? (The product of yet another initiative.) Actually it was more a case of, 'What would they get him to say?' They couldn't tell you the answers to your problems - only help you find them. First of all, they'd get you to realise that there's no use wasting time on regrets. You are where you are. The past is history. Don't look back, look forward. If you do find yourself looking back, then look on your mistakes as 'learning experiences' to help you on your way *forward!*

You're free now. Life is full of opportunities. Take them all now! Do something for yourself. Take a risk. Go for it!

Come to think of it, Ruth had said much the same thing to him in their last blazing row. Something along the lines of, 'For God's sake do something with your life! Stop drifting in a job you hate. You can't use having to pay the mortgage, (*because she took the house*), or providing for me as an excuse any longer. Take control of your life and do something positive! Do something for yourself! Show some bloody balls for once!'

So he had. When the opportunity had arisen to be awarded the prestigious DCM, (Don't Come Monday) award, with its generous pay off, he had 'carpe-ed' the 'diem' and set up his own detective agency. That was definitely doing something for himself. He'd never thought he could do it. Never thought he could make any money at it. (He'd got that right.) But it was something he'd wanted to do since he was very young; since he'd watched those old black and white films on the television with Sam Spade and Philip Marlowe in them. And then when he saw his very first 'Thin Man' film with William Powell as Nick Charles that clinched it. His own name had been 'Nick Charles', in fact it still was; 'Nick Charles Howard'. It was fate. It had to be. Except that it wasn't fate. And it didn't have to be. 'You can't do that!' he was told by people who knew better. So he didn't. He took the much easier, much safer way forward. Went to university, got a steady job, got married. And now look at him. They'd been right; those people who had known better. He'd tried to be a detective and failed. He'd been shutting the business down on Saturday. This case was only postponing the inevitable. Then he wouldn't even have a steady job. He began to wonder why he hadn't been beguiled by any of the British detectives he'd seen on television when he was growing up. But who had they been? Sherlock Holmes, Miss Marple, Father Brown and a few police detectives. No contest. Holmes was far too clever to be *his* role model. And an old lady and a priest? *'Do me a favour!'*

A condescending voice interrupted his thoughts. Richard Seaton was looking down at him over the partition, 'Shouldn't you be doing something? You're being paid to get results, not drink coffee.'

'I'm waiting for someone.'

'Of course you are,' said Richard as though he knew it wasn't true, before turning away muttering, 'waste of bloody space.'

'How's it going?' asked Ruth, suddenly appearing at Nick's side.

'Oh, hi. I was just thinking about you.'

'Nothing too disparaging, I hope.' She sat down opposite him.

Nick thought for a moment before answering. It had been himself he had been criticising, not Ruth. 'No you didn't come out of it too badly - surprisingly enough.'

Ruth almost blushed. Was Nick being nice to her? He realised how his comment may have been interpreted and went on quickly. 'Actually I've not done anything yet. I've spent the whole morning fending off questions about why I'm here, rather than asking any myself.'

'So have I. Seems like half of them think we must be back together.'

'You're right there. I think we should do something about that,' said Nick and he explained why.

'So what are we supposed to argue about?' asked Ruth

'You never used to have a problem finding something to argue about,' replied Nick with half a smile. They were already on their way.

'What do you mean?' replied Ruth, also realising that they were about to put on a show.

'You were always finding fault. You said I sneezed too loudly, coughed too loudly. You said I talked too loudly. You even said I breathed too loudly! *And* you said I never did anything around the house, which was just not true.'

'Yes it was; you did sod all. Until I had a go at you. We had to have a blazing row before I could get you to do anything!'

'Which you always started.'

'I did not!' said Ruth raising her voice very slightly.

'Yes you did! You'd say "Can't you see the house is filthy?" And that was it. If I said "no", you'd call me a dirty slob, and if I said, "yes", you'd call me a *lazy* slob for not doing anything about it. And the house was never filthy! You were obsessed with cleaning. The place was always like a ruddy show home!'

'No it wasn't. It was no cleaner than anyone else's. OK, it was. It was cleaner than your mother's, but hers was too big a job for "How Clean is Your House?"' referring to a reality T.V. programme whose presenters cleaned up disgustingly dirty houses.

'Don't you bring my mother into this!' shouted Nick. 'Our problems had nothing to do with her!'

'No! They were all to do with you!'

'Me?'

'Yes you!'

'What did I do?'

'Nothing. That's the point. You just stopped doing anything!'

'Sorry you've lost me,' said Nick, and he meant it.'

'You stopped trying; stopped putting *anything* into our marriage into our relationship; you stopped caring.'

'No I didn't.'

'Yes you did. You stopped buying me flowers!'

'Well, when did you ever buy me any?'

Ruth sighed noisily, 'There you go again. You have to make a joke of everything. I could never have a serious conversation with you.'

'We seem to be having one now!'

Ruth ignored him, 'Repeating the same jokes over and over again.'

'Now, what are you talking about?'

'Oh, let's see: offering to share the driving every time we went out – you'd drive there if I drove back. So you could have a drink. Amusing once maybe, but not every time we went out for ten years. Saying it couldn't be time to get up because it was still dark every morning, because the curtains were closed.'

'*Ouch!*' thought Nick. He remembered using that one again on Ruth just the other day.

'And if I said something was "neither here nor there" you'd say, "Where is it then?".'

Nick smiled. He did like that one.

Ruth seized on it! 'See!' she shouted. 'You still think it's funny! After God knows how many years you still think that's funny. Even now, I bet if I said I wasn't feeling myself, you'd ask me who I *was* feeling.'

Nick smiled again, yes he would.

'When were you last abroad?' asked Ruth.

'I've never been a broad. I've always been a feller!' Nick shouted back. This was great. It was like being in Morecambe and Wise tribute act. Then someone at a neighbouring table coughed. Nick turned and shouted, 'Arsenal!'

'See! I was right! There's no point talking to you, you balding, big-nosed, pot bellied, lanky, middle aged, cretinous moron!' She was standing now, leaning over the table at him, so Nick stood as well.

67

'How dare you? Middle aged? I'll have you know I'm in my prime!' he complained. Adding as she stormed off, 'And I still think you're confusing me with the Osmonds!'

She raised two fingers at him without turning round. *'She's right. That's twice I've used that in the last couple of days.'*

He looked round the restaurant. *'That seems to have done the trick,'* he thought. Everyone was looking at him.

'I hope that you enjoyed the show!' he said bitterly, before leaving. *'Isn't that a line from "Sergeant Pepper's"?'* he thought. *'I hope it didn't spoil the effect.'*

CHAPTER EIGHT

Back at his desk, he sat down and thought about how their show had ended. He had to admit she'd sounded genuinely upset and angry. But surely she hadn't meant those things she'd shouted at him. *'Pot-bellied?'* No, he was not having that. His stomach poked out very slightly over his trouser belt, but only very slightly. And *'Balding'?* He thought not: receding yes, with a bit of distinguished greying of the temples. But definitely not balding. *'Big-nosed?'* W...e...ll. And *'lanky?'* Yes, he had to give her 'lanky'. *'Cretinous moron?'* Still mixing him up with the Osmonds. (How many times had he used that joke in the last two days – he'd have to admit to the crack about repeating the same old jokes as well.) His phone rang. It was Ruth. 'Are you all right?' she asked.

'Of course why wouldn't I be?'

'I wondered if I went a bit too far, that's all.'

'Don't worry about it,' said Nick. 'I didn't take any notice. I think it worked though. You should have seen everyone's faces when you stormed off.'

'So you're not upset?'

'Not at all. Like I said, I wasn't taking any notice.

'That's good, because...'

'Yes?'

'I meant every bloody word you, moron!' said Ruth through clenched teeth, before ending the call.

Nick shook his head. *Now what had he done wrong?*

He tried logging on to the RWS network and was surprised to find that he could. An MD who could get things done – there's a novelty. He deleted all the various

69

welcome emails without opening them and then sent an email to Jane. 'I'm on the system. Any joy with getting me access to John and Maxine's accounts?'

There was no immediate reply so he pushed his chair back and thought again about the show he and Ruth had put on for the masses. Had she really meant every word? Probably - *he* had. Although he hadn't shouted at her that he thought *she'd* stopped trying; stopped caring as well, he remembered being vaguely conscious of that same feeling at times during their marriage. Who stopped trying first? He'd thought it was her. Now he wasn't so sure. He hadn't even known she'd noticed. Sensitive soul wasn't he? Ah well, too late now.

He spent half the afternoon trying to gain access to the locked grey metal cupboard behind his chair. Eventually he found someone in 'admin' who presented him with a set of keys to unlock it. Every now and then his thoughts drifted back to his and Ruth's 'put on' argument. Perhaps it hadn't been as 'put on' as he'd expected. There'd obviously been a few home truths spoken.

He sent an email to Ruth: 'Sorry. Can we meet later?'

He received an immediate reply: 'Forget it. No.'

'*Sod you then,*' he thought and started examining the contents of the cupboards. There were the usual 'management speak' text books. Titles such as 'People are Your Company's Biggest Asset' and 'Make Your People Feel Like Winners' screamed out at him. He resisted the urge to bin them and took out some files. Several of them contained exactly the same information as the folders he'd found in John's loft. '*So he'd thought these were important enough to create copies to keep off site. Why was that?*'

A couple of his old colleagues, who'd missed out on the show in the restaurant but had heard about it, paid him visits to check he was OK and ask him out for a drink. Although he couldn't go out for a drink, ('another time

70

perhaps') he assured them he was fine. 'She was always flying off on one. I got used to it,' he'd explained and they'd said, 'You're well out of it mate.'

At four o'clock BTO kicked into action again. It was Ruth again. He wondered if it were her turn to say 'sorry'.

'I've got someone I think you should meet,' she said, without even a 'Hello'' he noticed.

'Who?'

'Someone who says she has some information about John. She said I probably wouldn't like what she had to tell me. I told her I wanted you there, so *she* probably thinks we're back together now. I don't think she's heard about our performance in the restaurant.'

'Where is she?'

'She's stood by my desk. I've moved away to talk to you.'

Nick valiantly fought down the urge to say, 'She's not "stood", she's "standing",' and instead said, 'Where can we meet?'

'All the meeting rooms are free. I've checked. The whole meeting room corridor is empty. So no one will see us. We'll see you in Room 3. Can you come straight away?'

'Give me two minutes. I'll see you in there,' he said. He put John's files back into the cupboards and locked them. His lap top had already timed out and was password protected.

In Meeting Room 3 Nick was surprised to find Ruth waiting with a woman dressed in a cleaner's navy blue tabard. Nick thought she was probably in her late thirties. He was sure she was attractive. Her blonde hair framed her face in a long bob, her soft blue eyes shone intelligently.

Ruth noticed his reaction. 'This is Sally,' she said. 'She's a cleaner,' as if using the fact to make her seem less attractive to Nick.

71

Nick leant across the table to shake Sally's hand. 'Hello. Pleased to meet you. Can I get you a coffee or anything?'

'She doesn't have time for that,' said Ruth before Sally could open her mouth.

Nick looked at her, with a 'jealous?' look on his face.

Ruth reacted immediately. 'Sally's already told me that she has to get straight to work. She hasn't got time to sit around drinking coffee. Have you?'

'Well, no,' said Sally, before smiling at Nick and adding, 'but thanks for asking.'

'Right. So what is it you want to tell me?'

Nick couldn't help thinking that Ruth was coming across as very confrontational. Did she know what to expect, or was she just nervous?

'Take your time Sally,' he said looking into her blue eyes.

'Well, I heard that you were back today, sitting in for John Anderson, and that he was supposed to away looking after his mother or something.'

'That's right. He is,' said Ruth, a little too firmly, thought Nick.

'Well, it's just that I'm not sure that that's true.'

'Why's that Sally?' asked Nick.

'Well, because of what I saw last Tuesday evening. I wasn't going to say anything, but then I heard that Mr Anderson had gone away and I didn't want to say anything that might upset Mrs Howard.' She looked at Ruth, took a breath and went on. 'But if you two are back together then I suppose you've no need to be upset.'

'We're not back together,' said Nick, a little too emphatically in Ruth's opinion. 'What did you see that might upset Mrs Howard?' he asked, noticing how Ruth's posture had tensed.

'Last Tuesday evening it was. I was running a bit late; it was about seven o'clock. I was in the directors' suite, cleaning. I always leave them until last, as they tend to work later than everyone else.'

'They get paid to,' said Nick.

'Anyway, I went into Ms Hudson's office. I know I should have knocked but I thought she'd already left and there was no light showing under the door so I just opened it. She was still there...with Mr Anderson and they were...well...you know...'

'They were what?' shouted Ruth. 'At it? Having sex on her desk?'

'Well, no they hadn't got that far but I'm sure they would have done if I hadn't interrupted them.'

'So what exactly did you see?' screamed Ruth. 'I thought you said there was no light on!'

'I said that there was no light showing under the door,' said Sally holding her composure determinedly under Ruth's rage. 'There was a desk lamp on. I could see well enough.'

'And what did you see?' asked Nick.

'As I said, if I hadn't interrupted them they would have been...' she paused and looked at Ruth, as if to say "your words", 'having sex. She was leaning back over her desk with her skirt up round her waist and her hands undoing his trousers. His hand was inside her blouse.'

'You lying, scheming, little bitch!' screamed Ruth. 'You're just after some money aren't you? That's it. You're hoping the Company will pay you to keep quiet about it. You think they wouldn't want the scandal of their HR Director caught shagging in her office don't you? Well it won't work lady, and I'll tell you why. Because they won't believe you. Because John's with me. He loves me. He's not interested in Maxine fucking Hudson. He can't stand the woman. He's told me. He thinks she's a stuck up cow, with no bloody idea how this company or any other works.'

'I think you'd better leave Ruth. Don't you?'

73

'You don't believe her do you Nick? She's lying. She thinks she can get some money out of the company.'

Nick said nothing.

'Oh I get it! You *want* to believe her don't you? You want John to be cheating on me. You don't want me to have anyone else! You want me to be on my own. Lonely... like you! With nobody who cares about me. Well I will go! I don't need to hear any more of this crap.' She stormed out, only failing to slam the door because of the strong spring controlling it.

'I must apologise for my ex-wife's outburst,' said Nick calmly. 'She was, is, at least far as she knows in a serious relationship with John Anderson. What you told us has obviously come as a great shock to her. I've not seen her shouting like that for a long time.' Then he looked at his watch. 'Well not for about five hours.'

'That's all right,' said Sally. 'Like you said it's a big shock finding out your partner's shagging someone else. And I should know. I'm glad you were here. She might have attacked me otherwise.'

'I suppose she might,' said Nick. Had there been a twinkle in her eyes when she'd used the word 'shagging' or had it been in his?

'So what happened next?' he said. 'His hand was up her blouse I think.'

'I said "excuse me", and left'

'Very considerate of you. Then what?'

'I didn't know what to do, but I hadn't finished the other directors' offices so I went to do them. Ms Hudson found me in Ms Edwards' office.'

'What did she say?'

'She apologised to me. Said she was sorry I'd walked into that. That it shouldn't have happened. I said it was nothing to do with me. She said it was a "one off". She didn't know how it had come about. She said that one minute they'd been leaning over her desk close together looking at some document or other and somehow they'd touched and it had all started. She actually thanked me for coming in when I did. Said I'd stopped her making a big mistake. Then she said that she hoped she could rely on my discretion and that she would make it worth my while if I kept quiet.

'She offered to pay you to keep quiet?'

'I presume that's what she meant. I don't think she was going to offer me a job as her highly paid personal assistant. She said she'd need a couple of days. I presume to get some cash together.'

'Then what did you do?'

'I finished the cleaning and went home.'

'Did you believe her - when she said it was a "one off"? I mean'

'Not at all. I could see she was lying.'

'I see, well thanks for telling us. I can guarantee that no one else will hear about it from us.'

'That's good. I wasn't sure if I would get into trouble for telling you. I mean if Maxine and John come back.

'No need to worry. I won't be passing it on and you can be sure Ruth won't want it to go public.'

'I suppose not.' She gave Nick the full effect of her blue eyes. 'Can I ask you a question?'

Momentarily losing himself in her gaze, Nick brought himself back. 'What? Yes of course. Fire away!' Why had he said that? It sounded so stupid.

'If you and Ruth are not back together, why did she want you to hear what I had to tell her?'

'That's a good question. A bit of long story really. Er...look, can we meet up later? We can have a chat and I'll try to explain.'

Sally smiled. Her face lit up. Her eyes sparkled, like well... like ice blue stars thought Nick. *'Pull yourself together man. This is business.'*

'Yes, OK. I could meet you this evening after I finish work at seven.'

'Great!' *Was that too enthusiastic?* 'Where? Where would be good for you?'

'I live locally, so how about the Roundel? At say, seven-fifteen, if you don't mind me not going home to get changed.'

'Fine. Can I buy you something to eat? They do serve food in the evenings don't they?'

'That would be great. It'll save me having to start cooking when I get in.'

They both stood. He opened the door for her. He wondered if he should shake her hand but decided not.

'See you later then,' he said.

'I'll look forward to it,' she replied, knocking him dead again with her smile.

CHAPTER NINE

Back at his desk he tidied up, made sure the filing cupboard and desk drawers were locked and that he'd logged off and switched off the lap top. It was locked in its docking station so he didn't have to put that away. Then he went to report to Jane.

The tight ship was in evidence again as he was allowed into her office at five on the dot.

They shook hands again. *'Keeping it very formal,'* he thought. But then she said 'Let's sit over here rather than at the desk,' indicating a sofa against the wall to his right.' There were two cups and a vacuum jug of coffee set out on the coffee table in front of it.

They sat down and she poured without asking if he wanted any. 'You can put your own cream in can't you?' she asked pleasantly, although he noticed that there was no choice of milk. She took cream so everybody else did. It was as simple as that.

'Thanks' said Nick, adding a splash of cream to his coffee, which he then left on the table.'

Jane added her cream and held the cup and saucer on her lap as she asked, 'How was your first day? I've heard that you had a bit of a row with Ruth in the restaurant this morning. That's not going to be a problem is it?'

'Row? No...I mean yes. Well no, it's not going to be a problem because it wasn't a real row. I decided that it would be better if people thought that we were still not getting on and then if anyone had a problem with me asking questions, especially about what John had been doing they'd be more likely to go to Ruth and complain and even tell her the answers to the questions I was asking.'

'So the row was all an act? It sounds like it was very convincing.'

'We've had plenty of practice.'

'Apparently so; you could be heard from miles away. Let's hope it works. You and Ruth are all right then?'

'Oh yes,' said Nick. 'Couldn't be better – apart from being divorced of course.'

'Of course. And apart from your pretend row. Are you on the network?'

'Yes, logged on after lunch – no problem. I sent you an email. Any progress with getting me access to John and Maxine's emails and home drives?'

'Afraid not. Apparently even I don't have the ability to authorise that. It has to be the IT Security Manager and he's away at some IT Security Course or other. He won't be back for a couple of days. Do you want me to push it, or do you have enough to be getting on with?'

'No, I've enough to go at.'

'Tell me more,' said Jane, clearly intrigued.

'I've found some files in John's cupboards. Looks like they may be worth looking at in detail.' He did not yet intend to tell her about the copies he had at home.

'What's in them?'

'Well I've not had time to look through them yet. I spent all morning dealing with people who came to say hello and get the gossip on why I was back. I think most of them were secretly pleased that my Private Detective Company had gone belly up.'

'They'd probably been jealous that you'd had the courage to do something different and saw your apparent failure as vindication of their own lack of courage. Of course we know different.'

Nick was surprised by her comments: both in her appreciation of the courage it had taken for him to set up in such a risky business, and also in apparently acknowledging that many of her employees were not in their dream jobs. Had she been thinking about what he'd said that morning about employee empowerment being a load of bollocks? Or had she simply been giving him, what they had called on some course or other, 'a positive stroke'? (In other words a bit of flannel to make him feel better.)

He felt encouraged in spite of his thoughts – positive strokes still worked, even on him. 'One file contains descriptions of some major capital projects, with the budgets underlined,' he said.

'Which projects?'

'The Sludge Treatment and Combined Cycle Power Generation Plant...'

'A bit of a mouthful.'

'Not something I'd want in my mouth!' said Nick. And then went on,' The Regional M & C Project, some sludge storage projects; the membrane water treatment project...' He listed the others he could remember.

'I wonder why those projects,' said Jane. 'What's special about those?'

'No idea...yet'

'And what about the other files? What's in those?'

'I don't know. I've not had chance to look at any of the others,' he lied. 'Could be just more of the same.'

Even if he did nothing before he next met with Jane, he'd be able to show some progress just by updating her on what he'd actually already found in the other files he'd looked at. In any case he had some other news for her, and he didn't want to produce too much too soon. She could start to expect too much.

'But there is something else I've found out.'

'Something useful?'

'Oh, I think so,' he said pausing for effect. 'John and Maxine were in a relationship, an intimate one at that.'

'How do you know?'

'They were seen.'

'Who by?'

'I'm sorry I can't tell you that.'

'Why not? Need I remind you that I am paying you for this information?' Jane's tone had hardened – completely different to her 'positive stroking' voice.

'Without wanting to sound like a 'black and white movie detective', I have to protect my sources.'

'I can appreciate that but what harm can it do? I need to know if your source is reliable.'

'And *I* can appreciate that, but I promised that I wouldn't even pass the information on. And I've already broken that promise. So I'm afraid I can't tell you any more. I'm meeting her again later...'

'Her?'

'Yes "her". I shouldn't have let that slip but it only narrows it down to about half of your employees. As I was about to say, I'm seeing her later to get to know her a bit better and explain my involvement: without giving anything away – don't worry! I'll be able to tell if she's making it up for any reason.'

'OK, Nick. I'll trust you. You're the professional.'

The 'positive stroking' had returned. Was it sincere? Seemed to be.

'You've not touched your coffee!' Jane suddenly noticed.

'Cutting down.'

'*I* should really. I drink gallons of it during the day. I'm totally wired by the time I leave.'

'So what do you do to relax?'

'That sounds like the beginning of a chat up line!' Jane teased.

'What? No, it wasn't meant to be. I'm sorry ...'

'I was teasing you Nick. There's no need to worry. Although I'm sorry you don't find me attractive.'

'What? I didn't mean that. I do find... I mean.'

'Nick, relax; I was teasing you again. Still I'm glad you do find me attractive.' She paused to see if he reacted again, but he hadn't a clue what was going on so he kept quiet. Then she added, 'You could take me out though.'

Nick started to say something again, but she went on. 'Or I should say, I could take you out, since I'd end up paying for it through your expenses anyway.'

Nick frowned.

'Seriously, I would like to hear more about what you think about the Company's employee initiatives. HR are continually selling the latest thing on employee relations and we have new initiatives year after year. I've had my doubts for a long time but most of the board seem to be totally sold on them. They think they're essential to maintain morale and after all "a happy workforce is a productive workforce" - or so they tell me. Anyway, I believe that you are in tune with a lot of the staff – the older ones anyway,' she said with a smile. 'And I would like to hear more. So I was wondering if I could take you out to dinner somewhere – your choice and I'd pay. What do you think?'

'Oh...er...yes. OK. I suppose that would be fine,' replied Nick uncertainly. He wasn't sure that she'd like what he had to say, but on the other hand he didn't want to turn her down and risk offending her. Regardless of the gentler side of her nature, which he believed he'd seen over the last couple of days, she still had a fierce reputation.

'Good,' said Jane brightly. 'You're busy tonight aren't you, with your *source*. How about tomorrow evening? Say eight-thirty. Where would you like to eat?'

'Er...'

Jane lapsed into her natural position of authority and took control again. 'Tell you what. I know the perfect place. I'll arrange for a taxi to pick you up at eight-fifteen.'

'Oh, right, yes OK.'

'Right,' said Jane, resting her hand on Nick's knee for a moment before standing. 'I think we've finished for now.' Nick stood up as well.

'No need to come and report to me here tomorrow,' she said moving to her desk. 'You can bring me up to speed over dinner.'

Nick left a smiling Jane wondering what had just happened. Had she just made a date with him? Was she really interested in what he had to say about Company initiatives? Or was she just taking the piss?

He drove straight to the Roundel arriving with an hour to kill. So he parked up and went for a walk along a stream that ran nearby, mulling over the events of the day.

CHAPTER TEN

Nick arrived back at the Roundel at seven o'clock, ordered a coke from the bar and found a seat at a table from which he could see the door. Sally arrived a minute after half-past. She was wearing slim fitting jeans, a denim jacket, an open necked white shirt tucked into her jeans and a small gold cross on a fine gold chain around her neck. Nick felt his mouth go dry as he stood to allow her to notice him. He moved to meet her, directing her towards the bar. She had make-up on, not too much, but he was sure it was more than she'd had on before.

'You look...'

'Gorgeous?'

'Different,' finished Nick, cursing that he hadn't been quick enough to change to 'gorgeous' as she suggested. But before he could say anything else she said, 'I managed to finish a bit early so I went home to get changed and put my face on.'

'And a very beautiful face it is too,' he wanted to say but instead he stammered, 'Oh good. Can I get you a drink?'

He'd never been any good at chatting up women. He'd never felt totally at ease with them. Afraid that he'd misinterpret the signs, say the wrong thing.

'Diet coke please.'

He ordered two 'Diet Cokes'. If she was disappointed he hadn't complimented her on her appearance, she didn't show it.

They sat back down at the table with their drinks, and after a little small talk, mainly by Sally, they perused the menu and he ordered a mixed grill for himself and salmon for her.

'You were going to explain why you were at my meeting with Ruth,' Sally reminded him.

'So I was. Well the first thing to say is that what I'm about to tell you is completely confidential. You must promise me that you'll tell no one.'

'I promise,' she smiled and leaned forward as though she couldn't wait to hear what he had to say. 'It sounds all very "cloak and dagger".'

'It is. Except there's no cloak and no dagger. The fact is that when I left RWS, nine months ago I set myself up as a Private Investigator.'

'You didn't! How ...'

'Stupid? I know.'

'I was going to say "exciting".'

'It's not as exciting as you might imagine. Certainly not as exciting as *I'd* imagined. Anyway Ruth came to my office last Saturday to ask me to try to find John. She hadn't seen him for a few days and she thought ...well actually I don't know what she thought. I must ask her. Anyway she asked me to find him. And then on Monday it turned out that Maxine had disappeared as well and so Jane Edwards has asked me to try to find her as well. I'm simply working at RWS at the moment to get some background. Find out what they were both doing before they disappeared. Find out if they were doing something together. So your information was very useful. It confirmed that they were together. And, I suppose have probably disappeared together. The next step is to find out why, and that might help us find out *where* they've gone.'

'Wow! It sounds like a plot from a movie. You're a real-life detective? That's amazing. If there's anything else I can do to help...' said Sally obviously highly impressed.

'Thanks, I've been thinking about that. You said earlier that you were cleaning the executive offices?'

'That's right. That's my "patch".'

'So you have keys to all of the directors' offices?'

'Yes.'

'And If I wanted to get into any of them to look for...'

'Clues?' she suggested excitedly.

'Well yes, clues. Could you help me?'

'Oh God, yes! I'd love to help.'

'Are you sure? I don't think it would be physically dangerous, but I suppose it could get you into trouble if anyone found out that you'd helped me.'

'Could you not just ask Jane to get you in?'

'I might want to get into her office as well.'

'Why?'

'I haven't a clue, but you never know.'

'Wow! Well like I said, I'll do anything I can to help. It's much more exciting than cleaning. I'll give you my mobile number so you can get hold of me whenever you want.'

The food arrived as they were exchanging numbers and they reverted to small talk while they ate. Nick found out that she'd been separated from her husband for three months. She'd caught him 'playing away' and kicked him out of their flat. She had 'moved on' as they say. She worked as a teaching assistant during the day and had taken the cleaning job at RWS so that she could save up a deposit and buy a flat of her own somewhere off the estate where she currently lived.

After explaining *her* current circumstances, Sally returned to the subject of Nick and Ruth. 'So that's all there is between you and Ruth now? You're not back together - you're just working for her?'

'Yes, of course.'

'It's just that she didn't seem to like it earlier; when you smiled at me... as though she was...'

'Jealous? Yeah, I noticed that. I think she'd taken an instant dislike to you because she had an inkling about what you were going to say, and obviously she didn't want to believe you. But she was so aggressive to you and so quickly, that I think she *must* have already had a reason not to trust John. She must have had her suspicions already; the way she went at you, almost as soon as you opened your mouth.

'Understandable I suppose. But isn't it awkward; working for your ex-wife?'

'Well, I had my reservations when she came to see me. But I needed the money. I had no cases. The business was about to go under. It probably still will when this case is over.'

'I see. That would be a shame. I think it's fantastic that you've tried it though. Everyone should try to follow their dream.'

'That sounds very idealistic. What's *your* dream? Not cleaning at RWS, that's for sure.'

'No. I wanted to go into teaching, but... ' she hesitated. Was this getting too personal, too soon? She decided to go with it. 'I got pregnant, when I was still at school. Classic teenage pregnancy. Infatuated with an older boy. But he didn't want to know when he found out about the baby. Schooling went to pot. And then I lost the baby! That was the final straw.'

She paused, visibly upset, blinking back tears.

'You don't need to say anymore if you don't want to,' said Nick, grasping her hand.

'There's not much more to tell,' she said, looking down at their hands. 'I didn't go back to school; got a job in a shop instead. I managed to get some qualifications, met Dave and settled down for a while. Then I got a job as a teaching assistant. Nearest I could get to teaching. I was lucky really.

My Mum and Dad were very supportive. They could have kicked me out. That happened to friends of mine.'

She looked up and smiled; glad to have got it off her chest. 'Enough of that. What about your parents? Where do they live?'

'My Mum's eighty-three. She lives a couple of miles away. I think she's in the early stages of Alzheimer's. She's very forgetful and confused at times. My Dad died in his early thirties. Smoking killed him.'

'Cancer?'

'No, he dropped his packet of fags in the middle of the road, bent over to pick it up, and was hit by a lorry.'

Sally's jaw dropped. 'That's terrible! I'm so sorry,' she said.

Nick laughed, 'Not as sorry as he was – it was a full packet.'

She looked at him. Was he joking or was he being really callous about his own father's death?

'I was joking! You were right he died of lung cancer.'

Sally laughed and thumped him lightly on the arm, and then said, 'I'm so sorry. I shouldn't laugh. Lung Cancer's not funny.'

'That's all right. I made the joke. I presume you were laughing at that and not that my Dad died of cancer.'

She looked mortified that he should even think that. 'I...' she started to stutter.

'Relax I was just teasing. I'm the one who should be sorry for making you feel awkward. You don't know me well enough yet to understand my humour.'

'I'd like to,' she responded.

Nick had noticed that every time she looked at him, her blue eyes seemed to be smiling. He was hoping that it had meant that she liked him, but it had been so long since he'd been in this situation he couldn't be sure. Perhaps her eyes sparkled all the time. But now she'd said it. He was thinking about what to reply when a young woman in her early twenties arrived at the table next to them. A man, also in his early twenties, although he looked younger, dressed in jeans and an open necked checked shirt – not tucked into his jeans, had been sitting at the table for the last few minutes.

'Hi Babe,' said the young man, a huge toothy smile lighting up his whole face. 'Sit down then,' he added, when the young woman hadn't.

'Look, there's no easy way to say this.'

Nick and Sally exchanged a glance, '*Oh-Oh,*' they both thought.

'I'm ending it,' said the woman.

'What do you mean you're mending it? What's broke? Let me mend it for you, whatever it is. I'm good with my hands: you know I am,' he said with a salacious wink.

The young woman let out an exasperated sigh. 'Nothing's broke you idiot – except us. I said I'm...ending it, "not mending it". It's over. I'm sorry but it is!' She turned and left quickly holding her hand over her mouth trying not to cry as she left. The young man was stunned for a few moments before he leapt up. 'Hang on babe! Wait! We can sort this. Whatever it is!' and he was gone.

Nick and Sally burst out laughing. 'Shall we go?' he said. 'Can I give you a lift home?'

'I'd rather walk if you don't mind. I only live round the corner.'

'OK, can I walk you home then?'

'Anytime,' she replied, her eyes sparkling again. Nick tried to suppress a blush.

As they strolled slowly along, Sally said, 'That was so funny! I know we shouldn't laugh, that poor boy, being dumped like that! But thinking she'd said "mending it". I mean why would she?'

'I know, I barely stopped myself laughing out loud. I nearly wet myself.'

'So did I.'

'*And* they both said "broke" instead of broken!'

'What? What do you mean?' asked Sally.

'*You bloody idiot!*' thought Nick. '*Now is not the time for your stupid grammar pedantry. She's not interested in that. She's going to think you're a stuck up, pretentious prat!*' But there was no way out; he had to explain, which he did in as short a way as he could. 'They should have said "broken" that's all, not "broke". You can say "I broke" but not "I've broke." It's "I've broken". I'm sorry it's just one of the rules of grammar that's all, and sometimes it gets me wound up. Especially when people who should know better break them.'

'You always obey the rules do you?' There was a suggestiveness about her question that had Nick starting to blush again. He tried to overcome it by answering.

'Not always. I just like to know what the rules are, so that I can decide whether to break them or not.'

Sally stopped walking and stood in front of him, their bodies almost touching. 'And what do the rules say about coming up to a girl's flat on a first date? We're here by the way.'

Nick's mouth was dry. He swallowed - like that was going to help.

'Er... I don't know the rules on that one. Do whatever feels right I suppose.'

She leant in closer, her right hand pulled his head down so that she could kiss him gently on the lips. 'And what feels right?' she whispered.

By way of an answer he kissed her back, pulling her in even closer. Sally took his hand and said 'Come on, let's get some privacy.' She led him up a path leading to the main door of a block of housing association flats. As Sally pushed

89

the door open, doubts suddenly surged into his brain. What was happening? What was he getting into? He knew he wanted her. And he knew she wanted him – at the moment. But she was gorgeous and about ten years younger. He was batting way out of his league. Was she simply seduced by glamour of him being a "Private Detective"? That seemed to have really impressed her. What would happen in the morning, when she realised he was just an ordinary bloke? An ordinary *boring* bloke. They'd both feel incredibly awkward: *and* he might need her to help him gain access to those offices. Would he still feel able to ask her?

'Hang on Sally,' he said. 'I'm not sure we should be doing this.'

She turned and looked up into his eyes, 'Why not? Have you thought of one of your rules? I thought you didn't mind breaking them as long as you knew what they were.'

'That's just it. I don't know what they are.' His voice almost pleading for her to let him off the hook - unsure if he could resist her. 'You're beautiful, really beautiful,' he blurted out. 'And I...well I'm just an ordinary bloke. I have a business that's almost dead in the water, and God knows what I'm going to do when it finally goes under. Look, you've had a hell of a day, what with Ruth screaming at you like she did and accusing you of all that stuff. And I don't want you thinking I'm special just because I'm a Private Detective, because I probably won't be for much longer. I don't want you to do anything you'll regret in the morning.'

'Don't you think that's my decision?' she replied, still standing close to him.

'Of course it is but I'm not sure your judgement is sound at the moment. Don't forget, *I* know me better than you do.'

'Perhaps I just fancy a one-nighter.'

'You might, I know I do.' He shook his head. 'Christ! What I wouldn't give to go in with you right now! But I really like you, and I want to get to know you better. I don't want to risk that for the sake of one night. I guess I'm saying I don't want you rushing into anything you might regret later.'

'That all sounds very noble of you, but I still think it's my decision. But just so you know; it wasn't a one-nighter I was looking for. I really like you as well.'

'You do? That's great!'

'Does that mean you'll come inside now?'

'Look, I can't believe I'm saying this, but would you mind if I didn't? I... I just have great difficulty in believing that anyone as... well as gorgeous as you could really be interested in me. So how about we take a rain check? How about we wait a day or two? And if you still want me then, you can be damned sure that I'll be here.'

'It really means a lot to you doesn't it? Not taking advantage of me.'

He nodded.

'That is so sweet. And if it's just a ploy, then it's worked, because I want you even more now. But I'll wait a day or two, and so you know what you're missing...' She reached up and pulled his head down to hers and kissed him. Then she slipped her hand down his back and pulled him hard against her.

When she let go, she stepped back slightly, then reached up on her toes to give him one brief kiss on the lips, before saying, 'Off you go then Detective. See you soon.

Then she disappeared through the door.

CHAPTER ELEVEN

Nick walked slowly back to his car. Had he just blown it with Sally? Would she really think that he was a total loser – not accepting her invitation? Had she been hurt by it? Should he go back and tell her he'd changed his mind? No, it was too late for that.

He was about to turn on to a footpath that led to the car park when something hit him hard on the side of the head, like a sack full of wet sand with knuckles. Pain exploded in his right ear. He stumbled sideways and fell to the ground. He was kicked hard in the stomach. Instinctively he tried to bring his knees up to his chest and his elbows in, to protect himself. Still the kicks got through. He could hear himself grunting loudly in pain. Suddenly it stopped and a male voice growled. 'If you know what's good for you, you'll stop sniffing around...' Another kick came in and hurt even more because Nick had momentarily relaxed when the kicking stopped. He cried out louder; drowning out anything his assailant said. The kicking stopped again. Nick lay still, tensed up in case it started again. It didn't. Through half open eyes he saw bright orange trainers turn and run swiftly away.

He lay still for a while. He didn't know how long. Eventually, he slowly straightened his legs. His shins felt bruised. They'd taken a lot of the punishment. He rolled over on to his stomach and started to push himself up on to his knees. He felt someone take hold of him and he recoiled in fear. 'Steady mate,' said a voice as its owner helped Nick to his feet. A 'Good Samaritan' had stopped to help. Bizarrely, Nick wondered if any 'Pharisees' had 'passed by on the other side'. The 'Samaritan' went on. 'What happened mate? You been mugged?'

Nick nodded, still unable to straighten up fully. He didn't know what had happened but a mugging would be a good enough explanation for the 'Samaritan'. Nick stood up straight and tried to catalogue his injuries. His stomach ached. His ribs ached. His arms and legs felt bruised. Oh, and his head hurt. Let's not forget the head. He put his hand up to it and groaned.

'You're in a bad way mate. Better get you to hospital.'

Nick finally looked at his 'Samaritan'. He recognised him from somewhere, but for a moment he couldn't place him. Then it came to him. It was the lad from the next table. The lad who thought his girlfriend had wanted to mend something. He nearly laughed at the memory but it came out as a cough. At least no blood came up.

'I've seen you before,' Nick managed to croak. 'You were in the Pub.'

'Yeah, that's right mate. My name's Micky. I was the one you saw getting dumped! You were at the next table with that fit looking lady weren't you? Say, she didn't do this mate did she? That's one nasty fit looking lady if she did,' he laughed.

Nick managed a laugh too. 'No, I don't know who it was.'

'Some scumbag druggy probably. Let's get you to casualty.'

Nick protested, but the young man was insistent and helped Nick across the car par and into the passenger seat of his own car.

'You insured to drive my car?'

'Of course I am mate. What's your name? Can't keep calling you "mate".'

'Nick.'

'Right Nick mate. Don't you worry about nothing. We'll soon have you at the hospital.'

Nick winced at the grammar but let it go. He couldn't help but be moved by the fact that this young man driving to hospital had just been unceremoniously dumped by his girlfriend in public. He must have felt humiliated and must be still hurting and yet here he was taking the time to help Nick and drive him to hospital. As he began to find it easier to talk, he said, 'Sorry about what happened to you in the Pub. It was awful.'

'Bet you had a good laugh though. The way I thought she said she was "mending it" not "ending it". Bet you laughed yourselfs stupid!   What an idiot!'

Nick smiled and admitted they had laughed. 'But not until we got outside though,' he added.

The young man laughed. 'That's OK. I would of if I'd heard some idiot making a fool of his-self like that.'

'So did you catch up with her? If you don't mind me asking?'

'Yeah but she didn't want to listen. I'll let her cool off a bit and think about it. Then she'll listen, and I *will* mend whatever it is that's broke with us.' He laughed at his own joke.

Nick laughed too although it hurt, but he couldn't help thinking that Micky's girlfriend must have thought about it for some time *before* she'd decided to end it.

They arrived at the hospital and the 'Good Samaritan' helped Nick into the building and attracted the attention of a nurse to see to him. Then he handed Nick's car keys over and turned to go.

'Hang on Micky. You can't just go. Let me have your number. I'd like to thank you properly later.'

But Micky wouldn't hear of it. 'No need Nick, mate. No need.'

Nick managed to slip one of his business cards into the breast pocket on Micky's shirt with the words, 'You might need my services one day.' Then a puzzled Micky left, leaving Nick to appreciate that despite what sometimes seemed the case, the milk of human kindness had not entirely evaporated in the youth of today.

After an initial triage, to establish that he wasn't dying, followed by a forty-five minute wait, Nick was taken to a cubicle and checked over. He'd been lucky he was told. Nothing was broken and there was no sign of concussion. They kept him for an hour to make sure he was well enough to go home and then he was discharged with an instruction to rest and take the usual painkillers for any pain.

Back at his flat he poured himself a glass of Benromach ten year-old single malt, reflecting that since it had been a present from his sister and brother-in-law the Christmas before last, it was now a twelve year-old single malt. He put the bottle down on the coffee table in front of his sofa. Then he picked up his iPod and scanned his playlists. 'Too much bloody choice everywhere nowadays,' he muttered to himself as he put it on 'shuffle' and inserted into its docking station. Then he flopped down to feel sorry for himself and took a sip of his malt.

So what did he do now? His body ached, despite the two paracetamol he'd taken. The Police began singing 'King of Pain'. He didn't need any reminding so he used his remote to jump to the next track. Ralph McTell sang about the streets of London. He smiled as he remembered a spoof of the song he'd heard at a Folk Club thirty years ago: the chorus had ended with the words, I'll show you something that's supposed to make you blind. He couldn't remember who'd sung it but having McTell reminding him that there were plenty of people worse off than himself wasn't making him feel any better. Why would it? He'd been beaten up by somebody and he didn't know why.

Was somebody warning off his investigation? He thought that only happened in the movies. But what else could it have been about? And who would want to warn him off? John? Maxine? Richard perhaps? If *he* were involved then Nick thought he'd be favourite. But did it really matter? He'd had enough. He wasn't equipped to deal with this sort of thing. He'd take the hint and jack it in. He'd only been postponing the inevitable. Tomorrow he'd quit. He wouldn't get paid but he'd been planning to 'sign on' anyway.

Nothing ventured; nothing lost.

He poured himself another Benromach, and carried on wallowing. He didn't owe anybody anything: certainly not Ruth. She'd had her pound of flesh *and* all the blood that was coursing through its veins, when they'd divorced. He smiled at his reference to Shakespeare's Merchant of Venice. He'd not forgotten everything he'd learned – only all the useful stuff. No he certainly didn't owe anybody anything. And he'd been right not to go inside with Sally. How disappointed would she have been if she'd spent the night with him only for him to give up his 'glamorous' occupation so easily. No, he had to face it. He'd never be a 'Nick Charles', a 'Sam Spade' or a 'Philip Marlowe'. Every one of them would have been more determined to solve the case after getting beaten up. They'd have made them pay – whoever had had them beaten up. Even Miss bloody Marple would have refused to have been frightened off. He took another gulp of Benromach.

Paul Simon took over from Ralph McTell and was asking why he was so soft in the middle when the rest of his life was so hard.

What the bloody hell was going on with his iPod? Did it have some hidden function that he didn't know about? Had he pressed the 'ironic commentary on Nick's life' button without realising it? Well he didn't need it. He did know where the 'off' button was. He pressed it and continued brooding in silence.

All he'd ever wanted to be was a hard-nosed detective like Charles, Marlowe and Spade. So why wasn't he? He tried to think of reasons for his failure but could only come up with an excuse. But that was good enough for now. Because he'd never had a chance that's why! Certainly not working for RWS and certainly not married to Ruth. And not even as a detective: but that was because he'd never had the right sort of case. Well now he had the right sort of case. And he'd even been warned off! Now he had no more excuses. Now he really had the chance to *be* the tough guy. And he damned well would be.

From tomorrow he would start acting the part, and if they didn't like it, they could stuff it. He would be Nick Charles, Sam Spade and Philip Marlowe all rolled into one. He'd make the lot of them look like Miss Marple. If Jane didn't like his new attitude then she could sack him. At least he could go out in a glimmer, if not a blaze of glory.

He finished his drink, put his glass on the coffee table and went to bed.

He didn't even wash up. That was the 'new him' all right.

CHAPTER TWELVE

The next morning Nick arrived at his desk nursing a thick head. He didn't mind. He thought it would help him maintain his 'new self'; mean and moody. After all didn't all the old detectives drink too much? Nick Charles seemed to be permanently drunk in the 'Thin Man' films, although he'd have probably said he was merely a bit 'squiffy.'

He reviewed the situation. He had no visible bruising from his beating and he didn't feel too sore, so he wouldn't attract any attention on that score. If anyone did know about his beating then it would be because they'd organised it. Whoever was behind it, he wanted them to know that he was still on the case. If it had been John and/or Maxine then they would find out by whatever means they'd originally found out about him being on the case in the first place. And if that was through Richard, then he needed to let him know straight away.

He took his jacket off the back of his chair and went in search of Richard's office. It wasn't difficult to find – it had his name on it. Nick could see through the partially open blinds covering the glass wall of the office that his target was in, and alone. He swept past Richard's secretary who sat outside the office like an ineffectual sentry guarding the door, knocked and entered.

'Morning Richard. Got a moment?'

'Excuse me? Do you have an appointment?' said Richard looking up from the screen on his desk, his fingers poised above the keyboard, obviously annoyed to be interrupted.

'Nope. Didn't think I'd need one.'

'Well I'm afraid you do. I'm very busy. I'd like you to leave.'

'And I'd like to stay. I'm very busy too and I don't have time to go backwards and forwards waiting for you to give me an audience.'

'I don't like your attitude, you jumped up little...'

'What can I say?' interrupted Nick. 'I don't particularly like it myself. But it's the product of the countless behavioural courses that RWS sent me on. Perhaps you need to go on an "attitude appreciation" course?'

'Just get out!' said Richard. 'And you might as well pack up your things. I'm getting straight on to Jane. You'll be out of a job before you get back to your desk.'

'That's possible. Possibly even *probable*. *Probably* even probable,' grinned Nick. 'But I just wanted you to know that someone tried to warn me off last night. Warn me off my investigation that is – in a very *forceful* manner. I can show you the bruises if you like. And I also wanted you to know that it hasn't worked. I'm still on the case, and I will be until Jane takes me off it. That could be in a matter of minutes as you say, but I'll take that risk. I just wanted to reassure you that I won't be intimidated!'

Richard was clearly a little flustered, but recovered himself. 'I'm afraid you're confusing me with someone who gives shit about your wellbeing. I don't care if you've been attacked. I would presume that it's all part of the job. All part of the seedy world your type inhabits. And I really don't understand why you think I would care. Now get out. I have a call to make.

'Certainly. I've said all I came to say.'

Nick said 'Thank you,' to Richard's bewildered sentry and walked two doors along to Jane's office.

'I think Jane may want to see me,' he said to her secretary.

'Really? She's not said anything to me.' Her phone rang.

'Yes Jane,' she said into the mouthpiece. 'He's right here. Shall I send him straight in?'

She put the phone down and with a puzzled look said, 'You're to go right in.'

'It's a gift,' smiled Nick. 'The seventh son of a seventh son. I'm septic!'

As he stepped into Jane's office, he held up his hand and said, 'Don't tell me. Richard's just rung to demand that you fire me.'

'That's right. He said that you barged into his office and insisted on telling him that you'd been warned off your investigation last night. Beaten up he seemed to think. And that you insisted on telling him that you weren't going to give it up. He said you must have flipped or something and that you were definitely unstable. Is it true by the way?' a hint of concern in her voice. 'Were you beaten up? Are you all right?'

'Yes it is, but I'm fine now.'

'So why tell Richard? And why tell him like that?'

'The truth?'

'The truth.'

'Well, when I got back from hospital last night I was all ready to jack it in. But then I got to thinking "why the hell should I?" I became a detective because I wanted to do this sort of case. So I have to accept that getting beaten up is all part of the job. It must mean that someone is worried about the investigation and that must be John, Maxine or, given his position as head of Finance, Procurement *and* Audit, possibly even Richard or any combination of the above. Anyway, I also decided last night that I should start acting the part of the detective a bit more convincingly for my sake, if no one else's, so I thought I'd shake Richard up a bit; let him know that if he were behind my beating that it hadn't worked. See how he reacted.'

'And how did he react?'

100

'Too early to say yet.'

'I see. Well it's not the way we usually do things at RWS, but then we don't usually employ a Private Detective. Don't push your luck too far with Richard. I don't believed he's actually involved, and while I quite enjoy seeing his feathers ruffled, if push came to shove, I'd have to take his side I'm afraid. You still on for tonight by the way? Not too bruised from your beating?'

'Of course. Is that it? You're not going to fire me?'

'No, I'm not going to fire you. In fact I'm glad you're going to put a bit more commitment into the job. I was a bit worried you were just going through the motions; stringing me along to make the job last as long as possible with no idea what you were doing.'

'As if!' said Nick as he turned to leave. 'See you later.'

Back at his desk, with a coffee he'd picked up from the restaurant on the way, Nick had to admit that he had to start wading through the files again. It was mind numbing but it was not as though he had anyone he could delegate to.

He picked out the folder labelled 'Operations'.

From his time in 'Quality Assurance' looking after Operating Standards and Procedures, he knew the basics of the operating side of the business. The file had two sections – labelled 'Water Ops' and 'Wastewater Ops'. He knew that 'Water Ops' were responsible for the operation and maintenance of the Company's water treatment works which took raw water from rivers or reservoirs and treated it to meet stringent drinking water regulations, and then for the distribution of the treated water through the Company's water network to customers' homes, factories, shops etc. 'Wastewater Ops' were responsible for the operation and maintenance of the company's sewers which collected sewage from customer's homes, factories, shops etc, and delivered it for treatment to the required standard at the company's wastewater treatment works before being discharged to the environment. It was essential that the treatment works, and distribution and sewer networks were operated and maintained correctly so that clean water was delivered to the customer and effluent from the wastewater treatment works did not pollute the environment. And that required suitably trained staff with an adequate operating budget.

In the 'Operations' folder, Nick found details of operating costs and annual budgets for water and wastewater treatment, and their respective networks. The file covered the last five years of expenditure on an area by area basis. (There were ten water and ten wastewater operational areas within the business as a whole.) The budget was spent up every year, including the contingency and emergency revenue funds to cover exceptional circumstances – major operational incidents, such as extensive foul flooding, a very large water main burst, or a large contaminated water incident. There were some handwritten notes made by John, he presumed, but attributed to various area managers. They all complained that the new equipment with which they were supplied was not up to standard or that they were often told to 'sweat the asset' (run existing equipment into the ground before it could be replaced). A special note against a project, attributed to a manager called Peter Dodgson referred to a brand new wastewater treatment works that had been built in his area at Crossington, in the previous AMP period. It had used a new secondary treatment process, which the manufacturer (a wholly owned subsidiary of RWS) claimed would make the usual primary treatment process unnecessary. This had saved tens of millions on the project cost. However, the treatment process had never worked properly leading to multiple treatment failures and fines as well as extremely high maintenance costs for the treatment process. Nick decided he'd pay a visit to Peter Dodgson and get some more background.

There were a couple of more specialised OPEX items, (operating expenditure), one related to about five million pounds being budgeted for a security company to provide a fast response to any alarms on water treatment works or pumping stations and reservoirs. (In the current climate there was always a possibility that a terrorist organisation could try to contaminate the water supply or simply stop it by blowing up a works or aqueduct etc. This budget was a precaution against that.) A note said 'operational solution.' He'd have to ask Eddie Banks, the security manager, about that.

Then there was a note in John's handwriting regarding five yearly inspections on High Voltage Switch Gear that had not been carried out for the last sixteen years, because there was no one in the company qualified to do it. The note also stated that this was a regulatory requirement. A comment in John's handwriting said 'Not a huge cost: Simple incompetence/negligence?' Nick presumed, that should there be an accident caused by this switchgear then the company, and possibly certain individuals, would be held liable; hence John's comment about incompetence and negligence.

What was all this about? Why was John gathering all this evidence? Was Maxine in on it with him? And if so why? Were they simply concerned employees intending to 'blow the whistle' to put things right? Were they intending to try to sell the story to the media and make some money? It would certainly sell newspapers. What would be the effect if they did go public? Could the Company lose its licence to operate? The share price would plummet; that's for certain! Was that it? A takeover? The share price plummets and another company picks up a bargain? Could that be where Richard comes in? We might be getting

103

somewhere here Nick told himself. Too early to say anything to Jane though.

BTO interrupted his thoughts. It was Ruth. *'Let's hope she's calmed down!'* he thought.

'Hope you've calmed down,' he said.

'What? Oh yes, look can we meet? Have you got time for a coffee? I'm buying.'

'She's buying? Could there be an apology on the way?'

'Sure, see you down there in five minutes? On second thoughts, we're supposed to be at loggerheads. Best not be seen having a friendly coffee together. Is there a meeting room free?'

It occurred to Nick that he was *presuming* it would be a friendly meeting, but Ruth replied, 'Good thinking. I'll check and let you know. I'll bring coffees with me.'

Bringing the coffees? She *is* making an effort. Ten minutes later they were sitting across a meeting room table, a cup of coffee in front of each of them.

'I've been thinking,' said Ruth, 'about last night. I'm sorry for losing my temper like that.'

'It's not me you should be apologising to.'

'You mean I should apologise to Sally? I will. I'm not saying that I believe her. I mean I believe she saw something going on. Things happen on the spur of the moment. But I don't believe that John would go as far as Sally thinks he had. He'd told me before that he thought Maxine fancied him but he made it quite plain that she wasn't his type. I think that Maxine must have tried something on, grabbed him and kissed him or something, and Sally walked in before John pushed her off.'

'Sally said her skirt was round her waist!'

'She could have pulled it up herself. God knows she wears them short enough.'

'And John's hand was up her blouse!'

104

'It might not have been. Or it could have happened if he was trying to push her away - if she'd already undone a couple of buttons.

'Blimey! You really don't want to believe it do you?'

'It's not that I don't want to. I just can't believe it of John. He's not like that. He isn't...well, he isn't obsessed by sex! Not all men are, you know! I had a long think about it last night and I realised that Sally had no reason to make it up and that she must have misinterpreted what she'd seen.'

'It sounds farfetched to me,' said Nick.

'You don't know John as well as I do.'

'I should hope not,' he replied. *He* believed that Sally had seen what she thought she'd seen and that John and Maxine were heavily involved with each other. He didn't care too much if Ruth agreed or not. If she'd found a way to rationalise things and keep herself happy then that was all well and good. A happy Ruth was always easier to get along with than an angry one.

Ruth half smiled. She had started to relax, and said, 'So have you made any progress?'

'I've got a bit further through the files in John's cupboard. And, oh yes, I got beaten up and warned off last night,' he said, making it sound like a casual afterthought.

'Oh my God! Who by?'

'I don't know. I was hit from behind and then kicked on the floor a few times. I didn't see him.'

'Are you all right?'

'I'm fine now. A young lad took me to hospital. I've got a few bruises; that's all. Nothing broken. Whoever it was didn't do much of a job really. Mind you they did say there'd be more if I didn't stop sniffing around.'

'Really? It sounds like...'

'I know – like one of those films I always wanted you to watch. And before you ask, I don't know who was behind it.' He looked at Ruth waiting for her reaction as he added, 'although there are two obvious candidates.'

Ruth frowned and then said, 'What! No way! There's no way John would do something like that!'

Nick was tempted to say, 'Well you think there's no way he'd be screwing Maxine, and you're wrong there.' But he bit his tongue. Instead he said, 'Maxine and John are the only people I can think of. I'm looking for them, and if they've found out and they don't want to be found...'

'John would never do that. Maxine might. She's a cold hard bitch according to John. That's why she's not his type.'

'So you don't think Maxine and John are together? You think they disappeared at the same time as a matter of coincidence?'

'I don't know Nick. I just know that I trust John implicitly. I have to go now. You're supposed to be the detective. You work it out.' And with that Ruth stood up and left.

Nick sat for a moment or two. What did all that mean? Did Ruth really have such blind faith in John? Surely no one could be that blind. Or was the evidence starting to convince her and she just wanted more time – and space – to come round to it: to adjust to the fact that John was a scumbag and had run off with Maxine? Was she just clutching at straws that were slowly slipping from her grasp? Well, she wasn't his problem anymore. Those files in John's cupboard were. So he returned to his desk and carried on wading through the files while eating his lunch. He impressed himself with his determination to stick to the task. Much of what he looked at was almost 'Double Dutch' to him, but he was helped by the notes John had written at the top of some of the pages.

In the folder dealing with the Customer Services department he found spreadsheets showing the numbers of complaints by customers, mainly about their bills, but also about the quality of the water – it was dirty or cloudy or smelled of chlorine or something else – and about sewage getting into their houses. He found notes by John saying 'same date as previous sheet: different complaint numbers'. He looked more closely and saw that John's note was correct. There were two sets of spreadsheets covering the same time periods with two completely different numbers of complaints in all the categories recorded. He knew that the complaint figures were reported to the regulator. Why were there two sets of the figures? A real one and one for the Regulator he wondered? He'd have to contact someone in Customer Services – he made a note.

He needed some caffeine so he picked a cappuccino up from the restaurant; it was better than the stuff from the vending machine not far from his desk. He went to the toilet on the way and smiled to himself: he knew that within half an hour of drinking the coffee he'd have to go again. The exercise was good for him he told himself.

Another two coffees and three more visits to the toilet, (*should* he go to the doctor?), saw him through the remainder of the files. He found references to the customer call centre staff being outsourced to a third party company: a company owned by RWS. John's note said 'Why?' Similarly in the file labelled 'IT', he found references to the IT support being provided by the same company. This time John had made two notes. One said, 'WORST TECHNICAL BID - HIGHEST COST!' The other said, 'Why would an IT support company also provide customer call centre staff?' He would have to talk to somebody in Customer Services and IT.

Before leaving, he made a few phone calls and set up appointments for the following day. His first would be at Crossington with Peter Dodgson, but not until nine-thirty. He could have a lie in!

Now he had to go home and get ready for his 'date' with his employer.

'Oh! What to wear?'

CHAPTER THIRTEEN

Nick showered, and even shaved – he didn't usually shave twice in the same day, sometimes not twice in the same week, but he was out to impress Jane with his professionalism, and looking smart was all part of it. He hadn't a clue where they would be eating but he was guessing that it wouldn't be MacDonald's, so he elected to go for 'smart casual' - jacket, with an open necked pale blue shirt with a thin white stripe, and dark blue trousers.

The taxi arrived promptly at eight-fifteen.

'So where are you taking me? He asked the driver as he settled into the back of the car and struggled with his seat belt.

'The Halmesbury Country House Hotel, just outside of town,' came the reply.

'Nice,' said Nick. As country houses went The 'Halmesbury' was not particularly large but it had a reputation for very high quality food as well as top class accommodation – way beyond the limits of his own wallet. He wouldn't be needing the accommodation but he was looking forward to sampling the menu.

Jane had not arrived when he walked in and he was asked if he would like a drink while he waited. He thought that was a damned fine idea and went to wait in the bar. He discovered that Jane had already arranged for his drinks to be put on her bill, so he ordered a pint of the local bitter and found a comfortable armchair from which he could see the door. He looked around the room. It was all very elegant. A high ceiling, ornate coving, a chandelier shedding plenty of light, a large open fireplace, tasteful unobtrusive wallpaper, a thick beige carpet with a subtle pattern of clouds, and comfortable chairs and sofas made it all homely as well as elegant. Not any like any home that Nick had been in, but homely all the same. He was three quarters of the way down his pint when Jane entered the bar.

He had to admit she did scrub up well. She was wearing a classic black pencil dress, with a halter neck. It hugged her slender figure and he was surprised to notice a slit that revealed several inches of her right thigh as she walked across the carpet to greet him.

Nick stood to greet her. Jane held her hand out and he began to shake it as she moved closer and kissed him on the cheek. He was surprised by the kiss, but he supposed that nowadays it was quite the norm.

'Good to see you, sorry I'm a little late.'

'That's OK,' he replied. 'This is a pleasant enough place to wait.'

'Yes it is nice isn't it? Shall we go in?' she asked, turning towards the dining room without waiting for a reply. Nick followed, leaving his drink behind.

At the table Jane ordered a jug of tap water while they perused their menus.

'Can't have the MD of the region's water company being seen drinking the bottled stuff,' she said to Nick.

Nick looked through the menu and decided he's start with the parsnip veloute, (he was guessing it was a posh name for a soup) and roast pheasant for his main course. He'd never had pheasant and thought, '*May as well look like I'm game.*'

Jane ordered the parsnip veloute as well, (*'Good choice'*), and feather blade of beef for her main, with a bottle of Bordeaux. 'Should go well with your pheasant,' she said.

'Have you been here before?' she asked while they waited.

'No, I'm afraid not. It's a little beyond my pocket.'

110

'Good. It's a treat for you then,' she said with a smile. 'No need to worry about the cost tonight. This is a business meeting, though I see you're not wearing a tie.'

'Out of normal working hours. I thought I could be more casual.'

'Well you still look pretty good.'

'Thanks, you...er...' he faltered. He'd been about to say, 'don't look so bad yourself.' But that seemed a bit inadequate as she looked stunning.

'Look stunning?' she suggested.

'She knew already.' 'Absolutely,' he agreed.

'Absolutely stunning? Even better. Thank you Nick.'

He knew she was teasing him and he realised that he shouldn't be letting her get away with it – not if he was going to be the hard-nosed detective.

'I don't think you need me to tell you how good you look tonight.'

'Perhaps not. But it makes a girl feel good to hear it.'

'Anything else I can do to make you feel good?'

Jane raised her eyebrows in surprise at Nick's response.

'Perhaps, but for now you can tell me what progress you've made today –apart from upsetting one of my directors.'

'How is Dick by the way? I presume he wouldn't like being called that.'

'No he wouldn't,' replied Jane, allowing herself a smile. 'He's away at a conference for a couple days. He warned me to keep an eye on you while he was away.'

'Did he indeed? Jealous type?'

'What's he got to be jealous about?'

'Me of course'. Nick paused to give her just a moment to consider if he were being suggestive, before adding, 'Everyone thinks he's your right hand man. I presume he agrees and here you are dealing with me directly: openly excluding him from our meetings.'

111

'That certainly rankles with him. But *I'm* the MD. I don't have to explain everything to him. So, do you have anything to report?'

'I've completed a "first pass" through the files in John's cupboard.'

'And?'

'Projects with budgets underlined, comparisons with actual spends that were a lot less, sometimes tens of millions less – like the Sludge Treatment and Combined Cycle Power Generation Plant, the Water Treatment Membrane Plant. And others that were in the AMP submission but never happened. The Regional M&C Project, Strategic Sludge Storage Project, an OPEX allowance for a third party security fast response company. All approved expenditure for projects that didn't happen.'

'So the files contain details of projects on which the company has made substantial efficiency savings?'

'That's one way of looking at it. Others might be puzzled why the projects had been greatly down-sized or simply not done at all even though the Regulator had agreed they needed doing and had granted the money to RWS to execute them.'

'Presumably because an alternative solution was found. I think I'd have heard if the regional control system had fallen over or we had sludge coming out of our ears because we hadn't built some tanks.'

'Well let's hope so.'

'So why those projects? People don't usually gather information secretly on someone's successes.'

'The only thing I can come up with at the moment is that he, or they, believe the company has made huge profits by overestimating budgets and not doing projects they were given the money to do.'

'That would suggest a total lack of understanding about the way the system works. We are granted the money to provide solutions to meet environmental regulatory requirements and the like. We're also given incentives to make efficiencies. That means meeting those requirements by spending less money so that we don't have to charge the customer so much. As long as we meet those requirements – deliver the required outputs if you like - then we are meeting our obligations. And that ignores the fact that much of the money saved on the projects John has highlighted will have been spent on projects that were overspent, and there were plenty of those, I can assure you.'

'That's what I thought.' Nick thought that Jane had seemed a bit defensive but he threw another comment at her anyway. 'And there were notes on RWS giving the IT support contract to Kelsetex – a Group owned subsidiary – even though it made the highest bid.'

'We've already been rapped over the knuckles for that, and we were fined five million pounds.'

'I remember.'

'So they seem to have been barking up the wrong tree?'

'If what you say about the under-spends being genuine efficiencies or going into other projects then yes. Neither of them had been with the Company that long. Maxine was in "HR" so...'

'What does she know about anything?'

'You said it. And John was in "Audit", so would have been checking processes and information and data against spreadsheets and the like that he probably didn't understand at all.

'You don't seem to have a very high opinion of "HR" or Audit" or is it just John and Maxine?'

'I don't really know John or Maxine but I automatically doubt people who work for "HR".'

'So do a lot of people. But why should they disappear?'

'That's the million dollar question.'

'Any thoughts?'

'No. Have you?'

'No, I can't say that I have. Unless...'

'Unless what?'

'Oh I don't know. They've both disappeared without a word. Have they just given up? Or just run off together?'

'Why give up perfectly good jobs?'

'Perhaps they thought they were about to get found out.'

'Found out doing what?' asked Nick. 'Compiling a list of company successes.'

'Well from what you said it's pretty clear that they thought they were compiling evidence of wrong doing. Perhaps the way they went about it had broken some rules.'

'Possibly, but I don't think that's enough to explain their disappearance. Not yet anyway.'

'So what next?'

'Keep digging. I've got some meetings with people who I hope can shed some light on things. I've no doubt they'll just give me the detail that proves what you've told me about the savings being genuine efficiencies.'

'You mean you doubt me?' she said taking a sip of her Bordeaux. The first course had been eaten and they were waiting for the next.

'Not one bit,' said Nick. 'But I want my report to provide written evidence. I don't want anyone to doubt that you're pure and innocent.'

Jane looked at him over her glass. 'I hope you don't think I'm pure and innocent in everything.'

'Well, I've not found anything in the files to the contrary, so I'll have to take your word for it.'

'I wouldn't have thought a detective should take anybody's word for anything. Surely he needs hard evidence, firsthand experience you might say.'

The main course arrived and interrupted their flow. It was a minute or two before Jane said, 'If I'd asked around about you in RWS when we first considered bringing you in, what do you think I'd have heard?'

'That sounds like an interview question: "How do you think your friends would describe you?" Or "Do you your friends regard you as being an expert in anything?" I actually had to answer that one once by the way.'

'What was the answer?'

'The real one or the one I told the interviewer?'

'Both.'

'I told the interviewer that my friends regarded me as expert in current affairs. The truth was that they thought I knew everything there was to know about "Tom and Jerry". I wasn't too dishonest really. "Tom and Jerry" was on every week so it was very current.'

'Well, would you like to hear what I was told?'

'I don't know. Would I?'

'Summarising and translating, you came from a major civil engineering contractor and had a different way of looking at things. You were only with us for six years but your colleagues think that you're intelligent, witty, reliable, a safe pair of hands with potential to go a lot further than you ever did. Oh yes, and you're a bit of a cynic. How's that sound? Is it what you expected? More to the point is it true?'

Nick felt himself blushing slightly. He'd never been able to take praise, probably because he wasn't used to getting it.

'I suppose the bit about being a cynic is right. I've worked for a number of different companies and they all had a penchant for reorganising when things weren't going well. And it never made any difference. So I could never take the new initiatives or new organisational structures that were supposed to solve all of the Company's problems seriously.'

'I *know* all that. What about the rest of it? Is it true?'

'It's nice to hear, and is probably fairly near the mark'

'In that case, why did you not fulfil your potential? Were you overlooked?'

'Not *overlooked* as you mean it. I didn't want to go any further or higher than I did. So I didn't look for promotion. I did my job and a bit more usually but I didn't shout about it. I was invited to apply for higher jobs occasionally but I chose not to.'

'Why?'

'How many hours a week do you work?'

'Eighty or ninety.'

'There's your answer. Work/life balance they call it on those courses. It sounds like yours is way out of kilter.'

'Or *you're* lazy?' suggested Jane smiling.

'If you thought that you wouldn't have employed me. It's simple: I earned as much as I needed, and I preferred to spend my time at home rather than at work. Why put yourself through all the extra stress and agro?'

'I sometimes wonder myself.'

'So why do you? Put yourself through it?'

'It's just how I am I suppose. I have to strive to do the best... be the best I can.'

'Competitive then?'

'Yes, if you must know.'

'I must.'

'OK then. This wine must be strong. I don't usually talk about myself so readily.

Nick smiled. 'I'm a detective. I'm supposed to be able to get people to open up, and I've always been a good listener. But you don't have to say any more if you don't want to.

'No, it's OK. The fact is that I have a younger sister. We competed at everything. Of course I used to win every time - I was two years older. But she was father's favourite. The youngest one always is. They're always the baby of the family no matter how old they get. And Maggie was even more so. Father loved the way she never gave up no matter

116

how many times I beat her at everything. So she always won in the competition for his affection, which was what I really wanted. Then she had the accident - trying to beat me.'

'How did that happen?'

'We both loved horses and used to go for lessons every weekend. It was stupid. We were doing some show jumping stuff: you know, the sort of thing you see at gymkhanas.'

'Not really.'

'Anyway, I jumped a clear round and said to her, "I bet you can't do it faster." Well I don't know what happened. Whether something snapped inside her. Whether she was sick of losing to me or whether my goading had set her off, but she rode like an absolute maniac, like a bat out of hell. Everyone was shouting at her to slow down but she wouldn't. Then she took one jump, tried to wheel the horse round too quickly and fell off. The horse fell on top of her and crushed her. She's been in a wheelchair ever since. Of course she didn't blame me; she's far too sweet for that. But I blamed me and so did my Father. After that I worked harder and harder at everything to try to win his approval but nothing did it. I don't think he's even aware that I'm MD of a FTSE 100 company. But I can't stop trying.'

'Bloody hell. Well you need to learn to ease off or you'll work yourself into an early grave and all for the approval of a man who's never going to give it to you by the sound of things.'

'Perhaps you're right but that's easier said than done. Like I said: it's how I am now.'

'You know I was expecting you to say that you worked so hard because you had to; because you're a woman and it's always harder for a woman to get to the top. The "glass ceiling" and all that.'

'No, that's never been a problem for me. Glass is breakable: even toughened glass if you hit it hard enough with something sharp.'

'And you're sharp enough.'

'And hard enough?'

'I wasn't going to say that.'

'But it's my reputation. I'm a hard bitch. That's what they all say.'

'Do they?'

'Hadn't you heard? Be honest.'

'Well, to be honest...'

'Does that mean you're not normally being honest?'

'"Touché! Pussy cat!" That's a quote from "Tom and Jerry" by the way: The Two Mouseketeers, 1952. I told you I was an expert.'

'Obviously. It's interesting that you think that such knowledge would impress me.'

'Doesn't it?'

'Well, I suppose it shows an in depth appreciation of some 20th Century culture. Not adult culture, mind you. But you didn't answer my question. Had you heard that I'm a hard bitch?'

'To be h...Yes I had.'

'And what do you think now?'

'You're a very sharp, intelligent, driven woman.'

'You forgot to say attractive.'

'Perhaps I should have said "vain" or was that fishing for a compliment a sign of insecurity?'

'That could be perceptive, but on the other hand I've never gone fishing before. What does that tell you?'

Nick smiled; she'd somehow managed to turn a conversation about her childhood and the effect it had had on her, into fairly obvious flirting.

'That I could end up with a hook through my cheek?'

It was Jane's turn to smile but the waiter arrived to remove their plates before she could reply.

'Would you like to see the dessert menu?' he asked.

Jane looked across the table at Nick and said, 'I don't know about you but I think I've had enough to eat. Shall we go and sit somewhere comfortable and have a coffee?'

'Fine with me,' answered Nick.

'Good. Could you bring two coffees to the lounge please? And I'll be putting this on my room.'

'Certainly madam.'

'*Her room?*' thought Nick. '*Was that where she intended to land her catch?*' He told himself not to be so stupid and reminded himself that fish that were caught usually had their heads stove in. He followed Jane to the lounge where they sat on a two-seater sofa. His share of the two bottles of wine they'd had, had done their job and he felt suitably relaxed. He sat back and let his head fall back against the top of the sofa. His opinion of Jane had rocketed during the meal. She was intelligent, witty and (as she'd pointed out) physically, extremely attractive. The hard faced bitch reputation that she had was, as she'd explained, rooted in her childhood experiences and happened to be the only way a woman could get on in such a male dominated environment – just ask Margaret Thatcher. Actually she was quite soft in the middle, still craving the approval of her father.

Jane crossed her legs, revealing her thigh through the slit in her dress. She leaned back into the sofa half turning to Nick her upper arm along the top of the sofa, her hand behind Nick's head.

'I suppose you want me to tell you what I think about all of the initiatives RWS keeps running – employee empowerment and all of that guff,' said Nick. 'That was why you invited me to dinner wasn't it?'

'Not really,' said Jane. 'That's all bollocks really isn't it? I'd rather know how you're finding working for *two* women: one of whom is your ex-wife?'

'Oh! Well I've not seen much of Ruth since she heard about John and Maxine. She apologised for losing it and seems to have managed to convince herself that John is *not* screwing Maxine. Says he's not like that. I'm not sure if she means he's not the type to be unfaithful or is not that interested in sex. In fact I think she said something to that effect. Mind you, that would probably suit Ruth. The most excited I remember her getting in the bedroom was when an advert for a multi-headed steam cleaner came on the TV.'

Jane laughed out loud.

'Anyway,' said Nick. 'I think she's just letting me get on with it now.'

'And working under me?' Jane seemed to emphasise the word 'under' rather obviously to Nick.

'I think I could safely say that being under you is immensely stimulating,' he replied wishing that he could think of something a little more subtle, but then *she* started it. 'And I think you're more likely to pay me than Ruth is. I'm pretty sure she doesn't intend coughing up.'

'Well you've no fears on that score with me. I'm very happy so far.'

'That's good. As Simon and Garfunkel said, I'm just trying to keep the customer satisfied.

'Do you like old music?'

'Old? That's not old. It's only from the early seventies!'

'When I was about three years old!'

'I wasn't much older.'

There was a slight lull before Jane said, 'If you don't mind my asking, has there been anyone else? Since you split up with Ruth I mean?'

Nick smiled at his response before saying, 'To be honest,' he waited for Jane to acknowledge the phrase. 'No, why do you ask?'

'I just wondered if you ever got lonely. You'd been together for, what was it, fifteen years? And then you were suddenly alone. It seems natural that you might get lonely.'

'It's never been a problem. If I want someone to talk to, I just put the "Sat Nav" on in my car. Then I get nagged as well!'

Jane laughed. 'You know, I've enjoyed this evening. It's been nice to talk to someone without worrying about making an impression or trying to second guess their motives. I've not felt this relaxed with someone for years.'

'What about your husband?'

'Oh, he's about as interested in me as Ruth was in you by the sound of things. He's MD of major conglomerate based in London. That keeps him fully occupied.'

'He must be mad,' said Nick. 'Either that or he has some debilitating medical condition.'

'No, nothing like that. He'd just rather spend the nights in hotels in London than back at home with me.'

'No, he definitely needs his head examining,' said Nick reverting to 'eye contact' strategy.

'Charmer.'

'Nay lass. I just tell it like it is. I say, I just tell it like it is.

She smiled but said nothing. Instead she leant towards him and gave him a gentle, lingering kiss on the lips.

'Is your husband at home tonight?'

'I'm afraid so,' she replied, her mouth so close to his that they touched as she spoke. 'And I know that I said that he's not interested in me but I think even he'd notice if I brought another man home.'

'Damn it to blast!' said Nick as though thwarted by some criminal mastermind.

Jane smiled again, 'So it's a good job I've already booked a room upstairs.'

'So you have. My God! Did you plan the whole evening?'

'Not plan exactly but I thought there was a possibility it might end like this and I wanted to be prepared. Any objection?'

'Not at all,' replied Nick. 'By all means, let's spend the night together.'

'Don't tell me. That's another old song isn't it? The Rolling Stones. Didn't they do one about getting no satisfaction as well?'

'They did but they'd not met you'' said Nick smiling.

'And you say you're not a charmer. Shall we go up?'

By way of an answer Nick stood and offered Jane his hand to help her stand. He pulled her close and said, 'Lead the way.'

Another couple stepped into the lift fractionally before Jane and Nick and stood together in the middle. Nick and Jane separated and stood on opposite sides facing each other. Jane bent her right knee, slightly showing her thigh once again through the slit in her dress. They allowed their eyes to wander up and down each other. Nick felt the tension and anticipation rising. They arrived at their floor not a moment too soon for Nick, and Jane led the way to the room at a brisk pace. She had the key card out ready at the door but in her excitement it took her a couple of attempts to put the card in the right way round and get into the room. She pushed the door open hard and they stepped inside quickly, Nick closing the door immediately behind him just as Jane flung her arms round his neck and kissed him hard. They tried to undress each other frantically while they kissed. Jane undid Nick's belt while he pulled down the zip on her dress, slipped it off her shoulders and down to the floor. She stepped out of it. He swept her up into his arms and moved towards the bed only then realising that his trousers were round his ankles. He stumbled forward, managing to release Jane who stumbled sideways landing on the bed. Nick landed face down on the floor while Jane laughed hysterically.

'Bollocky bollocks!' he cursed, pushing himself up to his knees. His clumsiness had evaporated the frantic urgency of their desire.

'Hope you've not damaged anything important,' said Jane. 'Come here and let me examine you. See if anything needs kissing better.'

Nick yanked his trousers off as quickly as he could and clambered on to the bed. Jane pushed him on to his back and proceeded to examine him closely, deciding to kiss *everything* better, just to be on the safe side. Then he returned the compliment and they took their time caressing and kissing each other until they reached the point at which they could deny themselves no longer.

As they lay in each other's arms afterwards, they were disturbed by Nick's phone signalling that a text message had arrived. 'You can deal with that if you like,' said Jane. 'I'm going to the bathroom.'

He leaned out of the bed and grabbed his trousers and retrieved his mobile. It was from Sally: 'Are you all right? Do you still want to come over? xx'

'*Shit!*' he thought. '*Sally! I'd forgotten all about her. How could I?*'

He thought for a moment before replying, 'Really sorry. I can't. At my Mum's. She's had a fall. Have to stay over. Can come tomorrow if you still haven't changed your mind. Xx'

He deleted both texts and switched his phone off so that it didn't make a noise when Sally replied.

Jane came out of the bathroom and asked, 'Who was the text from?'

'My Mum,' he lied. 'She just wanted to have a chat. I told her I was tied up.'

'Tied up eh?' said Jane as she crawled towards him on the bed. 'Now there's an idea.'

'Haven't you had enough excitement for one night?' replied Nick.

'No chance. You can never get too much of a good thing,' said Jane as she kissed his lips, then his neck and his chest and carried on working her way down.

Nick woke the following morning to find himself alone in the room. There was a note on the pillow next to him, which read:

'See you at work. The room's all paid for and breakfast is included. Don't be late!'

It was signed, 'One very satisfied customer.'

Nick smiled. *'I should think she was satisfied. Not every customer gets that kind of personal service!'* He shuddered at the thought of the only other clients he'd had. They'd all been men. He switched his mobile back on. There was a message from Sally: 'Don't worry. I won't change my mind. XX'

'It's not only clients who are like buses,' he thought. *'It's lovers as well!'* He surprised himself at his casual attitude towards his sleeping with Jane after he'd made a commitment to do the same with Sally. Was that part of the 'new him'? He hadn't time to worry about it now. He showered and dressed. As he was about to leave he picked up Jane's note. Could he use it as a reference? No probably not.

He screwed it up and dropped it into the bin.

CHAPTER FOURTEEN

The excitement of the previous night almost caused Nick to forget that he had a meeting with Peter Dodgson at Crossington, but he remembered just as he left his flat, having taken a taxi back there to pick up his car. He drove in through the open site gates on time. '*I see security is just as tight as ever,*' he thought. He knew that it was company policy to keep all operational site gates closed at all times. He also knew that there were not enough people at the sites to repeatedly open the gates for the various visitors and deliveries that had to be made on a daily basis. Very few sites had automatic or remotely operated gates so they stayed open during normal operating hours – unless a 'bigwig' was due to visit. Obviously he wasn't a 'bigwig'.

He parked in front of a sign on a wall that said 'RECEPTION'. When he got out of the car a foul smell hit him. He looked around and identified the source quickly – the 'inlet works'. This was where the raw sewage entered the site. Mechanical screens filtered 'gross solids' from the inlet channel, (gross both in terms of size and in terms of well, just being gross - bearing in mind what is flushed down toilets into the sewers). The solids were then lifted out and dropped into an open skip where they'd remain until it was full. It would then be removed and replaced with an empty one. No wonder it stank. He walked in through the open door as quickly as possible, past the unmanned reception, and down a corridor looking for Peter Dodgson's office. On his right he saw a kitchen with electric cooker, microwave, kettle and toaster, then an old laboratory, almost derelict. On his left he passed one open door revealing two desks butted against each other, both covered in mountains of papers and folders. Eventually he arrived at another open door with a small plaque that said 'Works Manager' on it. Inside, a man in his late fifties, was sitting in his shirt sleeves, (Nick was pleased to see that he was wearing a tie), in front of tidy desk tapping at a keyboard.

'Morning Peter,' said Nick announcing his presence.

Peter looked up, recognition, taking a moment to dawn. 'Well hello there stranger. Come in and take the weight off.'

Peter and Nick hadn't known each other that well when Nick had worked for RWS, but Peter was one of those people who, once he'd met you, treated you like he'd known you all his life – unless he didn't like you of course, in which case he wouldn't give you the time of day or as he put himself, 'I wouldn't piss on him if he were on fire.' And that applied to just about anyone in 'Assets': the department that technically 'owned the operational assets on behalf of the company. They determined what equipment would be installed and, in the opinion of 'Ops', they never supplied equipment that was fit for purpose, leaving Ops to pick up the pieces. Peter was one of the old school managers. He had a relevant degree, (not, as he'd tell you, 'some Mickey Mouse one in Media Studies or Sociology'), and over thirty years experience with the Company, all in Operations. That was why he was so anti "Assets"'.

'Would you like a coffee?'

'Wouldn't say "No",' replied Nick.

Peter led the way to the kitchen, put the kettle on, and added a heaped spoonful of instant coffee to a couple of the cleaner looking mugs that he found on the draining board.

'So what brings you back to the Mother Ship?' he asked.

'Same as always: the need to earn a crust.'

'I thought you had your own business; as a Private Investigator, wasn't it?'

'Yeah, that's right. But that didn't work out. Simply didn't get enough work.'

'What sort of stuff did you get?'

'Just gathering evidence of adultery really - for messy divorces. Usually the man trying to catch his wife out hoping that would make the divorce cheaper for him.'

'No meaty murders, blackmails or "Maltese Falcons" then?'

'No, worse luck. Although to be honest I don't think I'd have known where to start. I think it was all just a pipe dream really.'

'Well to be honest, I thought that at the time but I really did wish you well. It would have been good to see someone escape, to work on something more exciting. So what are you doing now? You're not back on Standards and Procedures? Which have all gone to pot by the way, since you left. Back to the old ways of endless, pointless paper chases. At least when you were looking after it the paperwork wasn't interminable and the procedures could be understood.'

'I'm trying to pick up on what John Anderson was working on.'

The kettle had boiled and Peter added the water and milk and led the way back to his office. He talked as he walked, 'Why where's he gone?'

'That's just it nobody knows.'

'Perhaps they need a good detective to find him,' suggested Peter.

'I don't think they know one and I don't think they really care. Between you and me it looks like he might have done a runner with Maxine Hudson.' *'Bollocks! That's not the cover story! He's supposed to be away looking after his sick mother. Ah well, can't do anything about it now. And Peter hardly ever goes into head office anyway. Have to just go with it now.'*

127

'The HR director?'

'That's the one. Anyway, he was in the middle of a companywide audit of all sorts of stuff but he left it in a hell of a mess. Ruth, my "ex", knew that my business was going down the pan and she manage to wangle me a job trying to pick up the pieces of the audit.'

'Nice of her.'

'Considering she was living with John as well!'

'Didn't she ask you to find him for her?'

'You're joking! Her faith in my ability was limited to making a cup of tea. I think she only suggested me for this job thinking I'd make John look good. Oh, and she doesn't believe that John's run off with Maxine.'

'Where does she think he's gone then?'

'Haven't a clue. But we had one hell of a barney about it all in the restaurant at the office the other day. I'm surprised you didn't hear her yelling out here.'

'Might have been my day off.'

'Glad to hear that you can still get the odd day off.'

'Oh, I don't think of myself as being indispensable, not like some of them. The company certainly doesn't either – the way they've got rid of so many managers in the last couple of reorganisations. You know there used to be seventeen... no eighteen, operational areas and we're down to ten now. That means each manager has almost twice as many works and twice as many people to look after. How can you manage a workforce when you can't get to see them more than once a month? How can you manage them when you don't know what they're actually doing most of the time? In fact how can you manage them, when you don't even *know* what they're supposed to be doing? Like this latest crop of young managers; never been in Ops before, haven't a clue how it works, but they're here to "lead". At least *I* know what my people should be doing. I just don't know if they are or not. And the procedures we have now just get them to tick boxes to show they've done their scheduled tasks. And I *know* that they fill the sheets in at the beginning of the week, because sometimes they'll be off sick later in the week but the sheet's still ticked off for that day.' Sorry, that's a bit of a hobby horse of mine, and most of the other Ops Managers of my generation. Not that there are many of those now.'

'Just as well you're all supposed to be "leaders" now rather than "managers" then isn't it?' teased Nick.

'Don't you get me started on that!' said Peter in a mock-menacing tone. 'Fancy a fag break?'

'Why not? said Nick. 'I was never one to let not smoking stop me from having a break.' They went out of a back door and stood in the lea of the building, while Peter lit up.

'So what can I do for you?' asked Peter, exhaling a cloud of smoke away from Nick's face.

'Like I said, I'm trying to catch up with what John Anderson was working on and I've been looking through his files. There's one on the new treatment works here. I presume he came to talk to you about it?'

'Not quite. He invited me into head office. He implied he was too busy to spend the time travelling here and back.'

'And you went?'

'I had to go in anyway; monthly bollocking about my overspends. It didn't put me in a good mood for my meeting with him I'm afraid.'

'Shame! He'd written some comments about the Primary Tanks. Something about them being included in the AMP submission but not installed. I presume that's what he wanted to talk to you about?'

'That would be the Primary Tanks that are essential to the treatment process. The ones that we couldn't do without. The ones that Assets said we *could* do without. What a cock up!'

'So what's the story?'

'An extreme case of "value engineering".'

Nick pulled a face; this was not a term with which he was familiar.

'That's when the design lads in "Engineering" get together with the supplier and re-examine the original design to find "opportunities to improve the value for money". Put another way; make it cheaper. And as I said, this was an extreme case.'

'How come?'

'The original design, as you say, had the usual treatment stages in it and that was the design used for the estimates that were used for the AMP submission. But when it got to the detailed design stage, "Assets", in their infinite wisdom, decided on the say so of the supplier of the secondary treatment stage, Thorniley Water Processing, who *we* owned incidentally, that the new, totally unproven - on this scale anyway - secondary treatment process, didn't need primary tanks in front of it to remove most of the solids. I won't bore you with the theory. Suffice to say that it was supposed to save millions on the capital cost.'

'And what happened?'

'A complete success. The project people saved millions of course and they were all given a big pat on the back,' replied Peter venomously.

'And?'

'Of course it didn't bloody work. This new state of the art process couldn't handle the solids that weren't being taken out by the non-existent primary tanks. Compliance was an absolute nightmare. The EA were all over us. We tried to have some comeback against Thorniley's but they said the feedstock was completely different to what they quoted to treat. It's raw sewage for Christ's sake! So they wriggled out of it and lo and behold RWS sells Thorniley's with a full order book! Cost me a fortune in OPEX in the meantime, having to continuously clean out the secondary

130

treatment equipment. On top of that, the Company's been prosecuted for failing compliance, so that's cost thousands as well. Eventually even "Assets" had to agree that there was no way the plant would work without a primary settlement stage, so it was included in the next AMP submission and we got the money. And that's what you can see being constructed over there.' He waved his cigarette in the direction of some construction machinery behind an open mesh fence a couple of hundred yards away.

'So RWS got the money for the primary tanks twice?'

'That's right.'

'But is it? Right, I mean.'

'What do you mean?'

'Well if they'd already had the money once why didn't the Regulator tell them to just get on and build the tanks? How come they got the money twice?'

'Beats me. Perhaps it was just a case of demonstrating that they built a plant they thought would work, and in fact they could argue that it *did* work - until the solids bunged up the process. Perhaps they could argue like Thorniley's did, that the feedstock had changed. I know that if I were the Regulator, I'd have had none of it. I'd have told RWS to piss off and put it right.'

This all explained John's notes. Somehow RWS had effectively been granted the money for the primary tanks twice, because they didn't put them in first time round. But from what Jane had said about the way the funding worked, it was an honest attempt at an efficiency saving that hadn't worked - through no fault of RWS. Why *should* they have to pay for it? They'd ended up paying more in OPEX after all. It hardly seemed fair on the "Customer" – paying twice for the primary tanks, but that didn't mean it was illegal.

'You never fancied moving over to "Assets" and putting the "Ops" perspective on things?' asked Nick, in attempt to break the sense of frustration that had settled on both of them.

'And work with that shower of idiots? They're all "in compost mentis".'

'You mean "non compos mentis",' corrected Nick.

'No: "in compost mentis". They've got shit for brains.'

Nick snorted out a laugh. Peter carried on. 'Anyway, I'm an old dog and you know what they say about old dogs and new tricks.'

'*I* know,' said Nick. 'You can't teach an old dog new tricks. But he can still give you a nasty bite. You ought to think about it; move into "Assets" and give them nasty bites.'

'No, it's harder out here than it used to be but it's still a lot better than being cooped up in an office all day staring at spreadsheets and budgets. Shall we go in? It's a bit nippy out here?' Peter led the way back to his office and they sat opposite each other across the desk.

'Is there anything else you want to know?'

'Not unless you know about the Emergency Sludge Storage Tanks Project, and the Strategic Sludge Storage Project, and what was the other one? Oh yes, the Operational Sludge Storage Facility.'

'It looks like it's your lucky day young man. In the last AMP period, I was the Ops Rep on the steering group looking at sludge storage requirements for the AMP submission. All those you mentioned were projects that we put into the submission and got approved.'

'And were they installed?' asked Nick, knowing the answer already.

'No, *they* decided we didn't need them. *They* decided there were operational solutions that we should explore.'

'"They" being "Assets".'

'Who else?'

'But how would they know if there were operational solutions. They're not "Operations".'

'You don't need to tell me that, but they hold the purse strings.'

'So what happened?'

'Nothing. We just carry on with what we had before.'

'So you didn't need them after all?'

'I wouldn't say that exactly. We've been perilously close to running out of storage capacity on several occasions and have had to put sludge into some lagoons that we can't get it out from. And we're not supposed to do that anymore.'

'And what happened to the money that was earmarked for those projects?'

'Declared as CAPEX efficiency, I suppose. "Ops" never saw it.'

'Right, so all I have to do is talk to someone in "Assets" and they'll give me the answers.'

Peter shrugged.

'So how did you get on with John? I hope you weren't too short with him after your budget meeting.'

'Of course not; you know me. I'm used to talking to people from head office who haven't a clue what we do out here.'

'Thanks Peter!'

Peter grinned in response.

'Did he explain what he was doing; why he was looking at all these projects?'

'He just said it was some sort of audit. They're always doing them.'

'That's true. What did you think of him? Was he chatty at all?'

'Oh yeah; couldn't shut him up. Seemed surprised I didn't know all about him and your "ex". He emphasised that they didn't get together until you'd split up of course. Said he would never have an affair with a married woman.

133

But he was gushing about her, about how good they were together. It was quite embarrassing really. It's not as if I was remotely interested. Must be a "new man" thing - to talk about your wife or partner to other men like that. Not something I'd ever do.'

'Nor me. Well I've taken up enough of your time,' said Nick. 'It's been really useful. Thanks.'

'No problem Nick. It's been a pleasant change to talk to someone who doesn't want me to do more with less. And you know what they say: "A change is as good as a rest to a blind horse."'

Nick smiled and stood up and reached across to shake Peter's Hand.

'Well thanks again. Give me a nudge if you're at head office in the next couple of weeks, and we'll grab a coffee. I don't think I'll be there much longer than that. Take care.'

Nick drove straight back to the office. He had more meetings planned: meetings that would no doubt have the same results as the one he'd just had and confirm the notes John had made in his files. Then he would have to talk to someone in "Assets" who would no doubt be able to tell him exactly what had happened to the savings made from the projects in the files. He was sure that it would have been handled legitimately. RWS's systems, and the Regulator's for that matter, were too good to allow any dodgy dealings.

Of course the meeting he was really looking forward to was his next one with Jane.

CHAPTER FIFTEEN

Nick arrived back at his desk just after eleven o'clock. He had half an hour before his next meeting so he grabbed a coffee, checked his emails – there were none - and went to the toilet five minutes after finishing his coffee.

Then he made his way to the Customer Services building. Pauline Eccles, known to her friends as Jennifer, was seated at her desk in the open plan office that comprised the whole of the first floor of the building - the ground floor being taken up by the Customer Call Centre. Nick identified her by the name plaque that had been attached to the top her computer screen. She was in her late thirties, with dark shoulder length hair. She was also a little overweight, had far too much make-up on and smelled of a mixture of an almost overwhelming perfume and cigarette smoke. There was a photograph on her desk of two young girls aged about six and eight years old.

He approached from her right hand side and said, 'Pauline?'

She looked up. 'Ah you must be Nick. Call me Jennifer or Jen. Everyone else does.'

'Did you ever have freckles?'

'No more than any other kid. And no, the boys didn't all call me names.'

'Sorry you must get that all the time.'

'Not so much now. Only the older ones remember the "Scaffold"', she said smiling. 'I think I have everything you want to talk about in this file. Do you want to go and have a coffee while I take you through it?'

She picked up the file and her cigarettes and lighter. She couldn't smoke in the restaurant but she apparently went nowhere without them.

As they walked down to the Customer Services' Coffee Bar – a smaller version of the main restaurant - Nick tried to establish some rapport.

'How long have you been with RWS Jen?'

'About fifteen years. I joined from Uni as a graduate. Did the usual two year training development scheme. You know the sort of thing; six months here; six months there. Ended up in finance for a few years and then fancied a change so now I'm a Customer Services Manager.

'There's more than one then? Customer Services Managers, I mean.'

'Oh yes, I'm currently responsible for the regulatory reporting of all of our complaints – that's why you're talking to me – but I've also been Customer Communications Manager, Call Centre Manager, and a Business Development Manager.'

'Business Development: as in trying to bring in new business?'

'I know what you're going to say – water companies have a monopoly in their own areas. But OFWAT has been trying to encourage competition in the industry for years, and the Business Development Managers look for ways to supply water or treat wastewater in other regions. I think there are too many problems for it ever to take off. Water Quality being the obvious one.'

'What do you mean?'

'Well if RWS pumps water into another company's network to supply a particular customer, and it tastes different or is even contaminated, it will mix with the other company's water, and go to their customers as well as ours. So the host company ends up with thousands of unhappy customers through no fault of its own. An absolute nightmare. So I decided I'd be better out of that, and here I am. I'll have a latte please.'

They'd arrived at the counter in the coffee bar.

'OK. You go and sit down, I'll bring them over.'

Nick bought a latte for Jen and a tea for himself, wondering if tea would stay in his system any longer than coffee seemed to. He found her sitting at a table in a corner, away from the other customers. She thanked him for the coffee and took a sip. 'Ow! That's bloody hot! I always do that.' She put her cup down and glared at it as though it was the cup's fault she'd burnt her lips. Then she went on, 'In your email you said you wanted to know why there are two sets of figures relating to foul flooding for the same time periods?'

'That's right,' said Nick. 'It's something John Anderson had noted in his files and I've been tasked with picking up his work from where he left off.'

'Left off?'

'Yes, he's been given compassionate leave to look after his sick mother.' Nick remembered the cover story – the one he *should* have used when he spoke to Peter Dodgson. 'He could be missing for a while and they didn't want the work to stop. The only trouble is his files are not in the best state. But then he wasn't expecting to have to go off suddenly.'

'That explains why you're asking the very same questions that he asked.'

'I'm sorry you're having to answer them again, but at least you can just give me the very same answers.'

Jennifer smiled, 'Simple really. We redefined what qualified as a foul flooding incident and ended up with a lot fewer to report. Good news, for our rating in the Regulator's league tables.'

'Can we do that?'

'It's not as bad as it sounds. One of our guys was at an industry conference on sewage flooding and found that we

137

were a lot stricter in our definitions than some of the other companies were.'

'What do you mean?'

'Well, we said it was an internal flood if any sewage got inside a house. Other companies applied what their guys called the "boot test". If it didn't come over their boots then it wasn't a flood.'

'What about external?'

'Well that refers to flooding on customers' properties – gardens, drives, or whatever. We classed it as an external foul flooding if it got a metre from the manhole cover. In the words of our guy some other companies didn't classify it as an external flood unless they just about needed a boat to reach the house. And when we applied those criteria to our foul flooding incidents the numbers dropped by loads.

'Well they would, wouldn't they? What did the Regulator say?'

'Don't know; they haven't commented on the revised figures yet. But what can they say? We're just using the same definitions as these other companies now. If he doesn't like it he'll have to make them change their definitions and their numbers will shoot up. Either way we look a lot better by comparison.'

'I see. Well that sounds all perfectly reasonable – apart from the Regulator allowing the water companies to have such different definitions. That seems a bit odd; some might say incompetent. I hope he'll feel suitably embarrassed. Thanks for clearing it up for me anyway.'

'You sound disappointed.'

'Not really. It just seems pretty typical of the stuff in John's files – apparent anomalies that turn out not to be.'

'No problem, anything else I can do for you. This coffee's still too hot to drink.'

Nick thought for a moment.

'You said you were the Customer Call Centre Manager?'

'That's right: up until about three years ago, until it was outsourced to Kelsetex.'

'Was that why you moved on – because it was outsourced?'

'Partly, but I'd had enough anyway. We'd had ridiculous targets imposed by our director on the speed of answering phone calls. More than twice as quick as the Regulator required. The director wanted to be top of the response league but all it meant was that the call handlers were intent on only one thing - getting the caller off the phone as quickly as possible so that they could take another call; no thought for customer service, which I happened to believe was the most important thing. We even caught one call handler picking up a call from an old dear who'd asked, "Is that the Water Board?" and do you know what he answered?'

'No.'

'He said, "No, sorry madam, it's Regional Water Services PLC. Thank you for calling. Goodbye," and then he ended the call!'

Nick laughed but immediately apologised.

'It's all right. I laughed as well. If I hadn't, I'd have cried. But I decided then that I wanted to get out of that section. The outsourcing gave me the opportunity.'

'I see, so do you know what the point of the outsourcing was? I mean, as far as I can see, it's the same people answering the phones, in the same place and managed by the same people – apart from you that is.'

'Kelsetex is a company the group set up to provide call centre services to other companies. RWS is their first customer. They could never sell themselves to others if their own parent company didn't use them could they?'

'No, I suppose not, but is it cheaper for RWS?'

'How can it be? The people are paid the same and Kelsetex have to make a profit.'

'It must be more expensive for RWS then.'

'It is. But the extra cost to RWS is profit to Kelsetex and hence profit to RWS Group as well. So it doesn't cost "Group" any more money. In fact it enables "Group" to make profit from RWS that isn't counted as part of the regulated business, leaving RWS to make its allowed profit elsewhere.'

'So the group ends up making more profit from the water business?'

'Exactly.'

'Is that legal?'

'As long as RWS is not paying over the market rate. I think RWS will have to competitively tender the contract next time round, so other call centre service companies will have a chance to bid.'

'You mean like for the IT contract when Kelsetex got it despite being the highest cost bid with the lowest technical quality?'

'Exactly. Although since RWS were fined for doing that, I don't think they'll do it again when the customer service contract comes up for tendering.'

'Well, let's hope not. Anyway I think you've answered my next question, which was how come customer services and IT support are provided by the same company? I mean they don't exactly complement each other skills-wise. But from what you've said, IT and the Customer Call Centre were both moved into Kelsetex so that they can make non-regulated profit for the group from the RWS business.'

'Presumably, but like we said, they'll both have to get the contracts on merit in future.'

'I should think so too. Still you've confirmed what I already thought, so I can put another two of John's comments to bed. What did you think of John Anderson by the way?'

'Why'd you ask?'

'Curious, I suppose. He's with my ex-wife. Apart from when he's looking after his sick mother.'

'Really? He gave me the impression he was young, free and single. Well, free and single anyway.'

'Did he indeed?'

'Yes, he even asked me out to dinner.'

'Did you go?'

'I did as a matter of fact. My "ex" had the kids that night so I was free. And I try not to pass up a free meal. Should have stayed in and had a pizza.'

'Why's that?'

'He seemed to want to talk shop all night. If he wasn't pumping me for information about what we've just covered, he was bragging about how he was working on something important. I didn't understand him. He was only doing an audit. Mind you, he'd had a bit to drink by then.'

'Did he say anything else?'

'No. When I asked him what was so important about an audit, he clammed up. As though he realised he'd said too much. He still tried it on with me though.'

'Bloody hell! Did he?'

'There's no need to sound so surprised. I'm not that repulsive,' said Jenny, sounding genuinely angry.

'No, it's not that.... Of course you're not. Quite the opposite obviously.'

'Don't say any more. You don't want to get involved with this one as well,' he told himself. 'It's just that, like I said, he's supposed to be with my "ex" and the way she talks, they are the loves of each other's lives.'

'Yeah, well some blokes just can't control themselves.'

'I suppose not.' It occurred to Nick that she'd probably think the same about *him*, if she'd known about Jane and Sally, but he'd heard enough so he said, 'Thanks Jen, you've been very helpful. I'll let you get some lunch now.'

'Oh, I don't have time for lunch,' she replied standing up.

Nick shook her hand. 'You should make time,' he said.

'I wish I could,' she replied as she picked up her file and cigarettes and turned away.

Nick shook his head as he watched her walk away, not in the direction of her desk, but outside to the smokers' shelter. No doubt, after her 'ciggy break', she'd be snacking on rubbish, and that was why she was carrying that extra bit of weight, evidenced by the semi-inflated inner tube she seemed to be wearing around her waist underneath her blouse. Still, she'd been very helpful, although it looked increasingly as though John's notes were leading nowhere, unless his appointment with Ian Hughes in 'Assets' revealed something, which somehow he doubted.

His stomach growled. 'I know, I know,' he answered it. 'Time for lunch.'

CHAPTER SIXTEEN

As Nick ate his healthy lunch – a warm pasty – and flicked carelessly through John's files, his desk phone rang. 'Mrs Edwards would like to see you in her office right away, if you're available.'

'OK. Tell *Jane*, I'll be there in two shakes of a lamb's do-dah,' he replied. He finished his pasty on the first shake and was walking into her office as the lamb's do-dah stopped moving after the second.

She was sitting on the sofa with a buffet lunch for two set out before her on the coffee table. She had just poured out two coffees.

'Hi, I thought you might like some lunch. You've not had yours already have you?'

'No,' he replied, sitting down beside her.

'What are these crumbs on your tie then?' she asked brushing them off gently.

'That was just my starter.'

'Help yourself,' said Jane handing him a plate. Nick put a couple of sandwiches on his plate and started eating.

'How was the breakfast?' asked Jane.

'It was good. I didn't really do it justice though. I could have done with something to work up an appetite beforehand. But you'd already left.'

'I like to get to work before everyone else. I get more done that way. What about you, how was your morning?'

'Had a couple of useful meetings, one with "Ops" and one with "Customer". Both of them confirmed what was in John's files. I have a meeting with Ian Hughes in "Assets" this afternoon just to confirm more of the same. That should be a bundle of laughs. From what I remember of Ian, there isn't a more boring bloke in the company.'

'I'm sure you'll survive. Did you find the note I left for you?'

'Yes I did. I'm glad you were satisfied. I was thinking about keeping it to use as a reference, but I thought better of it.'

'That was your cue to say that you'd enjoyed it as well. I hope you don't try to satisfy *all* your customers that way.'

'Only the irresistible ones,'

'Charmer.'

'Nay lass. I just...'

'I know, tell it like it is.'

'Exactly.' Nick put his empty plate down and said, 'Any chance of some afters?'

'Nay lad, I've got a meeting in ten minutes, and we wouldn't want to have to rush our afters. We could get indigestion. How about this evening, could you manage some afters later?'

'I'll be starving by then.'

'I'll have to let you have two helpings then,' replied Jane resting her hand on Nick's thigh. 'In fact, I'll come to yours. I feel like slumming it after the luxury of last night.'

'Less of the "slumming it" if you don't mind. It's a little bijou that's all. You bringing dessert?'

'Nick darling, I *am* the dessert remember?'

'I like mine with cream.'

'I'll see what I can do.'

'None of that low calorie stuff mind you.'

'Of course not, you'll be working off the calories, won't you?'

'I hope so,' said Nick. 'But I think it's time to get back to work. I'm running out of euphemisms.'

'Not a sign of a lack of stamina I hope.'

'No, but I have to calm myself down before I meet Ian Hughes. He doesn't take kindly to any sort of frivolity.'

Nick stood up. Both of his knees went 'crack'.

'Goodness, you're cracking!'

'You're not so bad yourself love,' replied Nick.

Jane laughed, 'Getting the jokes out of your system before you meet Ian I see.'

As he walked back to his desk, Nick realised that he had just arranged to see Jane, (in fact more than just 'see her'), and he had already agreed to see Sally; in fact more than just 'see' her as well, unless he was seriously misinterpreting things. He turned round.

Without breaking stride, he said to Jane's secretary as he walked past her, 'She still in?'

'Yes she's on the...'

'Good.'

'Phone,' she finished as Nick knocked on the door and entered.

Jane was indeed on the phone. 'Richard, I've told you, everything's fine. I've got it totally under control.' She saw Nick. 'Look, I have to go. I'll speak to you later.' She put the phone down. 'I told you, you'll have to wait for afters.'

'Everything all right?' asked Nick nodding towards the phone. 'Anything a top class detective can help with?'

'Why, do you know one?' she countered. 'No that was Richard, he was worried about our next "load of bollocks", I think you call them. We call them employee initiatives. Since our HR Director is missing he's a bit concerned that there's no one driving it.'

Nick put his fingers in his ears, 'La la la,' he sang. 'I don't have to know anything about them anymore.'

'So why are you here, if you're not desperate for afters?'

'Who said I'm not desperate? But that's not why I'm here. I got so... motivated about our meeting later that I forgot, I have to go and see my Mum tonight. Remember she sent me a text last night.'

'Are you telling me I have to go hungry?'

'No, not at all. I was just going to ask if we could make it say, ten o'clock. If that's not too late for having your afters I mean.'

'No that'll be fine. I'll make it something special as a reward for your being such a devoted son.'

'Will it be hot?'

'Sizzling!' she said. 'So don't be late. I wouldn't want it to go off the boil.'

'I'm starving already,' said Nick. 'I'll see you at ten then.'

He went back to desk, texting Sally as he walked: 'I have to see my Mum again 2nite. Have to leave by 9.30. Can we meet early?'

'Two lovers in one night? That's more often than the buses,' he thought shaking his head, a broad grin running from ear to ear.

CHAPTER SEVENTEEN

In his usual efficient manner Ian Hughes had booked a meeting room for the whole afternoon for his meeting with Nick. He was never one to be accused of allowing insufficient time to perform a task. If a job's worth doing then it's worth doing in the minutest detail: until everyone else had lost the will to live. Ian had arrived early in order to set everything up. The table in front of him was covered with files. His laptop was open before him, numerous spreadsheets available at the click of his mouse.

Nick walked in whistling "Tonight's the Night", carrying a cup of coffee and an A4 pad with two sheets left on it. His whistling was almost inaudible, just a bit of air being pushed out between his teeth, because he couldn't stop grinning.

'Hello Ian! Good to see you again,' he lied determined to make a bright start.

'Hello. I've ordered coffee,' he said, nodding towards a flask, tiny little plastic milk pots with plastic milk in them, and plastic cups on a trolley in the corner. 'You needn't have bought your own.'

'Of course you have. I should have known you'd have everything organised.' *'Wouldn't touch the muck in that flask with a barge pole but then it would probably dissolve the pole,'* he thought.

Nick sat down opposite Ian. 'It's good of you to make the time to see me. I know you must be very busy. I hope I don't have to take up too much of your time.'

'That's OK. I've booked the room for the whole afternoon and I don't have to be away early. We can take as long as it takes.'

'Wonderful.'

'No problem. Shall we get started? I've sorted the files out so that you can see what was included in the AMP submissions for the projects with the projected spend profiles. They're in the file in front of you. Then you can see the actual spend profiles in the files to the right of that one. Then in the file over there,' pointing to a file at the end of the table, 'you can see details of the orders placed on each of the projects against the original budgets for those items. Then in that file over there,' pointing to the other end of the table, 'you can see the final out-turned cost of each project, and in the file next to it you see blah blah blah....'

Nick had already lost the will to live. His stamina was not what it once was. He was out of training: he'd not been in a meeting for months. Then he had a thought. He knew what would bring him round again. Another 'caffeine fix'. He'd finished his own; it would have to be that hot muck from the flask. 'Coffee Ian?' he asked, moving over to the trolley in the corner. 'Then perhaps you can take me through an example: follow a project through the files so that I can get my simple brain round it?'

'OK, just milk, no sugar.'

Nick filled two plastic cups with the hot, burnt mud from the flask, remembering to use an extra cup as insulation in both cases. Then he ripped the top of a pot of the plastic milk squirting it on to his tie. 'Bollocky bollocks!' he said. He poured what remained into a cup, and then opened another pot of milk, this time turning it round and squirting milk on to the wall. He decided to take his coffee black, and added a couple of sugars to compensate.

He put the two coffees down on the table and sat down next to Ian so that he could follow Ian as he took him through a project's progress through the files.

'Any particular project?' asked Ian.

'How about the big sludge project?'

'You mean the Sludge Treatment and Combined Cycle Power Generation Plant – project number WWS5016893.101?'

'That's the one,' said Nick, trying to sound enthusiastic.

Nick tried to focus and to maintain concentration by taking notes. It all seemed fairly straightforward. There was the AMP submission and projected five-year expenditure profile, then there was the approved budget and projected spends and then there was the actual spend and out-turn cost and there was the thirty million pounds or thereabouts saving on the AMP submission. 'And in this file,' said Ian, 'I can show you the individual orders and the invoices, against the budget for each item of equipment costing ten thousand pounds or more.' And he did. There were hundreds of them. 'But,' as Ian so rightly said, 'the Devil is in the detail.' '*And you must have sold your soul to the Devil,*' thought Nick.

Then Ian showed Nick another file – one of the 'blah blah blah' files - which showed the total investment made in the AMP period. In this one Ian showed Nick that other projects had overspent and that new projects, not included in the AMP submission, had been given approval as money had become available from projects on which efficiencies had been made.

Nick pulled over another file. 'What's in this one?'

'That, and those over there,' replied Ian, indicating a pile on a chair that Nick hadn't even noticed, 'have the detail of where the savings were made. If you look in there you can see how much was budgeted for design, procurement, construction, and commissioning, and how

149

much was overspent or saved in each area. Then if you're really interested, I can show you the same detail on the design and installation as I did on the equipment procurement.'

'Is there any point?'

'That depends on if you think there's anything gone astray in there.'

'Do you?'

'No chance. It's all accounted for.'

'Thought so.' Nick's phone vibrated in his pocket. He had a text.

'I need a comfort break he said, which was true. 'Be back in a sec.'

He left the room and went to the toilet two doors further down the corridor where, as well as taking his comfort break, he checked his phone. The text was from Sally.

'Early OK with me. Finish early 2day. How about 6? Where?'

'Pick u up at yours? Go for a meal?' he texted back.

His phone rang. He interrupted BTO after their first stutter. It was Sally.

'Hi, it's me' said Sally.

'I know,' said Nick. 'Not changed your mind have you?'

'No I just thought talking would be quicker than texting.'

'That's true. Shall I pick you up then?'

'Er, can we meet at the restaurant if you don't mind. I'll explain why later.'

'Sure, what do you fancy? Italian?'

'Yes, that'd be great.'

'OK I'll meet you at the Pizzeria in North Street at six.'

'Great. I'm looking forward to it.'

'So am I,' said Nick. 'See you later.'

'Bye!'

He went back into the meeting with Ian, wondering why Sally didn't want picking up from her place. Was there something or someone she didn't want him to know about? He'd have to find out. Much as he liked Sally he wasn't the kind of bloke who messed around with married women. All right he wasn't the type of bloke who messed around with *two* married women at the same time.

As he re-entered the room Nick had a thought: something in one of the files had just registered with him. 'Can I have another look at the file with the additional projects in it: the one that shows all the projects that money is being spent on?'

'You mean the AMP Current Spend File?'

'If you say so.'

Ian pulled the file towards them. Nick opened it and examined it for a few moments. 'So these are the projects that were in the AMP submission?'

Ian sighed; he didn't think Nick had been paying attention, 'Yes.'

'And these are the projects that were added to make use of the savings made elsewhere?'

A louder sigh, 'Yes.'

'And am I right in saying that the cost of these projects is nowhere near the total savings made from the original AMP projects?'

'If you'd been listening... look I can show you again. If you look at this....'

'Ian, I'm sorry. I *have* been listening,' he lied. 'But I'm not as into all this stuff as you are. Is the total cost of these additional projects much less than the savings made on the original projects or not?'

'Yes.'

'By how much?'

'About two hundred and fifty million pounds.'

'So where's all the money gone?'

'What do you mean, Where's it gone"?'

It was Nick's turn to sigh.

'I mean RWS has been granted a certain amount of money to do certain projects and it's not going to spend it all. So where's it gone?'

'Nowhere. It's efficiency savings. The Company keeps it.

'Two hundred and fifty million pounds?'

'Over the five year AMP period, yes.'

'Let me get this straight. Every five years the Company has to go to OFWAT with a proposed Capital programme consisting of hundreds of projects. And those projects come from having to meet new drinking water and sewage treatment requirements?'

'Amongst other things, yes. The requirement for the vast majority of our projects is entirely outside of our control. It's stuff we *have* to do.'

'And RWS does all of the cost estimates for the work?'

'Yes, with the aid of outside consultants occasionally.'

'And if RWS does the work cheaper, it gets to keep the savings?'

'Well, we never get all the money we ask for. OFWAT imposes efficiency targets. They give us less money than we need to do the work.'

'But RWS still makes savings on the amount of money it *is* granted. And if RWS does the estimating, what's to stop it over-estimating the cost to get more money?'

'There are Industry cost-estimating models that we have to use.'

'So how the hell does RWS, and presumably all the other water companies make such huge savings?'

'By being creative.'

'Creative?'

Yes, by being innovative. By finding different solutions to the problems. Doing things in different, less expensive way.'

'Value Engineering?' suggested Nick, throwing in the phrase Peter Dodgson had spat out.

'Yes,' replied Ian in a surprised tone. 'That's one of the techniques, although that comes later on in the project.

'So what's to stop RWS proposing more expensive equipment and processes knowing that they can find cheaper solutions?'

'We have to explain everything and justify our proposed solutions in our submission. They have to be feasible and sensible. If they're not standard solutions, then we have to put a lot more explanation into the submission; say if we wanted to use new technology.'

'Like the secondary treatment process at Crossington?'

'Yes,' replied Ian, surprised again at Nick's knowledge, but then went on. 'And I know what you're going to say.'

'You do?'

'Yes. You're going to say that it didn't work.'

'Well it didn't, did it?'

'Well, Ops couldn't make it work.'

'Because the primary tanks had been dropped from the design and the secondary treatment stage couldn't cope with the solids.'

'Yes, but they were very anti the new technology from the beginning. I think they could have made it work with a suitable cleaning regime.'

'They've *been* cleaning them! It's cost Peter Dodgson a fortune.'

'Oh, you've been talking to Peter have you? Well, yes there was an increase in OPEX but it saved a fortune in CAPEX. Anyway, they're getting their primary tanks now.'

153

'And RWS has been granted the money for them even though they were included in the first submission that was approved.'

'Why not? We tried some new technology that didn't work. The plant has to be made compliant so we needed the money for the primary tanks.'

Nick could see that he wasn't to get any further on that project so he tried going back to another big one he read about in John's files. 'Can we go back to the Sludge Treatment and Power Generation Plant?'

'What about it?'

'It came in at thirty million under budget. How did that happen?'

'Classic case of "Value Engineering". The engineers found cheaper, alternative equipment and found that they could reduce the amount of standby equipment.'

'And the project was definitely needed?'

'What do you mean? Of course it was. You'd know that if you'd read the AMP submission. It's all in there.'

'I have read it. It says the project was necessary because the agricultural land outlet for the sludge was unreliable.'

'That's right.'

'Well, the plant's been shut down for over a year, while another stream is added. *All* of the sludge is being recycled to land. Doesn't sound very unreliable.'

'Market's changed.'

'So why is another drying and incineration stream being added?'

'In case the market changes again.'

Nick looked puzzled. 'So over a hundred million pounds was spent on a plant that clearly wasn't needed so soon, and another shed load of cash is being spent on expanding it when it's *still* not needed?'

'It could look like that - if you didn't understand all of the nuances of the sludge recycling and marketing and issues of public perception.'

'And obviously, I don't.'

'Exactly,' said Ian, as though he had won an argument. 'If you knew anything about the AMP process and project management, you'd be able to understand it.

Nick struggled successfully to resist the urge to give Ian a slap. He knew Ian had a reputation for talking down to anyone who knew less than he did – unless they were more senior than him.

Nick decided to play along. 'Perhaps if I stay for another ten years or so, I might get the hang of it. Let me check my understanding as it is at the moment. It's the development of alternative and cheaper solutions and value engineering that produces the CAPEX efficiencies?'

'If the project gets the final approval to go ahead.'

'Doesn't it get that when it's included in the AMP submission and the Regulator agrees to it?'

Another sigh.

'No, if we were committed to doing exactly what we put in the submission we wouldn't be able to make any efficiencies, wouldn't even be able to do any value engineering, because we'd have had to have done all of the design before we put the submission together. The submission identifies what we have to achieve – like what water quality, or in the case of that sludge project, how much sludge we have to dispose of – and proposes a feasible solution with costs. If we can find an alternative, more economic solution, then that's all well and good.'

'And that could include not doing the project at all.'

'It could.'

'Like the three sludge storage projects.' Nick paused to call the projects' titles to mind. 'The Operational, Emergency, and Strategic Sludge Storage Projects, I think they were called. They were all in an AMP submission but none of them were carried out.'

'Yes. That's right. "Ops" looked at them and agreed they could change their operating practices and manage without them.'

'That's odd. Peter Dodgson said "Assets" decided the projects weren't necessary and that "Ops" were struggling to cope as a result.'

'What can I say? They *are* coping, and "Ops" agreed to it.'

'Peter didn't think so and he was "Ops" sludge rep.'

'It was the "Ops" Director who agreed. We didn't deal with Peter. Directors tend to have a better grasp of the bigger picture.'

Nick now felt like slapping Ian on Peter's behalf. He thought he'd better leave before he gave into the feeling, but then he saw something that he hadn't seen in John's files.

'What's this mean here?'

'Just what it says,' sighed Ian. 'They were a group of priority/feasibility studies done to determine if the proposed new additional or "discretionary" projects were worth doing. Some were. Some weren't.'

'It says "Consultancy Spend".'

'That's right the work was done by consultants; Hooley and Vaal'

'Why wasn't it done in house?'

'The powers that be decided that we had enough to do, delivering the current projects, so they employed consultants to do it. Made sense really. Apart from the time aspect, some of the consultants' staff had specialist expertise in environmental protection, and could advise which of the proposed projects would deliver the biggest bang per buck for the environment.'

'So someone in "Assets" managed the consultants?'

Another sigh. 'No, as I said they decided that we had enough to do already, so someone else managed the work.'

'And that's why there's no detailed breakdown of the spend in your file. Who did manage the work then?'

'I'm not sure. I think it was "Procurement".'

'Procurement? What do they know about the water and wastewater businesses?'

'Enough! They had the proposed projects outlined. All they had to do was give that to the consultants. They already knew which consultants were on our approved list and they have very strict rules about only using them. Been trouble in the past with people using unauthorised consultants.'

'What sort of trouble?'

'I wouldn't know. I've never done it!' replied Ian briskly. 'All I know is that Procurement took the management of consultants entirely under its remit. Nothing gets approved without the Director's approval.'

'Who's the Director?'

'Now that Martin Worsley's... gone, Richard Seaton.'

'Really? I'll have to go and have a word with my mate Richard then.'

'You know him?'

'Oh yes. Him and me are like this,' said Nick, crossing two fingers.

Ian frowned. 'You surprise me.'

'Oh, I'm full of surprises,' replied Nick already looking forward to grilling Richard Seaton. 'I think I have everything I need, for the time being Ian. I think I'd better get off and see if I can catch Richard before "close of play",' using a term he knew they loved to use in "Assets".

'Oh Richard won't be leaving for a couple of hours yet.'

'*He might when he hears that I want to talk to him*' thought Nick but he said, 'I wasn't talking about him. I wanted to catch him before *I* leave.'

157

Ian looked at his watch and raised his eyebrows; it was only a quarter to five.

'Anyway, thanks again,' said Nick rising from his chair and heading to the door. 'I'll put a good word in for you with Richard.' He left, leaving Ian open mouthed at the thought of someone like Nick Howard who was so obviously clueless about everything putting "a good word in for him".

What damage would that do?

CHAPTER EIGHTEEN

Nick sat in "Pizzeria Italia", (was that not tautological: weren't all pizza places Italian by definition?), mulling over why Sally had been so obviously reluctant for him to pick her up. Why didn't she want him to come to her place? She'd been keen enough the other night to invite him up. Had she been so keen because it was a rare opportunity? Did she have a husband, who'd happened to have been away that night? That must be it. There was no other explanation that he could think of. And after all, he was a detective - used to working things out.

Sally arrived bang on time and apologised for being late. *'Why do people do that? It's like apologizing when someone has walked into you because they weren't looking where they were going.'* She was clearly nervous. Something was wrong, but at least it looked like she was about to come clean. *'This could be a very short date'* thought Nick.

Sally smiled and looked Nick in the eye, 'Before we order anything, there's something I have to tell you, and if you don't want to see me anymore after that, then I'll understand. Really I will. It would be perfectly understandable if you didn't: want to see me I mean...'

'Sally, why don't you let *me* worry about whether I still want to see you *after* you've told me whatever it is?' said Nick, trying to calm her nerves. *'But if you're married, then I'll eat my pizza and it's "Goodnight Vienna" or "Goodnight Rome" or whatever the Italian equivalent is.'*

'It's about the other night.'

'What about the other night?'

'Well after we'd said goodnight, about ten minutes afterwards actually, there was a knock on my door and I thought it was you. I thought you'd changed your mind and wanted to come in to... well you know.'

'I did want to but...'

'I know,' she smiled. 'But it wasn't you. That's stupid, I'm sorry. You know it wasn't you. It was my "ex"; Dave.'

'Your "ex"? What did he want?'

'He wanted to tell me that I wouldn't be seeing you again.'

'What?'

'He said that I wouldn't be seeing you again, because you wouldn't want to see me.'

'What made him think that?' asked Nick: a question, which he was shortly to realize, was very stupid. The answer was obvious.

'He said he'd warned you off.' The look in Sally's blue eyes expressed hurt, sorrow, and a 'please don't let him put you off me' look, all at once.

Nick thought, *'Why didn't I work that out before she had to say it? Some detective!'*

'So it was Dave who attacked me, in the car park?'

'Yes, he's been hanging around my place on and off for months. He can't accept that it's over: that I won't take him back. Sometimes he comes up and knocks on the door and asks me to forgive him and swears he'll never look at another woman again. And every time I tell him to piss off!'

Nick was surprised at the language - Sally looked too weary to muster up such venom.

'So what did you do when he told you he'd beaten me up?'

'I smacked him. No, that's not true. I punched him, in the face. Then I kneed him where it hurts. Then I told him to "F Off" and never come back. And then I slammed the door in his face.'

160

'What did he do? asked Nick thinking that Sally's "ex" might have tried to beat the door down and beat her up.

'He skulked off. He wouldn't have the guts for a face to face fight with anyone. I was very surprised he'd manage to beat you up.'

'He caught me off guard. Came at me from behind.'

'He must have, but even then he must have been drinking to get the courage up to do that. Dave's never been one to put up a fight for anything. Apart from me anyway.'

'He must really care about you then and I can't blame him for that.'

'I suppose so, but that doesn't change anything. I never want to have anything to do with him ever again. I want to move on.'

'So is he *still* hanging about around your place?'

'I think so. I saw him yesterday. He may be there now. I'm not sure. I know he hasn't followed me here, because he doesn't have a car. I'm sure he won't try to beat you up again, especially if you saw him coming but I just didn't want...'

'Any unpleasantness?'

'Yeah, that's the word. And to be honest I didn't want to rub his nose in it. I mean he is a complete loser, and I am completely finished with him, but I didn't want... well I didn't want to upset him for no reason – I mean if you didn't want to see me again. You are all right aren't you? He didn't do any real damage did he?' said Sally, as if she'd suddenly realized that Nick might have been badly hurt, even though he was sitting in front of her looking perfectly all right.

'I'm fine. And if I do want to see you again?'

'Then he can bloody well go to hell, and you can come round to mine as often as you want!'

Nick smiled. 'I like the sound of that: coming round to yours as often as I like.'

'You mean it's not put you off?'

'No, of course not. Have you forgotten what I do for a living? Getting beaten up comes with the territory. You know, getting warned off when you're getting close to exposing someone.'

Sally's eyes widened slightly, 'Has that really happened to you?'

'No, not really. But it could, you never know.'

Sally had to check again. 'So you really do want to see me again? You're not put off?'

'Now that you've explained things, your "ex" seems a lot less dangerous than mine. Look at the mauling she gave you the other day! Has she apologized by the way?'

'Apologized? No, but there's no need, she was just upset. I remember how upset I was when I found out that Dave was cheating on me.'

'Enough of "ex's", shall we order?'

'I think I need to go and powder my nose first.'

'Your nose looks suitably powered to me,' said, Nick although he had thought there'd been tears in her eyes when he'd said that he still wanted to see her again - and to come round to her place as often as he liked.

While Sally was away from the table he thought things over. '*No, he had never been beaten up as a warning to drop a case before, and it hadn't happened the other night either. He hadn't been warned off this case. That was good news, in that it could imply that he wasn't dealing with violent people. But on the other hand, did it mean he wasn't getting anywhere? That he wasn't getting close to anything? Of course he wasn't; all he'd achieved was to discover that RWS was making efficiencies on its AMP submissions! But then he'd only been on the case for a couple of days. Perhaps if he did get close to something he would get beaten up as a warning.*' And as he had that somewhat disturbing and slightly exciting thought, Sally arrived back at the table.

162

They both ordered pizzas, from a girl who said her name was 'Debbie', if they needed anything. Nick only just stopped himself asking her what her name was if they *didn't* need anything. They both drank tap water because they were both driving. Neither ordered a dessert nor even a coffee, as a wordlessly exchanged glance into each other's eyes confirmed that they both wanted to get back to Nick's as soon as possible. (They didn't go to Sally's as they didn't want to risk winding up Dave, who might have ruined the mood. Next time, as Sally had said, he could go to hell.)

Back at Nick's flat things progressed quickly and easily and they were soon consummating their relationship in Nick's specially tidied bedroom. Afterwards they lay together naked in each other's arms chatting and dozing. Sometime later Nick opened his eyes and kissed Sally on the forehead, and reflected on his new relationship. He and Sally got on so well. It all seemed so natural. The way they had made love was so gentle, so smooth, so considerate: each wanting to ensure that the other was being fulfilled. With Jane, it was wild! She was out to enjoy herself which, to be fair, did guarantee that Nick was more than satisfied. But for Jane it was all about *her* pleasure, Nick's pleasure was a fortunate, (for Nick) by-product. Jane was carnal. Jane was ...Nick looked at the digital radio alarm clock on his bedside cabinet. Jane was going to here in half an hour!

'Shit!'

Nick sat up sharply, almost breaking Sally's neck.

'What the f...? What's the matter?' said Sally as she tried to sit herself up.

'Look at the time,' said Nick. 'I should be on my way to my Mum's by now. She'll be getting worried. She's a terrible worrier. I have to get going.'

Sally looked at the clock radio. 'Blimey is that the time? You're right, you'd better get going. But how about a kiss first?'

163

She leant into him and gave him a long, lingering kiss. He responded and very nearly got carried away. He pulled back just in time. 'Tomorrow?'

'Yes,' she replied. 'Dave can go to hell if he's hanging around. And *you* can arrange to stay the whole night. I want to wake up and make love again. Not wake up and have to dash off!'

'Sounds like a good plan,' said Nick.

'*Bloody hell,*' he thought, '*Are all women insatiable nowadays? Or am I suddenly irresistible? No, Ruth proved I wasn't irresistible.*'

Nick dressed as quickly as he could without appearing to be rushing – he was only supposed to be going to see his mother. Fortunately Sally dressed quickly as well. They were just about ready to leave when BTO told them they hadn't seen nothing yet.

'Can't wait for tomorrow night then,' whispered Sally, her arm round his waist trying to see who was ringing.'

Nick grunted, it was Jane! 'It's my Mum, she'll be wondering where I am. Excuse me; I'll have to talk to her.' He wandered as nonchalantly as he could back into the bedroom, pretending he was looking for something.

''I'm outside' said, Jane. 'What number do you live at?'

'*Shit! Shit! Shit!*'

He didn't reply for a moment. He looked out of the bedroom window onto the street below. There was Jane's Audi a couple doors down.

'I'm not back from my Mum's yet,' keeping the lies he was telling his two lovers as consistent as he could. 'Why don't you wait in the pub down the road? I'll only be about ten minutes. I'm just stuck in a bit of traffic, ("*At nine-thirty?*"), at some road works.'

''I'm not stepping foot in that place. I noticed it as I drove past. It looks like a right dive. It looks like the sort of place cockroaches would avoid. I'll wait in the car.'

164

'What? No!' he shouted.' He didn't want her to see Sally and him leaving.

'What's the matter for goodness sake?'

'I just don't want you sitting out there at night on your own. Like you said that pub at the end is a right dive. They get all sorts of pond-life going in there.'

'Is that the same pub you wanted me to wait in?'

'Why does she have to be so sharp all the time?'

'No, you're right that would have been a mistake. Tell you what, come and wait in my flat. There's a key above the door (*Or there soon will be*). You can let yourself in. I'm in 27a. Oh, will you be using the lift?'

'Why?'

'I er... want you to save your energy.'

'OK, tiger. Think you're going to be tiring me out do you?'

'If you play your cards right. I'll see you in about ten minutes.'

He ended the call, took a deep breath, remembered to take his spare key out of his bedside cabinet, and walked out into the lounge area. He glanced round making sure there weren't any signs that two people had been using the room, and then said, 'Right, we'd better get going.'

He shepherded Sally towards the door, picking her handbag up for her, with a silent *'Phew, that was close.'*

'Were you telling your Mum to save her energy?'

'What? Oh yes she said she was ironing! I ask you! At this time of night!'

'I thought she'd had a fall and could hardly move.'

'Exactly! And she still drags herself to the ironing board to iron her knickers.'

'She irons her knickers?'

Nick realized that there too much talking and not enough walking.

165

'I know, she's mad.' He pulled the door closed behind him and put the key on top of the door frame.

'What are you doing: putting your key up there?' asked Sally. 'That's not very safe. Anyone could find it.'

'Er... oh... I... er... thought I'd just do it until I can get a key made for you. Then you can let yourself in, if I'm not here when you come round... *if* you come round.'

'But you're coming back tonight aren't you? I won't be coming back before you do.'

'I'm just trying to get into the habit, so I don't forget.'

Too much talking again. 'Come on let's get going.'

He crossed the hallway and opened the door leading onto the stairs.

'Why aren't we using the lift?'

'It's better for you to use the stairs – the exercise.'

'We didn't use them on the way up,' replied Sally as she stepped through the door.

'I wanted to save *my* energy.'

'Glad you did,' said Sally reaching up to kiss him on the lips again. They walked down the two flights of stairs quickly and Nick was about to open the door out on to the foyer when he looked through the small glass panel in the otherwise solid, double skinned white metal door. Jane was still there, waiting for the dammed lift! He turned to Sally grabbed hold of her, pulled her close, turned her so that her back was to the door and kissed her passionately, whilst watching through the glass panel for the lift to arrive. Jane must have just missed it, and it must have had to go all the way to the fifteenth floor and back, as they had to come up for air twice. Eventually Jane stepped into the lift and the doors closed.

'Wow! I can stay the night you know. I could go back upstairs and just wait for you to get back.'

'What? Oh no it's OK. I don't know how long I'll be. I might even end up staying the night: guarding the ironing

166

board. I just wanted to say goodnight properly. Give you something to remember me by, and I couldn't kiss you like that out there in the streets.'

'You've already given me something to remember you by tonight. But I'll certainly remember that kiss as well.' She nibbled at his lips gently, and said, 'Come on, we'd better go before I ravish you here!'

Nick opened the door and they walked quickly out of the building and across to Sally's car. They kissed yet again, and Sally got in, while Nick got into his car which was parked immediately next to hers. She drove to the end of the road and turned left. He drove to the end of the road and turned right, then right again and right again, parking in the spot Sally had just vacated.

He took the lift back up even though he was only on the second floor. He needed to conserve his energy. He wasn't entirely sure he was going to be able to live up to the expectations that his phone conversation with Jane might have given her. He unlocked the door and heard some movement in the bedroom as he closed the door behind him. *'She's not hanging about,'* he thought. I hope I'm up to it. As he crossed the lounge floor he heard a strange noise. Was it a spray? No it was more like a squirt. As he stood in the bedroom doorway, he saw Jane sitting naked on his bed. There was an aerosol can of cream at the side of the bed. That's what the squirting noise had been, and when he saw where Jane had squirted it all Nick's doubts about being up to it disappeared.

'What no cherries on the top?' he said, as he moved towards the bed licking his lips.

CHAPTER NINETEEN

The following morning Nick woke to find Jane had again already left. There was another note: 'No sign of breakfast. This hotel is rubbish. Although I can't complain about the room service. Help yourself to the cream. X' There was a drawing below the writing. Nick examined it. Jane was certainly no artist. But was that supposed to be his... with cream on it and a cherry on top? The sketch brought back memories that made him smile and things start to stir beneath the duvet. Then he noticed, squeezed in, in tiny writing because of the lack of space beneath the sketch, 'PTO'. So he did. There he found another note: 'My office 10.45. Don't be late please. Have to talk.'

What could that be about? There was no more to discuss about the case – he'd brought her up to date last night, confirming that John had effectively done nothing more than discover how the water business worked. He could think of only one thing she might want to talk about – she'd had her fun and was ending it. Probably some guff about not being able to have a relationship with an employee or at least a temporary one. Not the done thing for a director of a FTSE 100 company. Actually, that probably wouldn't be a problem; after what he'd told her last night she no doubt believed that there was nothing more to find. She would be ending his contract as well. He felt a little disappointed that she didn't find him totally irresistible but it would certainly make things a lot easier. He was going to have to finish it himself anyway. True, the sex was amazing, absolutely mind-blowing, but he had to think of Sally. She said she was looking for a long-term relationship, and they seemed to fit together like two pieces of a jigsaw. He looked at the note from Jane again. There was a 'kiss' on it and a 'please'. She may be about to dump him but at least she'd learned some of what they called "the softer skills" in HR.

Nick went for his shower thinking that things had worked out rather well. Even if Jane did finish with him personally, and even professionally, he'd had a great time and had made a bit of money. She might even give him a decent reference. Then he could look for a proper job and see how things panned out with Sally. He could even introduce Sally to the joys of squirty cream.

Nick had made an appointment to see Richard Seaton at nine o'clock – the crack of dawn as he now called it. Richard's secretary had been very obliging, managing to squeeze Nick in before Richard's nine-thirty meeting. No doubt she'd be in trouble for that. He decided to begin politely and knocked on Richard's door before entering.

Richard glanced up only momentarily from his computer screen, before carrying on with what he was doing. Nick sat down, watching him across the large oak desk. He was prepared to wait. He was being paid. He looked around the office for a while, looked past Richard out of the window. Then he stood up and wandered across to the wall to examine the photographs and certificates on display. There was a First Class Degree Certificate in Accountancy and Management, ('*I ask you: who actually hangs their degree certificates up nowadays?*') a photograph of several past and present directors, Richard and Jane included, with the Grand Canyon in the background, (some teambuilding course that must have been!) and some others of Richard with various non descript people – one may have been a junior minister whom Nick almost recognised. Eventually he sat down again, gave a loud sigh, took out his mobile phone and started to play a game on it - with the sound activated.

Richard did his own loud sigh, with a bit more of a huff in it, turned from his screen and waited for Nick to turn off his phone. He looked at Nick with what could only be regarded as contempt, and said, 'Well?'

'Never better thanks. Well that's not strictly true of course. Twenty-five years ago I didn't have aching knees and I could run a half marathon in under an hour and forty minutes. But I've not felt better than I do now for quite a long time.'

Richard did not rise to the bait, instead he merely clarified his question, managing to combine the aforementioned contempt with arrogance, disdain, and a 'don't waste my time' tone in his voice. 'What do you want?'

'Well first of all I'd like to thank you for sparing the time to see me. I know how busy you are. (*Although I bet you were just playing "minesweeper" on your screen when I came in.*)'

'Get on with it.'

'OK. As I understand it, you directly manage the consultants who are charged with prioritising potential new projects and carrying out feasibility studies on them.'

'That's right.'

'A lot of money.'

'What was?'

'What the consultants were paid. Over ten million pounds I think.'

'It costs a lot of money to get the expertise sometimes. It saves money in the long run.'

'And can you prove that?'

'Prove what? That it costs a lot of money to bring in the expertise or that it saves money in the long run?' The disdain was still there.

'Both.'

'Yes.'

'Good. Can you prove it to me then?'

'I could, but why should I?'

'Because I'm being paid to try to discover what it was that John Anderson was looking into before he disappeared and I think I've reached the point at which he'd have asked for what I'm asking for now.'

'He didn't.'

'He didn't?'

'No, at least he didn't ask me.'

'Why do you think that was?'

'Well, if you had spent your time trying to find him, instead of hunting through his files, and if by some extraordinary stroke of luck you'd found him, then you'd be able to ask him.'

'In the first place, it was Jane who asked me to look into his files to see if he could have found anything untoward or at least anything he might have thought was untoward and...'

'And have you? Found anything untoward or might appear so?'

'No, not if you understand how the business works anyway.'

'So why are you asking *me* for information?'

'Because the information on the consultancy spend is not in the files I've looked at and it's the only area left for me to examine. And now that you've told me that John didn't ask for it I'm wondering why.'

'There are two possible reasons that I can think of.

'Do tell.'

Richard ignored Nick's playful tone.

'The first is that he knew there was no need to, because it was being managed by me and he reported to me, so he knew that I would be running a tight ship.'

Nick suppressed an urge to scoff. 'And the second?'

171

'That since he worked for me, in my department, he could probably get access to the relevant information without asking me. It wouldn't matter, because he wouldn't find anything untoward.'

'So you've said. But can I see the files anyway?'

'No.'

'Why not?'

'It would be a waste of your time and my time. There's nothing to find.'

'Delegate it to someone else then. You must have someone who works for you, whose time isn't as valuable as yours.'

'It would be a waste of anybody's time.'

'Humour me. That is humour me or I'll have to tell Jane that you're obstructing my investigation.'

'If you think you can threaten me by saying you'll tell "teacher" then you've got another thing coming. I know Jane a lot better than you do...'

Nick could not suppress a smirk. *'Oh, I don't think you do sunshine,'* he thought.

'I don't like the look on your face. This meeting's over.'

'Oh I'm sorry. Would you rather I pouted coquettishly at you over my shoulder?'

'Get out!'

'Just going!' said Nick as he rose and walked to the door, pausing only to pout coquettishly over his shoulder. As he passed Richard's secretary she was on the phone and he could hear Richard's voice loud and clear, 'Get me Jane!'

He sauntered back to his desk, making a call of nature on the way before stopping at a coffee machine for a top up. It was Jane's call now. If she had any doubts about Richard at all, or just wanted to back Nick's judgement then she'd get him access to Richard's files. On the other hand, if she really did trust Richard then she'd probably call off the investigation or at least this part of it. Then the question

172

would be, if there was nothing to worry about in the files, did she really care where John and Maxine were, and if not, would she end his contract totally, and use the opportunity as he already suspected, to end it with him in all areas? Whilst it would end his revenue stream he decided that, all in all, it would be better if she paid him off and 'binned him' off as the kids say.

CHAPTER TWENTY

As in all his dealings with Jane so far, Nick arrived bang on time for his end of contract meeting at ten forty-five. *'Have to keep up standards. Got that reference to think of.'*

Jane was sitting behind her desk – no informal chat on her sofa this time. Another indication of the "bad news" to come. He knew that Richard had been on the phone. He sat down opposite her and made eye contact. Would he win again? She looked at him and then looked down. It was no contest, he'd won hands down. She couldn't look at him while she was firing him. He must have made some impression on her. She must be going soft.

She looked up at him. Those eyes were back already, peering into his soul, but were they slightly watery? Surely she wasn't that upset. He thought about saying, 'Jane I know. The job's finished. You don't need me anymore. It's all right.' But he didn't. She was paid a fortune; she should be able to get rid of temporary staff.

'Nick, I...I don't know how to say this. I've never said it before.'

'Blimey you do surprise me. With the reputation you've got I presumed you must have got rid of loads of permanent staff, never mind temps.'

'I know it's going to sound odd. A woman of my age. A married one as well.'

'What the hell's being married got to do with the price of fish?'

'But like I said, it really hasn't ever happened to me before.'

'Just say, "Nick, you're fired." It's easy!'

174

'Nick,'

'That a girl!'

'I think I'm falling for you.'

Nick's jaw didn't just drop; it ran outside, jumped in the lift and went down to the basement.

'That is, I *think* I'm falling in love with you.' Her eyes were definitely filled with some watery substance now. 'I know it's stupid and I know that you probably think it must have happened before. I *am* married after all, but that was always a matter of convenience. Suited both of our careers. Something happened, or at least started to happen when you changed – you know when you declared that you were going to take the job seriously: be a proper detective. You seemed to grow up. For want of a better way of putting it, you manned up. I realized how I felt when I woke and watched you sleeping this morning. Normally I just get up and leave.'

Nick's face did a, "You do that sort of thing a lot do you?' look.

Jane went on. 'But this morning I didn't want to. I just wanted to stay with you. Lock the rest of the world out, and hold you. And I have never felt like that before. I promise you. And I don't know what to do. It's taking all my strength not to crawl across the desk and put my arms around you.'

Jane looked at him silently pleading with him to say something. He didn't. So she said, 'Say something... please!'

'Shit.'

Jane looked devastated as though Nick had just ripped her heart out and fed it to pigeons in the city centre.

'No, I don't mean it like that. I just meant "Shit, I wasn't expecting that".' In actual fact of course he had meant exactly as Jane had at first thought, but he didn't have the heart to break hers so brutally. 'I just don't understand how you could fall head over heels for someone like me. I mean

175

you operate in a different world. I thought I was just a bit of light relief.'

'I suppose you're right in a way. I think that's what I fell for. Most men try to impress me with their knowledge of the business world. They brag about their achievements, or they try giving me a smouldering look; try to look cool and masterful. And *you* quoted Tom and Jerry for goodness sake! You were so different and refreshing. I'm not used to someone who has no airs and graces - someone who's not out to impress; someone I don't have to compete with, who I can relax with. Look, I have to go out on site visits in the north of the region in a minute – good for staff morale apparently. And then Richard and I have to host a dinner in a local hotel for the local managers – even better for morale apparently if they can all get pissed on the company. That's why it's on a Friday. We all stay the night and drive home late tomorrow morning after we've sobered up. Can I ring you tonight? Can we talk?'

Now she was *asking* if they could talk, rather than telling him they were meeting. She'd suddenly put him in charge!

'No.' He said it far more abruptly than he'd intended but he wasn't anymore used to this than she was. He'd never been in charge in a relationship before – at least not a real one.

'I mean I have to go and see my Mum tonight. She's not well. Richard's going with you?'

'Yes he is. I'd have to spread myself too thinly at the dinner otherwise. We need to give the field managers at least the feeling that they have access to us directors. And I know about your mother. You told me. She's had a fall hasn't she? But surely I can still ring you. Tell me what time.'

'Yes of course. I'm sorry. I'm a bit surprised by this. I thought you'd be ending my contract.'

'Why on earth would I do that? Never mind. What time can I ring you?'

Nick took a moment or two to think about it. Early. Before he goes to Sally's. Get it out of the way, then he could enjoy the night with Sally.

'Six-thirty.'

'OK,' said Jane. 'I'll be at the hotel by then and dinner's not until seven-thirty. God, this is amazing. I can't wait to talk to you. I feel like a teenager.'

'Well you can't have one. Too many calories.'

Jane looked bewildered.

'Forget it I'll go. You need to get off. Drive carefully!'

'Thanks, I will.'

He could feel her eyes on him as he left the office. *Why did I say "Drive carefully"? Now she'll think I care a lot about her!*

Nick went to the restaurant and bought a cup of tea and sat down in a corner, away from the other customers. He had some serious thinking to do. It was un- effin-believable! What the hell was he going to do about this? Has he really had such an effect on a woman like Jane? Did he have some power over women that he had only just unleashed? It had certainly never surfaced before – or Ruth was immune to it? But then Sally was pretty keen on him! But no: that was bloody stupid. He hadn't suddenly become irresistible to women. It was pure coincidence. Like he said before lovers, (and clients), were like buses. Did he really have to think about it? Was there any competition? Surely Sally was the one for the longer term. They'd hit it off immediately. With Jane it was just sex. Mind you it *was* mind-blowing sex! And if she'd softened somehow, become a nicer person, because of her feelings for him. And perhaps Sally could be a bit harder than she looked. She had beaten up her "ex" after all. No that was stupid.

Sally was the one.

177

So what did he do about Jane? If he told her he was not interested then it could be the end of his contract and his only source of income. On the other hand pretending to be interested would hardly be the right thing to do. Was it possible to string her along without being dishonest? Should he end it anyway with Jane because of his relationship with Sally? He hadn't promised either of them exclusivity. But it was already implied with Sally, and would be with Jane if he wasn't very careful.

But then again was he presuming too much with Sally? Sure, they got on extremely well but they hardly knew each other. Was it too early to commit one hundred percent to her? A long-term relationship didn't necessarily mean 'forever' to everyone. Sally might only be looking for a couple of months of a steady relationship. He needed the answer to that question. That was it. He would try to find out from Sally how she felt tonight. He would put Jane off – tell her he had to think about it over the weekend. No, she couldn't see him over the weekend – he'd need the whole time alone to think about it. Then it could be a question of morals or money. But that would be for Monday. Meanwhile another light bulb went on in the dimness of his brain: Richard was going to be out of his office that afternoon, and Sally could get him access! He could try to look at the files that Richard didn't want him to see. No need to ask Jane. It'll be far more impressive if he sorts it out himself. With that thought Nick went out to his car to make a call to Sally in private.

'Hello, you' answered Sally. Nick thought her voice was as soft and smooth as melted chocolate: sexy melted chocolate. Was there such a thing?

'Hello gorgeous,' he replied. 'How are you?'

'I'm fine thanks,' then with a note of concern she added, 'are you still on for tonight? There's nothing wrong is there? Your Mum hasn't taken a turn for the...'

'No she hasn't. Everything is fine. I'm after a favour that's all.'

'Anything. Your wish is my command.'

'I'll remind you of that tonight,' he said a little too salaciously for even his own liking. 'But before that, you said you had keys for all the directors' offices. That includes Richard Seaton's?'

'Yes, why?'

'Could you let me in there tonight when you come into work? After all the secretaries have left of course. And if I get caught I won't let anyone know how I got in.'

'Of course it's no problem. I'll get on with the cleaning and give you a ring when the coast is clear. Is that OK?'

'That's great. I'll erm...'

'Show me how grateful you are later?' said Sally showing that she could be every bit as salacious as Nick.

'Your wish will be my command.'

'And I'll remind *you* of that.'

'Hope so. See you later.'

Nick felt like he needed a cold shower when he'd ended the call but had to make do with a walk back to his desk interrupted by the usual visit to the toilet on the way, which prompted another mental note to cut down on the coffee. Unfortunately the toilet break didn't derail his train of thought and his brain was overwhelmed by a maelstrom of visions of Jane throwing herself at him while he was engaged in trying to fulfil Sally's ever desire. His imagination lurched backwards and forwards between images of his making love to Sally and Jane doing things to him that he'd never even fantasised about before. He had to do something to pull himself out of it. He rang Ruth. There was no answer from her mobile. It went straight to voice mail. Either she was on the phone or it was switched off. He tried her desk phone. No answer. He decided to walk round to her desk. Doing something would keep his mind clear.

But Ruth was not at her desk, apparently she'd rung in sick so he returned to his desk and rang her house phone. No answer again. It went to voicemail. He told the answer machine that he was sorry she was ill and asked her to ring him when she felt up to it. *'Which could be never,'* he thought, as he put the phone down. He still didn't want to sit at his desk so he picked a file up at random and headed off to the restaurant, where hopefully the background noise would stop his mind charging into the battlefield of fantasies involving Sally and Jane.

Nick sat down at the same corner table with a cup of tea, (*'was tea any better than coffee?'*), and opened the file. He recognized it immediately and was pleased that there was something to follow up – something to occupy his mind. He went back to his desk to find the phone number he needed and rang it.

'Brian? It's Nick Howard.'

'Blimey, hello stranger. What can I do for you?'

'You got ten minutes? Fancy a coffee? I'm in the restaurant.'

'You mean the restaurant here? Are you back with RWS then? Back in harness?'

'If you come down I'll explain everything to you. There's a cappuccino in it for you.'

'Add a bacon butty to that and I'm on my way.'

Nick looked forward to seeing Brian Twigg. He was one of the good guys. Very good at his job: didn't play politics, just got on with things, *and* he wore a tie to work! He had taken over a lot of the work that Nick had done and Nick was hoping that he'd also picked up the responsibility for what was in the file in front of him. Then he'd get a straight answer very quickly. By the time Brian arrived Nick had a cappuccino and a bacon butty waiting for him. In fact, Brain seemed more pleased to see the sandwich than he was to see Nick, but Nick didn't mind. They chatted for five minutes. Nick explained how he'd been about to give up on his private detecting and get a proper job when this job had landed in his lap. He explained that he was working as temporary agency staff and that he'd been asked to pick up John Anderson's work. Then he asked if Brian was still playing cricket, (at the ripe old age of sixty-three), which he was. Eventually Nick started to nudge the conversation towards his real agenda.

'So how are things here?'

'Much the same,' came the reply. 'They're still trying to improve efficiency. But the only ideas they have are limited to using fewer people with less experience to do the same work. No, I tell a lie. We did get an email round from the MD asking us each to come up with ten things we didn't really need to do. Like anybody's doing stuff they don't need to. I think it came out of a seminar they held for managers on "Lean Management". I was there. I had to go; my boss wouldn't believe I had to wash my hair for some reason.' Brian stroked his bald head. 'The absurd thing about it was that the bloke they'd paid a few thousand to talk to us was as big as a block of flats. And he was talking about *lean* management - not that he seemed to notice the irony of it!'

'Some people have no self awareness.'

'I wouldn't care,' Brian went on, 'but they want us all to be leaders now: not managers. One of the directors actually stood up at a meeting and said that you can't be a manager *and* a leader, and that we were all leaders. We have to inspire our people. Communicate our goals and inspire our people to achieve them. It doesn't occur to them that you still need managers to make sure people are doing what they should be doing, when they should be doing it. Do they think that any hairy-arsed operators are interested in the company's mission statement?? All some of them want to do is come to work, do the minimum they can get away

181

with, get paid their lager vouchers and go to the pub to spend them. Sorry I'm ranting.'

'That's all right. I couldn't agree more. I ride a hobby horse with the same pedigree. It's one of the reasons I left, so the sooner I get my job finished, the sooner I can get back into the real world and the sooner I can start looking for a *proper* job. And with that in mind, do you know anything about this?' asked Nick as he opened the file and turned it round so that Brian could read it.

'Oh yeah. It was something Dave Newcombe was complaining about before he left.'

'Dave's left?'

'Yeah, he's retired.'

'Who's taken over from him?'

'That's just it: no one. His whole team has gone. All three of them. Dave and Bill have retired and Terry joined international. All of the HV authorised electrical engineers have gone. Dave was pointing out to his director before he went, that some of the High Voltage equipment had not been inspected for sixteen years when, according to our own procedures, it was supposed to be inspected every five. I'm not electrical so I don't know if it was a regulatory requirement for five yearly inspections, or whether that was the result of some sort of risk assessment done years ago by Dave and his team. Mind you, that might have made it a regulatory requirement. All I know is that Dave was adamant that the inspections had to be done.'

'So why didn't he do them?'

'He didn't have the resources. He was given other things to do – design of new plant, commissioning, responding to electrical breakdowns. There was only the three of them who really understood the HV side of things. Now they're gone.'

'So who's looking after the HV stuff now?'

'Good question. You know, A couple of years ago there was a power cut that knocked off the power to our biggest Water Treatment Works. Fortunately, Dave was in a Pub nearby that also lost its power, so he went to the works to see if everything was OK. He found that the standby genny hadn't started and the electrical maintenance guy hadn't a clue what to do. Fortunately Dave managed to get the genny started. The plant manager said there was only fifteen minutes' worth of water in the final holding tank left when the power came back on. If Dave hadn't gone to check off his own bat, half a million people would have been without water. Can you imagine the ramifications of that? I saw the Operations Director in the corridor a few days later and told him about the incident *and* that Dave would be leaving the company in the relatively near future leaving us with a big risk.'

'What did he say?'

'He thanked me and said that he was aware of the situation and was going to get people trained up to cover Dave's job when he left.'

'Did anything happen?'

'Did it bollocks!'

'Bloody hell. That's quite a risk the company is running with.'

'Damned right it is.'

'I'm going to have to write a report when I've finished retracing Anderson's steps. I'll have to include the stuff about the inspections. Do you mind if I include what you've told me about that power cut incident? I can leave your name out of it if you like.'

'You can mention me as many times as you like for all I care. It's all true so... '

'Thanks, Brian. Another coffee?'

'No thanks. Got a few things to do, then it's an early dart for me. It's "POETS" day.'

Nick smiled: 'POETS' day was 'Piss Off Early: Tomorrow's Saturday.'

'OK,' said Nick. 'Have a good weekend. Hope you score a ton!'

'It'll have to be all in boundaries if I do. Twenty-two yards has become a long way to run!'

Nick picked up the two cardboard cups and dropped them into a bin, and then headed back to his desk. Tea wasn't any better than coffee and he called in at a toilet on the way.

CHAPTER TWENTY-ONE

At his desk, Nick settled down to start writing up his report. His conversation with Brian had done the trick and taken his mind off the two women who were so desperate for him. He still had a couple of hours before Sally started cleaning and he could get into Richard's office. It was Friday – 'POETS' Day – so even the directors' suite would be emptier earlier than usual but that still left him with enough time to make a meaningful start on his report. Not that he had that much to report. Sure, there were the risks that Brian had just told him about and there were plenty of things that might look dodgy to the layman – money approved for projects that weren't done and even money approved twice for the same bit of kit. But it all seemed to be within the rules. The behaviour that hadn't been within the rules; like giving work to other group companies that were the most expensive and least competent had already been punished by the regulator. He was about to start his report when he remembered that he'd forgotten to ask Ian Hughes about a note John had made. It was about the methodology used for gathering information on the operation and maintenance required at the operational sites. John's note had queried why the data gathered by the detailed surveys hadn't been used to develop the costs used in the AMP submissions. He sent an email to Ian asking him the question. Ten minutes later he received a reply: 'Because they produced the wrong answers. Far too low. So we gathered a team of experts together to come up with the right answers. Same as previous AMPs.'

'Helpful as always. Sounds like a bloody fiddle to me. Perhaps I'll have a look at that later.'

He settled down to his report. The office around him slowly quietened as people observed 'POETS Day', and he worked at his report all afternoon, interrupted only by two visits to the toilet, until BTO stuttered into life.

'Hello gorgeous,' he said.

'Hello, handsome,' replied Sally. 'I'm in the directors' suite and there's not a soul about.'

Nick looked at his watch. He was surprised to see that it was already six o'clock. That was early for *all* of the directors to have left, but it was 'POETS' Day, *and* the boss was away.'

'I'll be right there.'

When he arrived outside Richard's office Sally was apparently diligently cleaning the secretary's desk. She stopped immediately took a quick look around before kissing him softly on the lips. 'This *is* exciting. His door's open. You can go straight in. I'll carry on "cleaning" here while you're in there if you want – like a look out!'

'Good idea. And I'll close the blinds so I won't be seen from out here.'

He entered the office and immediately closed the venetian blinds that were mounted between the panes of the double glazed glass walls. He didn't switch the light on as there was enough light coming in through the two large windows of the corner office. He went to the desk and sat down in the large leather swivel chair. The desk was clear apart from a photograph of Richard with his wife and two teenage daughters. At least Richard observed the "clean desk" policy promoted by the security manager. Nick took a moment to lean back and imagine himself as a director of RWS. The thought disturbed him and he shuddered. He tried to open one of the drawers in the desk.

'Bollocky bollocks!' he cursed. It was locked. He tried all of the others, followed by the oak veneer filing cabinet standing against the wall and the cupboards and drawers in the large oak cabinet. The only doors that were not locked were the glazed doors of the display section of the cabinet, but that only held text books and photographs.

He went back out to Sally.

'It's no use. I'm scuppered. All the drawers are locked. I can't get into anything.'

Sally smiled. 'It's a good thing I know where there's a set of keys then.'

'Where?'

'In the secretary's desk.'

'Isn't that locked?'

'The drawers are, but the tray at the top of the drawer unit isn't. Look,' she said opening the tray and holding out the keys for Nick. 'I've seen her lock papers up in his desk and then put the keys back in here.'

'You're a star!' he said kissing her. 'You'll have to think of a way I can thank you later.'

'I already have. And the sooner you get finished here the sooner you can start thanking me.'

'I'm already gone,' he replied as he opened the door to the office.

He sat down again in the swivel chair and tried the keys until he found one that worked.

'Aha! I'm in!'

He systematically went through each drawer but found nothing of interest: just copies of emails and reports of no interest. The same went for all of the other desk drawers. It wasn't looking good. He tried the dresser cupboards but only found bottles of spirits and glasses. He resisted the temptation and tried the drawers but they only had coasters, placemats, and other paraphernalia for having a

187

bit of a soirée when the plebs had gone home. But he'd saved the best 'til last. Or at least he hoped he had.

He opened the top drawer of the filing cabinet and found the usual hanging files. The main differences between Richard Seaton's and his own filing systems were that Richard's were meticulously sorted in alphabetical order by a secretary and each neatly labelled hanging file contained only one slim folder dedicated to only one topic. He quickly flicked through the top drawer. There were no topics that interested him but he checked a few at random to ensure that Richard had not intentionally mislabelled anything to hide the real subject. He hadn't. The same went for the second drawer. He was thinking that he was not going to find anything useful when he opened the bottom drawer and started running through the titles of the files. As he pulled the hanging files forward to access those towards the back of the drawer he noticed a folder lying face down on the bottom of the drawer. He reached in and pulled it out. On the front it said, 'PEARSON & TOOMEY CONSULTANTS.' He opened it and turned the pages. He found invoices and records of payments totalling several millions of pounds for work related to the AMP investment programme. It seemed that Pearson & Toomey were the consultants used for the prioritising of the AMP projects and the investigations into the feasibility of projects. There'd been a lot of work done and it had cost a hell of a lot of money.

It was not like Richard's secretary to allow a file to fall to the bottom of the drawer and he looked through the drawers to find the correct hanging file for it. He thought he remembered seeing it in the middle drawer. He was right, but there was already a folder in it. He pulled this folder out and found that it had the same title. Presumably the folder at the bottom of the bottom drawer had been lost and a second had been made. He opened the second folder and

188

saw invoices for the same work. The invoices were from a company called Hooley & Vaal; the name that Nick remembered seeing in Ian Hughes' file. He was puzzled, and took the folders over to Richard's desk to look at them side by side. It quickly became apparent that the folder that had been hidden in the bottom drawer had invoices for all of the same parcels of work as the folder that was correctly filed. There were two sets of invoices for each order, both adding up to several million pounds. Richard was definitely on the fiddle. Hooley & Vaal were presumably submitting legitimate invoices for work they had done. These were booked into the system and logged against the work on the investment programme, and duly paid.

Then there was a duplicate set of invoices for the same work and the same amount of money, but from Pearson & Toomey. You didn't have to be a financial genius, (so Nick was fully qualified), to be able to work out that there was an enormous fiddle going on. He looked for the authorising signatures. Richard Seaton's was there as he expected. The other was more of a surprise. It was Martin Worsley's. Nick thought about it: as directors covering Procurement, Finance and Audit, they'd had everything covered between them. No one else needed to be involved. They could place dummy orders, pay the invoices, and make sure that no audit discovered what was going on.

Beautifully simple.

This is it! Presumably this was what John and Maxine had found out. Next job was to photocopy both folders and then he could show them to Jane on Monday. She'd certainly made a big mistake allowing only two directors to have so much power and control; presumably because she knew them so well - or thought she had. He took both files and found Sally still "cleaning" the secretary's desk.

'What have you got there? Have you found something?'

'I think so. I need to photocopy it and put it back. And *then* I'd like to take a look in Maxine's office if that's possible.'

'Yeah, sure no problem. I'll take you round after you've done your photocopying.'

Nick photocopied the files using the copier provided for all of the directors' secretaries. Then he put the folders back exactly where he had found them, remembering to reopen the venetian blinds before Sally locked up. A couple of minutes later, Nick was in Maxine's office and Sally had resumed her cleaning/look out duty.

The HR director's office layout was very similar to Richard's: the same oak furniture. The only real difference Nick could see was in the photographs. There were no family photographs - only photographs of Maxine with various groups of work colleagues. No doubt, being in HR, Maxine would have said *they* were her family. As before, Nick looked through the desk drawers first and found nothing of interest. Then he tried the oak filing cabinet standing against the side wall just like in Richard's office. There were files full of HR policies, training initiatives' details, and personal HR records of Maxine's co-directors. Nick took these out for amusement as much as anything else.

The first one he opened was Richard's. He found that Richard had joined the company straight from Nottingham University with a first class degree in management and accounting and had been put through the two year long graduate training programme. As was the norm he'd spent six months in four different departments, before taking up his first permanent post in Asset Management. None of his four end-of-placement reports by his managers marked him out as a director of the future. Nick read on: after a couple of years in 'Assets', Richard had moved into finance as a 'client manager' – his client being 'Assets'. This meant he helped the asset managers and project managers with the financial part of their project proposals, as well as questioning their need from a financial point of view. Nick knew from his own dealing with asset managers, that their finance reps also felt quite at home questioning the technical requirements of projects as well. The lack of relevant knowledge or experience never held many people back from voicing an opinion, particularly the younger graduates, who thought that the six months they'd spent in a department on their graduate training programme had taught them all there was to know about that department. Richard had then moved into the finance section of the capital delivery department – the department charged with managing the design and installation of the approved projects that had come out of Asset Management. This had been a slight promotion for Richard but he made a bigger one next when he got the job of project manager in the IT department managing the delivery of IT projects within the company. Nick was only a little surprised by this. Although Richard had nothing on his CV to suggest any interest or experience in project management or IT, it was not unusual for this to happen. Nevertheless he looked through the interviewing records.

He wasn't surprised to find that the interview had comprised a series of meaningless competency based questions, which were centred on the softer skills of people management; questions which sounded great but had little to do with project management or IT. And all questions to which Richard had given bog standard but brilliantly sounding answers, as had all the other candidates. Richard must have had stand-out verbal and numerical reasoning test results. He must be a bright lad. The original copies of his tests were in the files. '*Oh dear,*' said Nick to himself. '*Not so bright after all.*' His results only put him on the fiftieth percentile. That wasn't good at all. Nick's own test results for an interview he'd done were both well in excess of the ninetieth percentile. He turned the page and came to the recommendation for appointment. Richard's interview score was very high, as Nick expected, but his two test results were both shown as on the ninety-fifth percentile! That's how he'd got the job. His results had been doctored. Now who had done that? Nick carried on looking through Richard's file finding that he moved only a year later into the audit department and a year after that into the post of chief auditor. More reasoning tests were required for this as it was a significant step up and Nick found that the results of these had also been doctored. Richard had been given more than just a leg up in his career, he'd been rocket assisted and more than once! Nick noticed that in both cases the HR officer reporting Richard's results and recommending his appointment had been Martin Worsley.

Nick picked up his file next and opened it. *'Now there's a surprise'* he said aloud. *'Richard and Martin joined RWS at the same time from the same university. They were best mates!'* As he looked through Martin's file he found that Martin had done better in his graduate placements than Richard and had been given very good reports by his placement managers. After completing his graduate programme Martin spent several years in group finance, completed his CIMA qualification (Chartered Institute of Management Accountants), but then as soon as he'd become a chartered accountant he'd joined HR as Recruitment Manager. Again, Nick knew that this was also not unusual. The HR role that Martin took on was two grades above his finance role and promotion was probably his main goal at the time. Graduates often saw the grade of the job as the "be all and end all". Whether it was coincidence that Martin had ended up in HR in charge of recruitment at the very time that Richard needed some surreptitious insider assistance Nick couldn't be sure, but it had certainly been in Richard's favour. He looked through the remainder of Martin's file. After a brief spell in the Customer Directorate he'd moved back into Finance, presumably to make some use of his qualifications and had risen rapidly, via a period in the finance department of the International Division, based in the Middle East, returning to take up the post of General Manager of Finance before ultimately becoming Finance and Procurement Director following another company restructuring – the post he was in when he died in the tragic accident that Jane had described to him at their first meeting.

Nick closed the file and cast his mind back to what Jane had told him about that accident. It had happened on a site in the Middle East, Martin and Richard had gone out to pay a site visit, to let the staff seconded out there know that they were not forgotten – that their efforts were *appreciated.* And to keep the client sweet of course. Was it a coincidence that Richard had been with Martin when the scaffolding had given way? They were very close. Martin had clearly helped Richard get on in the Company and get into the position where they were able to work together and pull the sort of stunts with invoices that Nick had found. They were in it together. That much was certain. Had they had some sort of big fall out? Or had Richard simply had enough of sharing his ill gotten gains with Martin. As Finance & Procurement *and* Audit Director, Richard was certainly in just as good a position to carry on with his embezzling, if not better. He obviously didn't know that Martin had kept copies of Richard's real test results on file or they wouldn't still be in Maxine's file. He wondered if Maxine had ever read the file. Was this one of the things they had on Richard? Why had Martin kept the results? Had he simply been careless or had he kept them for a reason? No, it can't have been that: he couldn't have exposed Richard without exposing himself. He must have merely been careless. He made some notes

193

from both files and then sat back and thought some more about what he'd just found.

Jane had been very upset when she'd told Nick about Martin's death and that rang a bell with him. He opened Jane's file. Yes, he was right. She'd also joined from Nottingham University. She must have known Martin and Richard since their university days. No wonder she was so upset when Martin died. And with her knowing Richard so well, how betrayed was she going to feel when she found out what was going on? He started to look through her file. As she'd told him the other night, she'd spent her early years after her graduate training programme in Operations and she'd been very quickly promoted – some would say so outrageously quickly that she must have slept with the Operations' Director – to the post of Area Manager. There were no shenanigans with her test results: ninety-eighth percentile on verbal and ninety-fifth percentile on the numerical reasoning. *'Strewth!'* thought Nick. *'That's probably higher than mine'* unable to admit even to himself that he knew that Jane's results were definitely better than his own.

His phone shouted that he ain't seen nothing yet and he begged to differ before he picked it up. If he still ain't seen nothing, what else was in the files? It was Jane. He looked at his watch. It was almost seven o'clock. She was late but he'd forgotten she was calling.

'Hello, sorry I'm late. We got stuck on site longer than we expected. They're a very vociferous lot up here. They wouldn't shut up. Still, no doubt they'll claim it on overtime, under the heading of "giving the MD a hard time". Sorry, now I'm rabbiting when I haven't got much time. Nerves I suppose. Where are you?'

'At home,' lied Nick.

'Look, I'm sorry about earlier. You must think I'm a right nutter - or a bunny boiler like that Glen Close character in that film.'

'Basic Instinct,' prompted Nick. *'Bloody hell! Was she? That hadn't even occurred to me. Was this her way of warning him not to reject her?'*

'Yes, that's right. Anyway I'm not, so you've no need to worry.'

'But I am!'

'Like I said I haven't got much time. I have to go to dinner in a minute. I just want to say I'm sorry. I shouldn't have blurted out my feelings like that this morning. Can you forget I said it?'

'Not really. It's out there now, to use a well known cliché.'

'I suppose it is. Well, can you pretend to forget it? I mean don't feel under any pressure to feel the same way and just see how it goes? I'll just try to let you be in control.'

'Can you let anyone be in control?'

'I'll try. Look, don't say anything now. Think about it over the weekend. If you think it's too heavy for you I'll understand. I'd better go now. I've got to be at dinner in fifteen minutes.'

'A couple of things before you go. I suppose Richard has told you I wanted him to let me see his files on the consultants he's been managing on the AMP Investment programme?'

'What? Oh, yes he has.'

'Good. I hope you've told him to let me have a look at them because...'

'No, there's no need. I'm sure Richard is completely trustworthy. I've known him for years. You can forget it. I think you've done as much as you can do with the files. It's not that you've found anything illegal that needs looking into further.'

195

'But I was just going to say that...'

'Nick, there's no need to look at Richard's files. I can vouch for him one hundred percent.'

'But when you took me on you implied that you didn't entirely trust him. In fact you insisted that I report only to you and not to him.'

'Yes I know, but that was only because if anything had been going on, then it was probably in his department. So he could have been held responsible to some extent for not being in total control. *And* he wasn't in favour of hiring you, or any other detective in the first place. I thought he'd be bloody awkward or even unpleasant if he was in meetings with you. It wasn't because I thought he was dishonest.'

'So if he didn't want to employ a detective, what did he want to do? Nothing?'

'Yes. He said what did it matter if a couple of employees had decided to run off with each other?'

'How did he know they'd run off with each other?'

'He didn't. He was just surmising they had, as they'd disappeared at the same time. Anyway, it looks like he was right. You've found nothing in the files that John had looked at, so it looks like my worries were totally unfounded.'

'That's why I wanted to look at Richard's Files.'

'There's nothing in Richard's files! I've told you.' Jane's voice was raised in anger: she was not accustomed to anyone arguing with her – not even her lovers. 'I'm sorry,' she added. 'It's been a long day. Really, there's nothing to see in Richard's files. So you can forget about them. What was the other thing?'

'Other thing?' Nick was still reeling from the sudden anger in Jane's voice. Was she unstable? Was this another symptom? Was this another indication of her parlous state of mind? Could she really be a 'bunny-boiler'?

'Yes, you said there were a couple of things. But you'll have to be quick.'

'Oh yes. Did you have any luck getting me access to John or Maxine's email accounts and home drives?'

'Oh, no, sorry: I should have told you yesterday. I did try but the group security manager said it's against company policy, especially with you being temporary staff. He said that I could have access, so I've had a look but both their email accounts and home drives have had all their stuff deleted. And IT have said they can't retrieve any of it. It's all gone I'm afraid.'

'OK, it was worth a try. You enjoy your dinner. Don't get too bladdered: you might promise them all a rise.'

'No chance. I'll see you on Monday. And Nick... thanks.'

'What for?'

'For not telling me I'm a nutter and driving off into the sunset.'

'I wouldn't do that.'

'No, of course you wouldn't. You're too nice for that.'

'Some would say "soft". But you're right. I wouldn't; not until I've been paid anyway.'

'Oh, right. Bye then.'

'Bye,' said Nick, feeling not only a little guilty that she had not taken his last comment as the joke it was meant, but also determined to end it with her on Monday as gently as possible. The mere fact that she had mentioned the possibility of being a "bunny boiler" made him think that perhaps she really was, and that she was subconsciously threatening him. And that sudden outburst of hers was another factor. He thought back to their dinner date and how quickly she'd clearly become intent on getting him into bed – and how passionate she'd been. Not what he'd been expecting at all. Was that some sort of indication of an unstable personality? Perhaps it wasn't simply that she found him so incredibly physically attractive after all. He

197

smiled at that thought. Nobody would find him 'incredibly physically attractive' – 'not repulsive' perhaps, but his looks had never been his greatest asset. He had no idea what that was exactly, unless it was his encyclopaedic knowledge of Tom and Jerry: the Fred Quimby Years. He almost slapped his own face to bring his thoughts back to where they should have been. Was Jane unstable, prone to seek male approval by seducing them in some attempt to compensate for never getting her father's approval? Or had she just felt a bit randy on the night and taken advantage of Nick? But if that was the case why had she suddenly become totally besotted by him? Had she done this sort of thing before? With Martin Worsley for instance? Was that why she'd been so upset when she'd talked about his death? A darker thought invaded his thoughts: had he rejected her? Had she had something to do with Martin's death? But then why would she send Richard out there with him? He'd only have been a witness to any foul play? Unless he wasn't at site when it had happened or unless he'd been involved? Had Richard replaced Martin in her affections? Or had he hoped to but she'd rebuffed him? Was that why Richard had been so hostile to the idea of bringing Nick in? Did he see him immediately as a potential rival? Did Richard have unrequited infatuation for Jane?

Nick almost slapped himself again. He'd let his mind run riot, as though he was having his own brainstorming session in which 'no idea is a bad idea'. Bollocks, a bad idea is a bad idea. And he'd just had loads of them. Was it really true he wondered that they weren't allowed to call them brainstorming sessions anymore? Something to do with causing offense to people with a particular type of mental disorder? That they had to call them brain-showers now? His mind was off again! Thoughts piling in with no control; more like an exercise in word association than a structured thought process. He needed a break. He realised he was starving. Perhaps his brain was deprived of Omega-3 oils or something and that had caused him to lose the ability to think coherently. One thing was certain - it was time for food. He'd think about all of this again over the weekend- as Jane had suggested. Then he'd present his evidence to her on Monday in as professional and objective a manner as he could and then tell her he'd done all he could.

And then he'd send her the bill.

He checked his watch. It was well past seven o'clock. It was time he took Sally for something to eat, but first he tried phoning Ruth. It was about time he gave an update, especially now he had something to report and get paid for. There was no answer from her mobile or her landline. He put the files back in the filing cabinet and locked it. Then he went to find Sally.

'I'm all done. Are you ready for something to eat?'

'I'm starving,' she replied. 'And I've just about rubbed the veneer off this desk. I just have to put my stuff away, and then I'm ready. Nick followed Sally to the small room where her cleaning equipment was kept. They were alone in the building, and he suddenly decided it would be a shame to waste such an opportunity. He'd never made love to anyone in an office building. He'd heard rumours that a couple had been discovered in a storeroom a few years ago, and another couple in a car in the car park, and then there was John and Maxine of course – discovered by Sally. But he and Sally were alone. They could not be discovered. He stepped inside the room and closed the door behind him. They were surrounded by vacuum cleaners and floor polishers. Sally had her back to him as she sorted out various cleaning paraphernalia stored on a free standing shelving unit in front of her.

'Now then young lady,' he said slipping his arms round her waist from behind. 'Do you think it's wise, allowing

199

yourself to be caught unawares all alone in a deserted office building?'

He bent his head and kissed her neck. She cocked her head to one side to expose more of her neck. He continued to kiss her neck as his hands moved over her. All thoughts of Jane and Ruth were banished. He took hold of her hips and tried to turn her round but she resisted. Instead her hands glided past his and took hold of her tabard and skirt and pulled them up over her hips revealing her firm cheeks not covered at all by the thong she wore. As his right hand started to caress her buttocks, Nick briefly wondered if all of RWS's cleaners wore such sexy underwear and then remembered that some of them were old enough to be his mother. Fortunately the disturbing thought was driven from his mind when Sally's hands began to caress him. Soon they were making love with complete abandon with no regard for their surroundings. The shelving lurched violently from side to side, as Sally hung on for balance. Aerosol cans and bottles fell from the shelves; a vacuum cleaner was knocked over as they staggered sideways trying not to fall to the floor. When finally they were spent, Sally turned round and kissed Nick and said, 'Look what you've done to this place. How the hell am I supposed to explain this?'

'I'll help you tidy up. It won't take long. As long as you don't bend over in front of me. I might not be able to control myself again.'

'Who says I want you to? But let's get tidied up first.'

It took only a few minutes to put the room back together and Nick was driving them out through the site gates minutes later.

'Do you mind if we get a get a takeaway instead of going out for a meal?' asked Sally as they pulled out on to the main road. 'I'm suddenly feeling a bit tired for some reason. I think I need an early night.'

'Of course. Are you feeling all right?'

'Of course I am you idiot. I was just making an excuse for saying I'd rather go to bed than go out for a meal.'

'Good, so would I.

'There's a good chippy round the corner from me. Will that do you?'

'Perfect.'

They arrived back outside Sally's flat with fish and chips and a bottle of wine.

'You can't have fish without a bottle of white wine,' Nick had said when he'd seen there was an off-licence next door to the chippy.

As Nick took an overnight bag – his old sports bag – out of the boot, he couldn't resist looking round to see if Sally's "ex" was lurking anywhere.

Sally noticed. 'Don't worry. Dave's not around and even if he was he wouldn't dare bother us – not after what I did to him the other night. He's probably in hiding somewhere ashamed to show his face: getting beaten up by a girl.'

'What about me? I was beaten up by someone who was beaten up by a girl.'

'He attacked you from behind but perhaps I had better teach you a thing or two.'

'You've already done that.'

'Oh I've got a few more tricks up my sleeves yet,' said Sally.

Nick thought it prudent not to point out that "tricks" was a term used by prostitutes to refer to their customers and instead said, 'I've always been a quick learner.'

'Let's go up and start your homework then.'

Sally proved to be a talented and committed teacher and Nick to be a very willing and devoted pupil, with his lessons carrying on through the night: his interest being further stimulated by the discovery that Sally had been a gymnast until her late teens when an injury had forced her

201

to give it up. She hadn't lost her flexibility though as Nick was only too grateful to find out.

They inevitably slept late the following morning and it was not far short of lunchtime before they were both finally dressed and ready to go out, so it was just as well that it was Saturday. Nick tried ringing Ruth again but got no answer and he decided he would go round to her house to see if she was there. Sally said she'd go and do some shopping so that she could cook a meal for Nick that evening. 'I'll get a nice piece of steak. You could probably do with the red meat, after your exertions last night, I know I could.'

'Sounds great. I'll see you later, said Nick kissing her on the lips gently. 'I'll be back before five.'

CHAPTER TWENTY-TWO

Nick parked at the kerb outside his 'ex' house in which his 'ex' wife lived on her own, now that her 'ex' boyfriend had disappeared. He looked up at the house and tried to conjure up some memories – good or otherwise. It was surprisingly difficult. They all seemed to merge into a general feeling of dissatisfaction and disappointment. He sighed loudly and got out of the car and walked up to the three bedroom house; beautifully presented throughout, with a larger than average private garden to the rear mainly laid to lawn: an ideal family home. That was roughly how it had been described when he and Ruth had bought it. Well there'd been no family. That had been one source of disappointment. But only one. There'd been plenty of others. Best not to dwell now. He didn't want to be in a melancholy mood when he met Ruth. He needed to appear confident and professional – he was working: for the second Saturday in a row. Unprecedented in his current career. He rang the bell. There was no answer. He rang again. Her Audi A3 was in the drive. Walking anywhere was not an option for Ruth. She had either gone away on holiday without telling anybody or she was inside.

The only reason for her to go away was to be with John. That was highly unlikely as Nick was pretty sure John was with Maxine. So she was probably in the house. Nick bent down and pushed the letterbox open shouting, 'Ruth! It's me.' Stupid thing to shout really. Who ever shouts, 'It's not me. It's someone else.'? There was still no answer. One more try before he started to think about breaking in to see if she was all right.

'OK Ruth. It's *not* me! It's someone else. And that someone else has something to tell you.'

He saw Ruth walk through the kitchen doorway into the hall towards him.

'Stop shouting! The neighbours will hear. You'll ruin their weekend. They thought they'd got rid of you.'

'*A little harsh,*' thought Nick. '*I never had any trouble with the neighbours – apart from the regrettable incident when their cat somehow got under the back wheel of the car as I reversed out. Oh, and when I lopped a branch off the ash tree and it went through their greenhouse roof. Fair point Ruth.*'

'Well if you don't answer your phone or your doorbell what do you expect?'

'I expect you to take the hint and leave me alone.'

'I was concerned about you.'

'First time for everything.'

'Are you going to open this door before I seize up?' asked Nick ignoring Ruth rather clichéd jibe.

Ruth took the final couple of steps to the door and opened it.

He straightened up making a show of using his hands to push his back straight.

He received no sympathy from Ruth. 'I could do you an Ashiatsu Massage on your back if you like.'

'What on earth's that?'

'You do it with your feet, so I'd have to stand on your back.'

'No thanks, I think I'll give it a miss.'

'Pity,' said Ruth. 'I have a new pair of stilettos I'd like to break in.'

'Charming! Can I come in?'

'I suppose so. Go through to the lounge.'

Nick followed orders and Ruth followed Nick. The lounge had not changed since he'd moved out. The same chestnut brown leather three piece suite took up most of the room. He couldn't help thinking that if he'd still been living there, Ruth would have had him redecorate the room by now. The wallpaper was looking a bit tired and dated. No one had dado rails anymore.

'Well?' said Ruth, standing with her arms folded.

Nick just resisted the urge to say 'Yes thanks,' and instead said, 'I may have found something. Something that John and Maxine might have found. Something...'

'I told you. John and Maxine were not together. I'm sure of it.'

'OK, whatever. I've found something that could explain... that is I've found something interesting. First of all I have to tell you that Jane hired me to look into what John was working on because she suspected that he and Maxine...'

'I told you...'

'Yes I know, but they disappeared at the same time so Jane has made the assumption that they were working together.'

'On what?'

'Well she thought that they may have been on the fiddle somehow.'

'Bloody nerve! How dare she? The...'

'Anyway I think I have found evidence of some fiddling but it's not by John or Maxine.'

'What do you mean?'

'Well it looks like someone has been embezzling money from RWS.'

'Really? How?'

'I found two sets of invoices for the same work. Consultancy work, that wasn't managed by anyone in either "Assets" or "Engineering". So no one in those departments would pick up on it.'

At some point during the conversation Ruth had sat down on the sofa and Nick had seated himself in an armchair facing her. He waited for a reaction to what he'd just said; instead he heard a slow clapping coming from the doorway. He turned as John Anderson stepped into the room.

'Well done Nicholas. You've discovered all that much quicker than I expected. In fact, if truth be known, I didn't expect you to discover it at all. You weren't supposed to. I thought I was going to be able to work things through and reach a satisfactory conclusion without you ever knowing what was going on.'

'What the bloody hell are you doing here?' demanded Nick staring boggle-eyed at a grinning John before turning to Ruth and simply raising his eyebrows in a 'What have you got to say for yourself?' kind of way.

Ruth looked up at John as if asking his permission to answer. John was leaning against the doorframe with his hands in his pockets looking so nonchalant that only his face shrugged his indifference to whether Ruth explained things or not. She was obviously agitated by Nick seeing John and launched into her explanation.

'Look, I know how it looks...'

'I certainly don't,' interrupted Nick immediately. 'How long's he been here? You're paying me to find him – remember?'

'Yes, I know. If you'll be quiet for a minute, I'll explain.' Ruth paused, and Nick half expected her to ask him if he were sitting comfortably before she began. He settled back in his armchair.

'John came to see me last Friday...'

It took only a moment for the penny to drop with Nick. 'Last Friday! That's the day before you asked me to find him! Has he been here the whole time?'

Ruth tried to re-establish her control of the conversation but it was obvious she felt caught out in a major way. Only John maintained his blasé appearance.

206

'Yes it was, and yes he has. If you'll just let me explain.' This time she didn't give Nick chance to respond and she rushed on. 'As I said John came over last Friday evening in a terrible state. He was afraid for his life!'

Nick looked round at John. He seemed to have made a remarkable recovery. Nick's look seemed to have galvanised John into reaction. He took his hands out of his pockets and entered the room. He walked across and turned round so that he could see both Ruth and Nick. He had his back to the living flame gas fire, which wasn't on. He stood with his legs slightly apart and his hands clasped behind him – like he was some landed gentry warming himself in front of an enormous log fire in a Bronte novel: except that he was wearing M&S denim jeans, (Nick had some exactly the same) and an open necked shirt also from M&S. So the landed gentry look didn't quite come off, but he didn't let that faze him. 'Shall I take over, darling?'

Nick felt sick, but he said nothing. Ruth felt upset but she nodded.

'You're on the right track Nick. As I said; very impressive.' He stopped and turned to Ruth. 'Would you like to go and make some tea sweetheart? You've heard all this before. And I think I'm going to need one – this is going to take some time.'

'*Sweetheart! Darling!*' Nick couldn't believe the mush John was coming out with. He remembered how he would sometimes address Ruth as the 'Oasis of my desert' but that was a joke. He had also called her 'dear' once but only once. She had made it clear that she found the term extremely condescending. '*And "darling" and "sweetheart" weren't?*' But she happily went out to put the kettle on.

'As Ruth said, I turned up here last Friday evening quite literally in fear of my life. But I need to go back further than that. You have probably worked out by now that Maxine and I – yes we were *working* together, but that's all – had

207

found out about the embezzling. How did you find out so quickly by the way? *I* just happened to stumble on it.'

'It's my job. It's what I do.'

'So you know who's doing the embezzling?'

Nick had only one name to offer. 'Richard Seaton.'

'That's right. Well when we found out about it...'

'We? Tell me again – why were you working with Maxine on this?'

'Hers was the first department that I audited,' answered John without pausing to think about it. 'She knew I'd be auditing Richard's departments as well, and asked me to report to her on that as she felt there was a conflict of interest for Richard with him being the Audit Director as well as acting Finance & Procurement Director. She didn't expect me to find anything; it was just that she thought it would look better if Richard wasn't involved in vetting the reports on his own department. She said she'd cleared it with Jane, although they decided not to tell Richard as he was bound to be offended.'

'Wasn't he bound to find out anyway?'

'Not really. He wasn't going to be audited personally – only his departments. He was far too busy to notice. I was working well below his radar. In fact that's how I met Ruth. As you know she was in Finance and was very helpful.'

'I'll bet she was.'

'No need to be like that Nick. You and her were separated by then.

Nick knew that was true but he didn't feel inclined to apologise, especially when John had just said "her" instead of "she". He took a moment to look at John from a different point of view. What had Ruth seen in him? He wasn't extremely good looking. But he wasn't ugly either. Nick had to admit that John was in better shape than he was. There was no hint of even a small belly hanging over the belt that held his denim jeans up. And he was not averse to turning on the charm – however sickly it might be. Nick had already witnessed the "darling" and "sweetheart" terms that morning.

John went on, 'So it was during the audit of Richard's department that I found the irregularities. Or put it another way that Richard was stealing from the company.'

'And how did you find it out?'

'I told you. I stumbled on it. I'd heard him on the phone saying something that aroused my suspicions. He was too busy to worry about what I was doing so I embarked on my audits. I decided to audit most of the departments as a bit of cover for what I was really doing. Eventually I found what I was looking for.'

'Did you find any evidence that showed how Mike Shaw had been on the fiddle? Was it the same fiddle as Richard's?'

'No. I don't know what Mike was up to. Do you?'

'No,' said Nick making a mental note that he needed to look into the Mike Shaw affair, even though it had apparently been put to bed when Mike had committed suicide. Had Mike been in on it with Richard and lost his nerve, or had Richard had something to do with Mike's death? The brainstorming was about to start again so he shook his head and pulled himself back to his conversation with John just as Ruth returned with the tea.

'Ah thank you darling. You're a star.'

Ruth smiled her gratitude for John's appreciation before giving Nick a 'See, *John* doesn't take me for granted,' look, as she placed the tray down on the coffee table in the centre of the room. John leant over and picked a mug up before continuing.

'Anyway, when I found the evidence of Richard's embezzling I took it straight to Maxine, obviously.'

'Obviously,' agreed Nick. 'And she took it straight to Jane, obviously.'

'You know very well she didn't. She told me she wanted to think about the best course of action over the weekend.'

'And then what happened?'

'I got a call from her on Sunday evening; asking me to come over. She said she had a proposition for me.'

Nick raised his eyebrows.

'Not that sort of proposition.'

'Not everyone has a mind like a sewer,' chimed in Ruth.

Nick was sure that John and Maxine were lovers – Sally had caught them at it. He was also pretty sure that they were already lovers when John had started his auditing and that they might even have embarked on the auditing to dig up some dirt but he let it go for now.

''I went over to her place and no, I didn't already know where it was, she had to give me directions. When I got there she had the files all over her dining table and she'd opened a bottle of wine. She said it would oil the cogs. Help me look at the bigger picture, think outside the box, all that sort of stuff. She said that what she was about to suggest would shock me, but asked me not to dismiss it out of hand. And she kept the wine coming. She said that what I'd found was dynamite, to find that a director had such a huge fiddle going on was staggering. She said it would be the end of the Company; the regulatory bodies had made that clear after the Mike Shaw case had been uncovered. She said they'd lose their licence to operate, that it would be absolutely devastating for everyone who worked there... if it got out. She said that making it public was not necessarily the best thing to do, but that I deserved some reward for all the hard work I'd done. I agreed with her – I'd had most of a bottle of wine by now. That's when she came up with her mind boggling idea. That we should ask for money for the information we had.'

'You mean blackmail.'

'That's one way of putting it.'

'Is there another?'

'Maxine persuaded me there was - with the aid of the wine. She said that bringing the Company down wouldn't do anyone any good, but that Richard couldn't be allowed to go on profiting from his stealing. She proposed that we give him information that we'd found in return for a reward and him swearing to resign so that the embezzlement stopped. That way everyone would be a winner.'

'Except the Company. They've lost millions.'

'Exactly: past tense. And no one's any the wiser. Going public would be the worst thing for the Company.'

'I can see how you'd need a bottle of wine to go along with that logic.'

'I'd had more than a bottle of wine by then and it all sounded perfectly reasonable and the right thing to do. And Maxine even tried it on with me, to try to draw me in further. Get me more committed.'

'And you resisted of course,' Nick commented sarcastically.

'Of course I did. Ruth means far too much to me to risk losing her.'

'So you told Ruth what was going on?'

'No, I couldn't take that risk.'

'You mean you didn't trust her,' challenged Nick looking for Ruth's reaction.'

'Of course I trusted Ruth. I'd trust her with my life. That's why I came here on Friday. I meant I couldn't risk her getting involved in case it went wrong and the Police got on to us.'

'Go on,' said Nick, a little wearily - as though he'd really heard enough, or didn't believe what he was hearing.

'As I said, we agreed that Maxine would go to Richard to tell him what we knew, and how much we wanted to keep quiet and hand over our information.'

'Why not you? You'd found it. Or why not both of you?'

211

'Maxine thought Richard would show her a little more respect as she's a director. She said he might not want to deal with someone as low down in the organisation as me.'

'That could be true.'

'And we thought it would sound a bit more threatening if Richard knew Max had an unknown accomplice.'

'So what happened?'

'That's where it turns nasty.'

Nick leant forward, paying more attention. 'Go on.'

'Max went to see Richard, Wednesday of last week – the fifteenth. She told him that she knew all about his embezzling. He denied it of course, as you'd expect, but Max ignored him. She told him that she had an accomplice but not who it was. She'd told him that we wanted two million to keep quiet and give him what we'd found. She gave him twenty-four hours to think it over. Then she left. And we waited.'

'Where?'

'Where what?'

'Where did you wait? Ruth told me you didn't come home that night.' It stuck in his craw to refer to his old house as John's home.

'At home. Max went to her place. I went to mine, and stayed there.'

Nick wondered if Ruth had noticed that John had begun referring to his partner in crime by the more intimate "Max" and he also remembered the three weeks' worth of post that he'd found on John's doormat. He hadn't been home that night.

'Max went to work the next day. I rang in sick. Richard offered to meet her, and she suggested they met at her place. Her idea was that I'd be in another room listening in case Richard tried anything. But he refused and said they could meet in his office at eight, when everyone else had

212

gone home. Max agreed thinking that nothing could happen there. There is security on the site.'

'So what happened?'

'I don't know exactly. Obviously something happened. I haven't heard from her since.'

'How do you know she hasn't done a runner; double crossed you?'

'A combination of things.'

'What things?'

'The first was when I rang her on her mobile at about nine o'clock on the Thursday night.'

'Why? What happened?'

'When I rang she answered by saying "Hello darling." Max would never call me darling. There was no reason that she should,' said John with a half-smile at Ruth. 'She was trying to warn me. So I ended the call. Then Richard sent me an email from her RWS account to my RWS account. That's something *she* wouldn't have done. And that's another thing. He must have forced my name out of her.' He had a grim look as he paused.

'Why? Wouldn't it have come up when you rang her mobile?'

'No, we had phones we only used for communicating about this. And my name would have come up as "secret squirrel".

'Very professional.'

'So he must have beaten my name out of her *after* I ended the call. She was obviously still trying to protect me when she called me "darling"'

'What did the email say?'

'That she'd lost her phone and that Richard had agreed to pay and that I should come over and celebrate.'

'So what did you do?'

'I sent an email back saying great but that I couldn't come that evening because I was with Ruth. Oh, and I added "I wonder who answered your phone."'

'I don't suppose that fooled him.'

'I don't suppose it did but I had to say something. Saying Max's phone was lost wasn't convincing either. But we were all trying to think on our feet, and I'm certainly not used to dealing with a violent man with a hostage. Anyway, then I got another email asking me to go round to Max's to celebrate at six the next evening, and I agreed.'

'This was Thursday?'

'Yes.'

'So where did you stay on Thursday night? I presume not at your place now you knew Richard knew about you.'

'I went to a Travel Lodge. I had to think things over in safety.'

'Why didn't you go to the Police?'

'Greed I suppose. I was still hoping to be able to salvage something. I had something else on Richard now. Apart from that it would have meant admitting attempted blackmail'

'You're a cool customer.'

'Stupid you mean.'

Nick didn't disagree.

'You're right. I should have gone to the Police,' John went on. 'And *now* I've got Ruth involved.'

Ruth gave John a reassuring look. 'Don't be silly. We all make mistakes.' Nick's jaw dropped. She'd never been that understanding with his mistakes.

'Thank you darling,' said John. Nick couldn't believe how overtly sickly sweet they were with each other.

'So what did you do on Friday?' asked Nick tersely, trying to interrupt their sweet talk.

'I rang RWS asking to speak to Max just in case she'd turned up for work; just in case I'd got it wrong. Then I checked that Richard was at work before I went round to Max's house.'

'That was a bit risky. Richard could have had someone watching it.'

'I was very careful. I sat outside for ages watching the place before I went in.'

'How did you get in? Did you have a key?'

'Of course not. I had to break a window round the back. I could see someone had almost trashed the place and I wanted a closer look.'

'Did you find anything?'

'Only that the whole place had been searched. There was stuff all over the place. All the drawers and cupboards had been emptied. I found nothing, but then she wouldn't have kept anything at home anyway.'

'Where would she have kept it?'

'She had the incriminating evidence with her at all times – just like me.'

'So what were you looking for then?'

'I don't know really. Just to see if I could find evidence of anything nasty happening to her I suppose. Like I said he must have hurt her to get her to give him my name.'

'So you came here?'

'I had nowhere else to go and I thought Ruth deserved an explanation.'

'Very noble of you. But before you go any further, can *you* explain why you came to me the following day playing the damsel in distress, asking me to find John?' said Nick looking directly at Ruth.

'Look, I'm sorry I had to lie to you but we knew that Richard would expect me to be upset. He'd asked me on Friday morning if I'd seen John and he'd seen then that I really didn't know where he was. We realised that we had to keep Richard believing that I still didn't know when I went into work on Monday. So I asked you to find John to show Richard that I was looking for him. I suppose we were trying to be too clever, but it's not as though either of us have done this sort of thing before. To be honest...'

'It's a little late for that.' Nick paused. The penny dropped, and he said, 'you didn't expect me to find him, did you?'

'No, but that's not as bad as it sounds. I mean it's not that we thought you'd be a bad detective but how could you find John when your client was hiding him? No one would think that John was here if I'd employed a private detective to find him. And then Jane got involved and employed you to look for him as well as looking into what he'd been working on.'

'She had an inkling that Maxine and John might have been up to something,' said Nick. 'In the end that led me to finding out what Richard was up to, and from that I guessed that they must have been blackmailing him.'

'Yes that was very impressive, like I said when you arrived.'

'Cut the flannel, what happened when you turned up here?'

'Not much really. Ruth went through the roof to start with. As you can imagine.'

Nick could.

'She thought that I'd simply been on the raz for three days. Quite understandable.'

'But I shouldn't have hit you darling.'

'No, it was absolutely reasonable. And you did let me explain.'

'Explain? How?'

'I told her the truth. That Maxine and I had found out that Richard was embezzling money and that we had tried to blackmail him.'

'And you didn't turn him in?'

Ruth looked surprised at the question and then recovered. 'Of course not! I love John. I couldn't just turn him in.'

'Blackmail's a major crime Ruth. It ranks right up there with murder.'

'Don't be stupid! Of course it doesn't. That's the trouble with you Nick. You' were always too judgemental. You think that bad grammar should be a capital offense.'

Nick was tempted to argue with that, but knew there was plenty of evidence supporting Ruth's accusation. Anyway, this wasn't the time.

'So what did you do?'

'Nothing. I came to see you to buy some time really. To make sure Richard didn't think of looking here. We spent a lot of time thinking.'

'It must have been a bit awkward when Sally came forward. There must have been trouble in paradise then.'

'Not really,' said Ruth, before John could answer. 'It was obvious as soon as John said it; Richard must have paid Sally to lie so that I'd give John up to him if he *did* get in touch with me. I couldn't tell *you* that, so I had to come with the explanation that I thought she was simply mistaken.'

'I *was* surprised you came up with that load of crap.'

'Well now you know,' said Ruth.

Yes he did. He knew that Sally wasn't being paid by Richard because she'd let him into Richard's office.

'So now what? asked Nick.

'That's up to you,' answered John. Before Nick could reply he went on. 'As I see it you have three options.'

Nick couldn't help but be impressed by John's coolness. Here he was, having admitted to conspiracy to blackmail and he was spelling out Nick's options, not his own. But he had to disagree. 'I can only see one option. I'll have to tell Jane and the Police.'

217

'It's true, that's one option. You could turn me in and bring down Richard at the same time and probably ruin RWS in the process.'

'And ruin my life as well!' interjected Ruth.

'*Like that's supposed to bother me!*' thought Nick

'*Or* you could simply walk away and let Ruth and I...'

'*Ruth and me!*' screamed Nick's internal grammar police.

'...do whatever we decide.'

'A bit difficult that one. I can't just ignore what I've found.'

'There is another option.'

Nick would have raised an eyebrow if he had the necessary muscle control. Instead he frowned.

'You could come in with us,' said John, as though he were inviting him round for tea.

That option was so unexpected that it took a moment to register, then Nick half snorted half laughed out loud.'

'WHAT?'

'I said you could come in with us.'

'I heard what you said. I meant what on earth are you talking about?'

'Think about it. We have information that's worth a fortune...'

'Information that may have got Maxine Hudson killed.'

A silence descended on the room. It was the first time that had been said out loud.

'Don't be ridiculous Nick! This isn't an episode of Law and Order UK. Richard Seaton is a crooked businessman, not a murderer,' said Ruth.

'Whatever Richard Seaton is or isn't,' said John, heading off another set to between Ruth and Nick. 'We know that we need to be careful. He must have forced information out of Maxine somehow. That much we do know. Whether he's murdered her or not, I don't know. None of us do.'

Nick started to say something but John went on. 'We also have another advantage if you join us and that's *you!* He doesn't know that you've found me. I'm sure we could use that to our advantage somehow. And he doesn't need to know you're in on it, so you'll be totally safe.'

Nick liked the sound of being totally safe, but it was still complete nonsense. 'You say that but what if we do get caught?'

'I thought you were supposed to be the fearless hard-nosed detective now,' sneered Ruth. 'You're obviously still soft in the middle.'

Nick stared at Ruth. How had she come up with that phrase? It was if she'd been in his flat when he'd had his "epiphany". He couldn't let her get away with that. He needed a witty but vitriolic response.

'Piss off Ruth,' he spat.

'Come on you two, calm down. It's a lot for Nick to take in, Ruth. He's bound to have some reservations.'

'Yeah, like how are you going to get the money without Richard getting hold of you?'

'I was rather hoping you'd have some ideas about that. I've already been in touch with him.'

'You have?'

'Yes, I rang him. Don't worry; I didn't ring from this landline, I rang from a new pay-as-you-go mobile. I told him to get the money ready by tomorrow and that I'd be in touch with instructions. I... *we've* been trying to think of a foolproof plan ever since. And I think we might have one. There's only one of him. He had the advantage of surprise over Maxine. She didn't know what he was capable of. And she's only a woman. Sorry Ruth, but you know what I mean. Richard wouldn't have had any trouble overpowering her, especially if she wasn't ready for it. Look Nick, I can explain our plan and you can tell us what you think, maybe even suggest improvements.'

John stopped talking giving Nick a chance to think, but ready to rebuff whatever objections Nick came up with. Nick's brain was racing. John was clearly off his head. That was the first thought to go careering across his mind's eye. But there was a lot to think about, not just about John's proposal, but about other events. Events that had happened before he'd got involved. Events that may or may not be linked to what was going on now. And then there was Jane. How did she fit in to all of this? Should he tell her or keep her out of it until it was all over? He didn't trust John. John had clearly lied to Ruth about his affair with Maxine, not to mention not telling her about his plans to blackmail Richard in the first place. On the other hand in John's own words, 'he knew what he was capable of.' He could manage John.

No, he couldn't give a definitive answer. He had work to do first, but he did have one question that he had to ask.

'Ruth, don't you have any qualms about getting involved in blackmail? About stealing from the company you work for? This is more than nicking a few pens or post-it notes you know.'

'Of course I know that. I'm not stupid. As far as the blackmailing goes, we're blackmailing a thief, possibly a violent nasty one, who's hurt Maxine. He deserves to lose the money. And as for stealing from the company, we're not.'

Nick frowned.

'*Richard's* already stolen the money from the company. We'd be taking it from him and like I just said; he deserves it. Anyway how could we give the money back to the company without it all going public and ruining the company? They're better off not knowing it's gone.'

'That's an impressive piece of rationalising. I almost feel like agreeing on the strength of it but I'll have to think it over. You'll have to give me a few days,' said Nick.

John was surprised that Nick hadn't come up with a million objections or questions. 'So what do you want to do?' he asked.

'I'll have to go away and think about it.'

'How do we know you won't go straight to the Police?'

'You don't. As you said, it is one of my options. But I could have done that before I came here this morning. The only difference is that I know *you're* here now. And if you're that worried about it you could go and stay somewhere else. All I can say is, that for Ruth's sake – she is my client – I'll let her know what I decide before I do anything.'

He stood up to leave. 'Strange being back here,' said Nick as he looked around the room, before adding, 'Even stranger being the one to leave,' glancing at John as he walked towards the door. Ruth followed him to the front door and as he opened it she whispered, 'Meet me in the "Pay the Difference" cafe in fifteen minutes.'

Nick frowned and smiled simultaneously, 'OK,' he replied as he turned and walked down the drive to his car. "Pay the Difference" had been just about the last joke they'd shared together, while they were still married. She'd misquoted the local supermarket's catchphrase when she'd served something up for dinner and it had stuck. They'd referred to the supermarket as 'Pay the Difference' ever since.

'*I wonder what she wants,*' he thought as he drove away.

CHAPTER TWENTY-THREE

As instructed, Nick was seated in the aforementioned cafe fifteen minutes later with a coffee in front of him waiting for Ruth. When she arrived he offered to buy her one, but she refused.

'What can I do for you?' he asked.

'I'm not sure how to start.'

'In that case can I ask you a question?'

Ruth nodded.

'Did you believe that load of crap about Sally being paid to lie about seeing him and Maxine together?'

'No,' replied Ruth dropping her eyes to the table.

'No? Then why haven't you turned him in?'

'I didn't know what to do for the best. The best for me that is.'

'What do you mean? If you turn him in then he'll be put away and you'll be rid of him. Isn't that what you want?'

'Of course I want rid of him but I began to think I could have more than that.'

'Oh bloody hell! Not you as well!'

'What do you mean?'

'You want to blackmail Richard and get the money without John don't you?'

'Am I that obvious?'

'It was the only option left that we hadn't discussed.'

'So what do you think? Will you help me? I know you don't like John so that shouldn't stop you.'

'It doesn't.'

'Good. What I'd really like to do is get the money for myself – well for me and you – *and* drop John in it at the same time.'

'You've been watching too much television. I don't see how that can be done; even if I were up for it.'

'I know it sounds crazy, but since John turned up last Friday normal behaviour seems to have gone out of the window. He's been plotting how he can still get his hands on the money ever since, and I started getting into it myself. And then when Sally came out of the woodwork and he came up with that cock and bull story saying that she must be being paid to lie, I started plotting on my own. I think I deserve something after the way I've been treated. I was going to approach you about it even if you hadn't turned up this morning.'

Nick was speechless. The morning had been the most surreal of his life. First he had found the missing person he'd been employed to find. He'd had a successful case! Then John had proposed the most preposterous scheme he'd ever heard of, which was now being "out-preposteroused" by his ex-wife. They were both mad! He was now convinced that he had to go to the Police. But there was Jane to consider. Should he tell her first – give her some warning at least - about the proverbial that was about to hit the fan? And then there were the other questions that needed answers. The Police would no doubt look into those, but he'd rather follow them up himself. He was getting to enjoy this detective lark, and he wanted the satisfaction of presenting the completed case to the Police.

'OK, I'll think about it.'

'Brilliant! When will you have made your mind up?'

'For Christ's sake! I don't know Ruth! Have you any idea what this morning's been like for me? It's been totally bonkers. I feel like my head's about to explode.'

'OK, I'm sorry. I'll ring you on Monday.'

'No. I'll ring you, when I'm ready,' he said firmly.

Ruth was about to argue but saw the look in Nick's eyes and thought better of it.

'Right, well I'd better go and buy what I told John I was coming here for.'

'Some "Pay the Difference" stuff?'

Ruth smiled, 'Yeah. "Pay the difference"; "Can't Tell the Difference" The packaging's nicer though.'

'Sometimes the packaging's the only difference.'

Nick was left to contemplate how profound his last statement was when applied to his current options. It didn't take him long to realise that it wasn't at all.

'Load of bollocks,' he said out loud finishing the dregs of his coffee before heading to the toilet for his usual post-coffee visit.

CHAPTER TWENTY-FOUR

He spent the afternoon looking through the project files, the invoices for Pearson & Toomey and Hooley & Vaal, and the HR documents he'd copied, as well as thinking over the morning's events. By half past four he had a headache. Neurons had been flying backwards and forwards between the analytical and the creative parts of his brain all afternoon. Now they were getting lost on the way. It was time to go and see Sally. She would be able take his mind off things and soothe his troubled soul.

A bottle of wine helped but it was mainly Sally's touch and the fact that she took him at his word when he said he'd had enough of the job and didn't want to talk about it anymore, which soothed him.

That and the lovemaking.

The following morning, after some more soothing, Nick was ready to have the awkward meetings that he had planned.

It was a grey dank day as he drove to his first meeting; the sort of weather that would probably match the mood of the meeting, but it had to be done. He pulled up outside the 1950's three bed-roomed semi-detached house just as the rain started to fall. As he walked up the drive his eyes took in the overall impression of the house front. It was in reasonable condition. The eaves could do with painting but apart from that it looked well looked after. Perhaps the family inside weren't struggling financially. Perhaps the life insurance policy had been honoured, even though the inquest had concluded that the man of the house had been found to have committed suicide.

Nick rang the doorbell. A woman in her mid-thirties opened the door. She had short dark hair and was wearing blue denim jeans and a cream t-shirt. She was carrying a tea towel. Nick had obviously disturbed her in the kitchen.

'Mrs Shaw?' he asked.

'Yes,' replied the woman taking care not to open the door fully, keeping one leg wedged up behind it.

'Hi, my name's Nick Howard. I work at RWS. I've been looking at... well, I was wondering if I could have a word... about Mike.'

The woman was clearly surprised by someone from her husband's company turning up on her doorstep on a Sunday morning almost twelve months after he'd died. The surprise quickly turned to annoyance as some memory was triggered.

'Look, I don't know what you want but everything was said at the inquest. I have no more to say, especially to anyone working for RWS.'

Nick cursed himself for not ringing ahead and arranging the meeting. How could he have been so stupid?

'I don't really work *for* RWS. It's more that I'm working at RWS. You see I'm a private investigator. Someone's gone missing. Two people actually and I've been employed to look for them.'

'What's that got to do with Mike?'

'It looks like they might have uncovered something. Something very similar to what Mike was accused of being engaged in and I... '

Mrs Shaw must have decided she didn't want to discuss this on her doorstep as she said, 'You'd better come in,' and opened the door fully to allow Nick to step inside. She seated him in the lounge and went to the kitchen to make them both a cup of tea. He could hear children playing in the back garden; a boy and a girl he thought, about ten years old. There was a photograph of each on the mantelpiece along with one of Mrs Shaw with, he presumed, the late Mike Shaw. The widow brought the tea in and sat in a chair by the unlit gas fire.

'Beautiful children,' said Nick looking towards the photographs on the mantel.'

'Thank you. So what is it you want exactly?'

'I'd like to ask you some questions about your husband; if you knew what he was working on, how he seemed before he died. That sort of thing.'

'Why?'

'To be honest Mrs Shaw,' said Nick noticing that he'd used that phrase again but unable to take it back. 'I'm not sure I know myself. I think it may help me understand why the two people I'm looking for have gone missing.'

'How?'

'I think they found out that someone is embezzling money from RWS.'

'You mean like Mike was.' There was anger in her voice, perhaps because her husband had committed suicide because of his crime or because he'd been accused of the crime. Nick waited.

'Oh, just ask your questions.'

'Thank you Mrs Shaw. Can I call you ...?'

'Mrs Shaw's fine.'

'OK. Did Mike ever discuss his work with you?'

'Yes, he usually told me every evening what he'd been doing. A lot of it was the same from day to day and he didn't go through that every time. He'd just say "Same old, same old" if there was nothing interesting.'

'And just before he died?'

The widow took some time to think, dredging up memories of a painful time. 'He'd been at RWS for a long time and was the senior auditor. There were regular audits to do and he worked unsupervised most of the time. The only time he really had any discussions with his boss was

227

once a month when he reported on progress with the auditing. Even then the meetings were often cancelled.'

'Who was his boss?' asked Nick, already knowing the answer.

'Richard Seaton, the director.'

'What did he think of Richard? Did he ever say?'

'He thought he was a prat! But as I said, he didn't see him every day so it wasn't really a problem. Of course he got a bit pissed off when the monthly meetings were cancelled. He used to say if the director couldn't be bothered, why should he? He thought that half the audits the team did were worthless. No one took any notice of them. The resulting actions were never carried out and management never did anything about it. So he started auditing other stuff off his own bat.'

'What sort of stuff?'

'I don't know really. To be honest, I never really understood what he was talking about, but I knew it was important that he had someone to talk to about his frustrations at work, so I never let on. All I know is that he was enjoying doing whatever he was doing for the last couple of months. He seemed almost excited when he got home some evenings. If "excited" is a word you can use about auditing.'

'Excited? How?'

'He'd talk enthusiastically about his work. Saying that he'd nearly worked it out, and that he just had to prove it.'

'It?'

'I don't know.'

'But he was definitely excited about something? Did you tell all this to the Police?'

'Yes, they said that they had proof that he was embezzling money and that he must have been excited about working out how to do it.'

'What was the proof?'

'They had copies of payments made from RWS accounts into an account in Mike's name.'

'Did you know anything about the account?'

'No, of course not. They said it was all done on line. There was fifty thousand in it apparently. Put in only a couple of days before he... died.'

'Did you talk to anyone from RWS?'

'Yes Jane Edwards came to see me with Richard Seaton. They said they were very sorry and that they'd managed to get the Police to agree to keep the reason for Mike's suicide quiet for my sake and the sake of the Company.'

'What did you think of them?'

'Jane was very nice. She seemed genuinely upset. Said if there was anything she could do...'

'And Richard?'

'Mike was right. He was a prat. He'd been the one who'd produced the proof and confronted Mike. He said that Mike had made some elementary mistake and that was why he'd found out about it almost immediately. He said he'd given Mike the opportunity to come clean himself, to tell Jane and the Police. And that it would have made it easier on Mike. He told me all that as though he'd been doing *me* a favour! He tried to sound like he was sorry about it all, but he didn't convince me. He clearly thought that Mike deserved what happened to him.'

'But you don't think Mike was guilty do you?'

'No.'

'I heard that you'd left Mike when you found out what he was accused of. It doesn't sound like you did.'

'Of course I didn't. I heard that myself, but it was just a vicious rumour. Why would I leave him if I knew he was innocent?'

'What do you think happened then?'

'I think whoever it was found out that Mike was about to expose them and they framed Mike and made sure that Richard Seaton would find the evidence quickly.'

'So why did he commit suicide if he wasn't guilty?'

'I don't know. Apparently he been drinking, which he never did. I suppose it all looked very black. He couldn't see a way out and that made it worse for him because he knew the truth. Normally he'd have been angry and wanted to fight. It must have been the drink. He'd had nearly a full bottle of whisky.'

'How did he...?'

'He set fire to himself in his car in a city car park.'

'Oh my God. I'm so sorry.'

Mrs Shaw took a moment to compose herself. 'Apparently some psychologist said the fire was Mike's way of trying to cleanse himself.'

Nick said nothing. He waited for Mrs Shaw to speak.

'I'm sorry,' she said when she'd composed herself again. 'Was any of that any use to you?'

'Thank you Mrs Shaw. Yes it was. If it's any consolation I agree with you. I don't think Mike was embezzling from the company. I think whoever it was - whoever framed him and drove him to suicide - is still doing it. And I intend to prove it.'

'Will you let me know when you do?'

'Of course I will Mrs Shaw.'

'Julie.'

'Of course I will Julie. I'll tell you as soon as I can.'

Then he added, rather pointlessly he thought, 'And if there's anything I can do...' before he stepped out of the front door and walked back down the short drive. The rain had stopped but Nick's mood was darker. He couldn't make his next visit in this mood so he took himself off to 'Pay the Difference' and bought himself two sausage rolls, a bag of crisps and a bottle of their cheapest water.

CHAPTER TWENTY-FIVE

Having consumed his version of comfort food sitting in the supermarket car park, Nick set off for his next meeting. A meeting that could prove to be more upsetting that his last. Losing a husband was bad enough. But was it as bad as losing a son?

Mrs Worsley lived in a relatively small bungalow. Small that is for someone who had as much money as she must have had, or at least that's what Nick thought as he rang the doorbell. She was the mother of a director of a FTSE 100 company, who had died in an accident whilst on Company business. The payouts must have been enormous. Nick gave himself a mental slap. It wasn't her fault her son had been killed. The money would be no consolation at all. At least he'd remembered to phone ahead this time. He was expected.

The woman who opened the door was probably in her late sixties or early seventies. She was still very fit and could have easily passed for being ten years younger. She was dressed in black slacks and a grey cashmere sweater. Her hair was a kind of gun metal grey with whiter highlights. She showed Nick straight through to the sitting room as she referred to it. Already sitting by the fire was an older lady, whose hair was completely white. Martin's mother, ('You must call me Joyce,') introduced the older lady as her mother.

'Please don't mind my mother,' said Joyce after they'd settled themselves down with cups of tea. 'She's quite deaf. Hardly hears a thing.'

'No I'm not,' piped up the older lady. 'You don't speak clearly that's all.'

'Although she does seem to hear everything you don't expect her to.'

'And I heard that as well! And I'm not just your mother you know. I do have a name. Agnes Burton. Like the stately home Burton Agnes but backwards. I think my parents thought I'd grow up looking like the back end of a big house.'

She laughed away to herself.

'My mother reverted back to her maiden name after her husband – my father- left her. She loves her name,' explained Joyce.

'Good afternoon Mrs Agnes. I mean Mrs Burton. I'm pleased to meet you,' said Nick.

'A young man with manners. How refreshing! And I'm pleased to meet you too – for the moment.'

'How can I help you?' asked Joyce keen to get the meeting back on track. 'You said it had something to do with my late son.'

'Late? Who's late? Are we expecting someone else?'

'No mother. We're not expecting anyone else. Why don't you carry on with your reading?' said Joyce picking up an e-book from the coffee table in front of her before switching it on and handing it to her mother.

'Your mother, I mean Agnes reads e-books?'

'They're a godsend. She's always been an avid reader and they're so easy to use - we can make the font as large as she wants, so she's not having to hunt for her reading glasses all the time. But that's not the reason you're here.'

'No, sorry. I was wondering if you could tell me something about your son Martin.'

'Could I ask why you're asking?'

'Sorry, I should have explained on the phone. I'm working for RWS at the moment and... well... to be honest...'

Before he had chance to chastise himself for the use of that phrase again, Agnes piped up again. 'Does that mean you're not usually honest?'

'I do apologise Nick. Mother! Don't be so rude!'

'It's quite all right Joyce. It's a phrase I hate myself. In fact I picked Jane Edwards up on it the other week just like Agnes did to me.'

'You said that to Jane Edwards? How did she take it? Bit your head off I suppose.'

'No she took very well really. Even tried to correct herself when she did it again later.'

'My, you must have made quite an impression on her.'

'Do you know her then?'

'Yes, slightly. My son knew her a lot better obviously. In fact he was almost besotted by her. She was the reason he never married.'

'Really?'

'Yes, they met at university, and became very close in their first year. They were both on the same course or at least had a lot of the same lectures. He'd never met anyone like Jane. He used to talk to us non-stop about her whenever he came home. She was so confident, so full of life, so focussed on what she wanted to be. Martin was from a much humbler background, a typical northern council housing estate. She'd grown up to have anything she wanted. When she showed an interest in Martin he was hooked for life. Martin was a nice enough lad, quiet, even shy but he was very bright. Exceptionally so. Should have gone to Oxford or Cambridge really. But he thought he'd have to wear a cap and gown to dinner and say prayers in Latin and he couldn't face that. Anyway I think it was his sheer intelligence that first attracted Jane to him. After the first year he tagged along like a faithful puppy; although he didn't talk about her as much. He was never interested in

233

another woman, even when she dated other men. Even when she married!'

'And did Martin know Richard Seaton at university as well?'

'Richard? Yes.'

'And how did he get on with Richard?'

'Fine I suppose – eventually. At first he thought Richard was a rival for Jane's attention but when that didn't amount to anything he got on with Richard a lot better. Of course they all joined RWS at the same time.'

'And Martin remained devoted to Jane?'

'Yes. As I said, even when she married! Ridiculous. We tried to talk to him about it. Suggested he see other women but he would have none of it. Still, he seemed happy enough. He did very well at RWS as you know. Became a director. They all did. Like the three musketeers, we used to say. He bought this bungalow for me after my husband died, and moved me over from Darlington. He said that he was never going to be leaving RWS so I didn't need to worry about him suddenly moving away, and leaving me on my own. Of course Mother had to come too.'

'I didn't *have* to come. I came because I wanted to. I'm not an invalid,' said Agnes looking up from her e-book. She looked at her watch. 'Would you like to stay for dinner Mr Howard? We're having a Sunday roast – with dolphin nose potatoes.'

'Dauphinoise as you well know Mother. And I'm sure Nick has better places to be.'

'I don't blame him. Bloody garlicky spuds with roast beef. Whatever next?'

'I'm sorry Nick. Is there anything else? I just seemed to have chatted about nothing so far.'

'You've been very helpful Joyce. Did Martin ever talk about work?'

234

'No not really, I think he thought, quite rightly, that I wouldn't know what he was talking about.'

'Well, did he never talk about leaving RWS? Did he never want a change or even a bigger job? Managing Director somewhere else?'

'We did suggest that to him. Said it wasn't good for him to stay at RWS just because Jane was there. That it was holding back his career. But he said he couldn't leave and that's all there was to it.'

'Couldn't leave? What did he mean by that?'

'I took it to mean that he couldn't bring himself to leave Jane. I know it sounds ridiculous, but...'

'Loyal of him. Or could it have been the money, if you don't mind my asking? He must have been on a good salary.'

'Well, yes he was, although he was always keen to point out that he wasn't on nearly as much as the directors at a lot of companies – especially those bankers in the City, down in London. Mind you, he must have been on more than he let on because he had a lot more money in the bank than we expected. And then there were all those shares and bonds and things. I don't really understand it all, but Richard Seaton put me in touch with someone who could sort it out for us.'

'Well thank you for your help, Joyce. What will you do now? Now that Martin's gone? Will you stay here or move back to Darlington?'

'Oh, we'll stay here. We have friends here now. More than we have in Darlington. Mind you, we still have to decide what to do with Martin's own place. He had a lovely flat - sorry he insisted we call it an apartment - in the city. In fact I've not even tidied it up since it was burgled. Shocking really, it was months ago, but I just couldn't bring myself to face it when it happened it was so soon after he died. And since then... well I've just been doing other things.'

'Martin's place was burgled, just after he died?'

'Yes the place was ransacked. Every drawer and cupboard was emptied. The contents were thrown all over the place. Things *were* taken. We know that. But I didn't have an inventory of Martin's belongings so it was impossible to say exactly what was stolen.'

'Were any other apartments burgled at the same time?'

'Not that I'm aware of. Oh, do you think that someone heard he'd died and broke in because they knew the place would be empty. How callous some people are.'

'It was probably just coincidence. Thanks again Joyce. And thank *you* Agnes. It was nice to meet you. Sorry to disturb your afternoon. I'll leave you in peace now.'

Nick stood up and looked out of the window. He couldn't let a whole conversation with two elderly women pass without a comment on the weather. It just wouldn't be British. The sky had darkened since he'd arrived; trees were swaying in the wind. It looked cold.

'Look at that weather,' he said. 'It's getting distinctly back-endish. It'll be Christmas before you know.'

'Of course it won't, you big doily,' came the reply from Agnes. 'Not unless you've lost the use of all of your senses and can't see the Christmas cards in the shops in September and hear the interminable Christmas songs playing from October onwards. And then there's the adverts on the tele, telling you about another chance to see the "1973 Morecambe and Wise Christmas Show". How on earth is it going to be Christmas before you know it? How will you not know about it weeks before it happens? And it's on the same date every year. How can it surprise you?'

The younger woman stood there horrified at the tirade her mother had just delivered to their polite guest.

'I am *so* sorry. Mother! How could you be so rude?'

Nick was laughing. 'It's quite all right, Joyce. I think your Mother has just given me a glimpse of myself in the future. And to be honest...' he winked at Agnes. 'It looks like fun.'

Joyce showed him to the door, apologising again for her mother's rudeness, and he reassured her it was quite all right. He said his goodbyes and hoped that she enjoyed her dolphin nose potatoes. She waited for him to get into his car and drive away before she closed her front door.

Although it was Sunday afternoon, Nick decided to pay his office a visit. He was still paying for the place and he had a lot of thinking to do. And who knows how many potential clients had left messages on his answer machine?

CHAPTER TWENTY-SIX

'Bollocky bollocks!' cursed Nick as he sat in his swivel chair behind his empty desk. *'No milk!'*

Should he go and buy a coffee from round the corner? No he'd only have to get up for a couple of Nelsons if he did. He should concentrate on the job in hand. This was the first time he'd ever worked on a Sunday in his current career and he ought to make it as productive as possible. He scoured his drawers for some paper and a pen. He needed to write his thoughts down. He could have really done with a whiteboard on the wall. Instead he found a couple of A4 envelopes and a biro from the local bookies'. The pen, which was only three inches long but would have to do, must have been left in the drawer by the previous tenants. He hadn't been in a bookies' for over twenty years. He felt that he needed to draw a diagram of some sort and had what he thought was a brainwave; he slit the envelopes open along the side and across the bottom and opened them up thereby making two A3 sheets of brown paper. He was sure that Jane, with her in depth knowledge of "office speak," could tell him exactly what the sort of diagram he wanted to draw was called. *'Was it a "spider diagram"?'* he wondered. But enough prevarication! He wasn't in his old job at RWS; he shouldn't be putting off the work because it was so tedious or pointless, or tedious *and* pointless. This was important and interesting. He picked up his pen, fiddled around with it to get it comfortable in his hand; not easy with it being so thin and short.

'Sod the spider diagram. You can't beat simple lists.'

He started to fill the paper in front of him with a list of thoughts and facts as he knew them as they came to him.

Some things were clear to him.

Richard is embezzling copious amounts of money from RWS via the consultancy 'contract' with Pearson and Toomey.

John and Maxine found out

Maxine approached Richard. She has not been heard from since, (apart from the bogus emails).

He had some decisions to make.

Do I simply turn all this evidence over to Jane and the Police? - the right thing to do.

     Pro's: Richard gets his just desserts.

     Con's: My job is over and the money stops.

Do I go along with John's suggestion and take part in the blackmail scam and earn a lot of money? Risky but it should be manageable. Anything goes wrong, can always say I was setting up both John and Richard to catch them in the act.

Could go along with Ruth's suggestion - would result in me receiving even more money and John gets nothing. Risk covered as above.

There were other things to consider. He started another list.

Sally: Are Ruth and I right to dismiss John's claim that she was paid to lie to encourage Ruth to give John up if he got in contact?

She did come forward with her evidence at a propitious moment; at a time when John may well have, indeed had, contacted Ruth.

But she did help me gain access to Richard's office. Surely she wouldn't have done that if she was in Richard's employ?

Or is Richard so over confident he didn't think me capable of discovering the evidence, and told her to let me in? (v unlikely)

Or has he pissed Sally off in some way so that she didn't feel any loyalty to him? (possible)

Or did he simply pay Sally for a "one off" job – the lying – and so as far as she's concerned she's no longer working for him and was happy to help me?

He thought about his time with Sally. How she was with him. How they were with each other. He couldn't believe that she could be lying to him. He wrote another fact down at the bottom of his first list.

John and Maxine are having an affair.

Then there was Martin Worsley and Mike Shaw. His conversation with Mike's widow had almost confirmed his own suspicions. He wrote again.

Mike stumbled on Seaton's crimes and Seaton found out. Then he killed Mike, made it look like suicide. Seaton framed Mike.

Seaton supplied the evidence to steer Police well away from Pearson and Toomey invoices.

Easy for him - being the Finance & Procurement Director at the time.

Can I find tangible proof?

Martin Worsley was a little different. Martin had died whilst on a business trip with Richard. While Nick did believe in coincidences, was this taking it a bit too far?

Was Martin involved in the embezzlement? Yes – his signature was on some invoices.

He had a lot of spare cash. Bought that bungalow for his mother and grandmother, as well as keeping up a luxury apartment in the centre of the city.

If Martin were in on it, why had Richard killed him?

Was he getting pangs of guilt because of his devotion to Jane?

Was that feeling finally overcoming his greed?

Had he been about to come clean to Jane?

If he had to put money on it, Nick would have bet that it had been Richard who suggested that he and Martin go to the Middle East together to visit the Company's sites out there. He could ask Jane about that. But could he ever get any proof about what had really happened out there?

No, but once this was all in the hands of the Police, no doubt they could.

He stopped writing. Thinking of Jane; what was he going to do about her? He had already resolved to tell her the following day that he wasn't in love with her. He'd have to find a way of doing that gently. It really was unbelievable - the way she had suddenly fallen for him. It certainly indicated a rather unstable mind. Even if Sally hadn't been around he'd like to think that he'd still have been able to turn Jane down. He couldn't believe that he would have been able to keep her satisfied - no matter how great the sex was. He couldn't help but think that what she ultimately wanted was someone who would be the dominant one in their partnership, someone more assertive and dynamic. Someone she could look up to, someone who she could seek approval from. A replacement for her father. And if that role was not fulfilled, or the approval not forthcoming, then woe betide any family bunnies. He'd like to think he would have resisted the temptation to take advantage of the great sex on offer until the bunnies were finally in the pot. He'd like to think he would have resisted. But he knew he wouldn't. It was a good job he had Sally.

That reminded him, it was time to go. He folded up his opened out envelope and put it his jacket pocket. He knew what he was going to do now - and he would do it tomorrow. It was late afternoon, and he'd earned an evening, (and a night), with the lovely Sally.

CHAPTER TWENTY-SEVEN

When Sally opened her door to him, Nick could smell a good old fashioned Sunday Roast on the go. He slipped his arms around her waist and pulled her close.

'You smell nice,' he said.

'That's the dinner, as you well know,' she replied gently thumping his chest. 'That reminds me, we're having chicken. Would you like stuffing?'

'Before or after dinner?'

'It'll have to be after unless you want everything to burn.'

'Spoilsport. Actually I need a "Nelson. And I mean now.'

'You always do. OK, give me your jacket and go.'

Nick walked quickly off to the bathroom doing a 'Groucho Marx' walk that went totally unnoticed by Sally.

When he came out, Sally was reading the opened-up envelope, on which he had written his thoughts. Her face told him that she wasn't happy.

'This is your writing? This is what you think?' The tone of her voice told him that his reading of her face had not been wrong.

He was beginning to grasp what she might be unhappy about. 'Yes, but...'

'You really seriously considered that someone had paid me to lie about seeing John and Maxine at it in her office?'

'No, not seriously. I mean it was only a passing thought. It wasn't even my idea. Ruth said that you must have been paid. I didn't believe it for one second.'

He avoided mentioning John. He didn't want Sally dragged into anything until it was all done and dusted.

'There are, let's see; five points on this list suggesting that I might've been paid. That's more than a bloody second! And only one of them says I *probably* wasn't paid.'

'They were just random thoughts!' Nick protested.

'Random thoughts that you thought were worth writing down! Because you were giving them serious consideration. You don't trust me do you? Not one hundred percent!'

'Of course I do! Implicitly,' pleaded Nick, in the hope that a posh word would add credence to his claims.

'And that's why you haven't mentioned that you've found John. Haven't mentioned that he asked you to join in his little blackmail scheme.'

'Don't be stupid. I've only just come through the door. Give me chance.'

'Stupid am I? Don't you dare call me stupid!' screamed Sally. 'You had no intention of telling me did you? Did you?'

'To be honest...' –'*How must that sound?*'- 'No. I haven't decided what to do and I didn't want to involve you. It may not exactly be legal.'

'What a load of crap! Well you can piss off! Go on, get out! Now!'

'Come on Sally, let me...'

'Get out!'

She took a step towards him as though she intended to punch him. There was pure violence in her eyes. He opened his mouth to speak again.

'I said "Get out!"'

Nick decided it was time to leave and give Sally chance to calm down. He turned towards the door.

'No! Wait!' she shouted, before marching off to the bedroom. Nick remained rooted to the spot wondering what was coming next. Had she changed her mind? Had she been joking? Was she going to call him from the bedroom? No, she wasn't. She came storming back with his jacket, which she threw at him, along with the screwed up envelope covered with the thoughts that had got him into so much trouble. He failed to catch either.

'I don't want you to have an excuse to come back for your jacket. Pick it up and get out.'

Nick did as he was told and left feeling somewhat crestfallen and angry at the same time. Crestfallen because he really felt something for Sally and it looked like he'd lost her. And angry both at himself because he'd not been more careful with his notes, and at Sally because she wouldn't listen to reason. There was only one thing for it. He'd have to go home and get pissed.

He threw the door open at the bottom of the stairs out on to the outside world. He caught a movement in the corner of his eye. He looked round. There was a figure lurking in the shadows by the area where the communal waste bins were kept. A cloud of cigarette smoke obscured his face but he wouldn't have recognised it anyway. But he did recognise the orange trainers the man was wearing. He remembered seeing them as they laid into him the other night.

It was Sally's "ex". He walked towards him.

'Excuse me mate, got a light?' he asked, fumbling in his pocket as if about to take out a packet of cigarettes.

The man grunted a response and held his cigarette out for Nick to take a light from it. Instead, as soon as he was close enough, Nick wedged his forearm under the man's chin and thrust him hard against the wall.

'Dave isn't it? Sally's "ex."'

Dave grasped at Nick's arm trying to pull it off his larynx. He couldn't breathe - let alone answer the question. He smelled of cigarette smoke with a hint of a damp caravan.

'You beat me up the other day, but I'm willing to let that go, because I'm a nice man,' growled Nick. 'I can understand that you were upset to see your "ex" with someone else. But I'm telling you it's time for you to move on now. It's not healthy for you to hang on to the past. So leave Sally alone. Stop hanging around here and don't ever touch her or me again? OK?'

Dave tried to nod but Nick was holding him against the wall too tightly. Nick realised that he was turning an unhealthy colour so he relaxed his hold on Dave slightly. Dave gulped in air and coughed a few times. Finally he nodded and croaked, 'OK, fine.'

'OK, fine, what?'

OK, I'll leave her alone. I'll stay away.'

Nick released his grip completely and was about to speak when Dave saw his chance and tried to catch Nick with a right hook, but his judgement was way out, probably due to the lack of oxygen reaching his brain for the last couple of minutes. He was far too close, and Nick intercepted the punch with his left arm before hammering Dave against the wall with his right forearm under his chin again.

'You don't frigging get it do you? Let me spell it out to you. If you go anywhere near me or Sally ever again I will kill you. I don't mean I will beat you up a bit I mean I will actually kill you. Do you understand?'

Dave nodded.

'Do you believe me?'

Dave was unable to shrug his shoulders but he managed to convey his scepticism with a facial expression. Nick now had a problem. Dave didn't believe his threat to kill him. Why had he had to ask? His anger with himself and Sally had fuelled his initial confrontation with Dave and his aggression had been heartfelt. Now it had gone on too long and he felt that he was in danger of losing

245

momentum. He wasn't used to being aggressive. And he was sure that Dave had faced a lot worse. He had to play the hard-nosed detective for a bit longer. That was it! That's exactly what he would do.

He still had his forearm on Dave's throat as he leant in closer.

'You don't know what I do for a living do you?'

Dave shook his head as much as he was able.

'I'm a Private Detective,' said Nick, making sure he spat the 'P' of 'Private' in Dave's face. 'And I picked up a gun at a crime scene. The Police don't know I've got it but they know who used to own it. That means that I can kill someone with it and they'll think they know who did it - and it won't be me. Now do you believe me?'

It sounded ridiculous and he instantly regretted saying it, but Dave nodded.

'Good,' said Nick. He had to do something to wipe out Dave's memory of his pathetic threat. He released Dave from his forearm and punched him below the belt as hard as he could. As Dave crumpled in front of him he grabbed his head and pulled it down bringing his knee hard up into his face. He felt the cartilage in Dave's noise crunch against his knee. Then he let him fall to the ground.

'Seems I lied about being a nice man,' said Nick, as he turned and walked away feeling totally revolted by his outburst of brutality.

He arrived back at his flat still feeling disgusted with himself. In the past, when he'd had this sort of day, he used to joke he was going home to kick the wife and screw the cat. Unfortunately he had neither. He knew that he should get something to eat but instead he went straight for the whisky bottle. It wasn't a single malt - he didn't deserve a single malt. In fact, he thought he should have been drinking cheap cider straight from a plastic two litre bottle. That's what the pond-life who beat people up in the street

246

drank. But he was better than them. He was drinking cheap whisky *and* he was using a glass. As he drank, his mood sank further. He mulled over the weekend and became more and more of a victim. First he'd had to talk to those two nice ladies; the one who'd lost her husband and was bringing up two children on her own, and the one who'd lost her son and was looking after her aged mother on her own. That was real suffering, which *he'd* had to witness. Then he'd discovered that Ruth had asked him to find John when John was already staying at her house! Because she didn't think he'd be any good and wouldn't be able to find John. Well she'd almost been right there. He hadn't really found John, he'd stumbled over him. Then he'd had to listen to them talking about their plans to continue to blackmail that Seaton twat. And they'd asked him to join in! And he was thinking about it! And then to cap it all, Sally had thrown him out. But then that didn't cap it all. The pièce de résistance was the beating up of Sally's 'ex'. It wasn't as though he was a threat to anyone. Sally herself had thumped him for goodness sake. No, he'd simply been taking his frustration out on him. That was the same excuse as the yobs used wasn't it: frustration? Frustration that they couldn't get a job, frustration that they had no hope. Frustration that their girlfriend had just kicked them out? Oh no, that was *his* excuse. And whose fault was that? Seaton's and Ruth's and John's; that's whose. If Seaton hadn't been embezzling, then John couldn't have been blackmailing him, and Ruth wouldn't have asked him to find John, and they wouldn't have asked him to help them blackmail Seaton, and he wouldn't have had to write all his thoughts down, and Sally wouldn't have found them and she wouldn't have kicked him out, and then he wouldn't have beaten up Dave, and...

It wasn't his fault; it was theirs!

He knew what he was going to do. Everything had conspired against him and it was all pointing one way. He dialled Ruth's number. As soon as she picked up, he didn't wait for her to speak, instead he said immediately, 'It's me. I'll do it. I'll help you. I'll be there at nine tomorrow.'

Then he rang off.

His glass was empty, His bottle was empty. His head was empty. It slumped forward on to his chest and he slept the sleep of the 'just'.

The 'just finished a bottle of whisky'.

CHAPTER TWENTY-EIGHT

He awoke bright and early the next morning, without the brightness. His head felt like someone was applying a tourniquet, twisting it tighter and tighter. All of his senses were overactive. The dim light from the street outside that normally made barely any impression through his curtains on his room, made him squint with the glare. His breathing was too loud. His mouth tasted like a gorilla's armpit. His neck ached, his back ached, and his legs ached. When he straightened his legs his knees 'cracked' and even that sound reverberated through his brain.

Apart from that he felt fine. He looked at his watch. Then he sat up and rested his elbows on his knees and let his head drop forward, not that he could hold it up anyway. He looked at his watch again and this time read the time. It was half past six. He wanted to shake his head to clear it but was afraid it might fall off. Instead he forced himself to his feet, and dragged himself over to the sink. He filled a pint glass with water and drank it all. He brought it up instantly, and a lot more besides. He drank some more water, and when he was as sure as he could be that he wasn't going to be sick again he took a couple of painkillers and went for a shower.

Half an hour later he was showered, shaved, and dressed, and looked almost human - even if he felt nothing like it. He made some tea and managed to eat a slice of toast. He drank some more water. He needed to rehydrate. His brain had dried out and shrivelled up to the size of a pea. It was bouncing around in his head like a dodgem car. That's why it hurt so much. At least that was his theory about hangovers, and he was in no state to think of another one now. So he drank more water; slowly, very slowly. And even more slowly he began to be able to think clearly.

He went over the events of last night. He was still disgusted by his beating up Sally's 'ex' but he couldn't do anything about that now, and anyway, he owed him one. More pressing was that he'd agreed to help Ruth and John with their blackmailing scheme, and he needed a plan. A plan that would satisfy them *and* Jane! He thought he remembered saying that he'd see Ruth and John at nine. That gave him about an hour to come up with the said plan. He found some A4 lined paper and started to write down ideas. An hour later he'd come up with the best plan he could and he read over it one last time. He was sure it was rubbish. He'd never done this sort of thing before. He was bound to have missed something or miscalculated something. But it was all he had. He screwed the piece of paper up and put it in the bin in the kitchen. He didn't want this one to fall out of his pocket.

Nick rang the doorbell at his 'ex' house at ten minutes after nine. Ruth opened the door. 'You're late!' she declared. Then having looked at him she said. 'You look like it as well. The late Nick Howard, I mean. Death warmed up doesn't begin to cover it. Come in, before the neighbours call an undertaker.'

Considering the state of her life, and even with *his* somewhat diminished powers of observation, Nick couldn't help noticing that Ruth seemed to be in a remarkably good mood. It could only mean one thing; She'd found comfort in a man's arms. Well perhaps 'comfort' wasn't the right word but she'd certainly found a little 'divertissement' that had raised her spirits. John's smug expression confirmed Nick's deduction when he met him in the lounge. He had to admit that Ruth was, as one of Dashiel Hammet's characters might have said, 'a piece of work'. She planned to double cross

John and cut him out of the money and yet she'd still slept with him and had her wicked way. That's modern women for you.

'Any chance of a cup of tea before we start?' asked Nick.

'Sure you wouldn't like a "hair of the dog"?' goaded Ruth.

'You know I'm not an animal lover. Tea will be fine.'

'Coffee for me darling,' said John. 'Need it to stay awake; didn't get much sleep last night,' he added, only just refraining from winking at Nick as Ruth disappeared into the kitchen.

'I'm not surprised,' replied Nick. 'As I remember she snores like a trooper.'

Ignoring Nick's comment, John said with copious bonhomie, 'So you're coming in with us? Good man. I have a plan that I'm sure you'll be impressed with.'

'Well *I* have a plan that we're going to follow, or I'm out of it.'

Ruth returned with the drinks at that exact moment.

'Has John told you his plan yet? I think it's very good.'

'Not had chance yet sweetheart. Nick says he has a plan that he'd like us to consider.'

'He has? You have? Is it really likely to be any good? I mean with the state you were in last night. You'd obviously had a skinful when you rang me, and I don't suppose you stopped there.'

'You're right on both counts,' replied Nick. 'But as I've just told lover-boy here, if you want me in, then it has to be my plan.'

'You sound like a little boy threatening to take his ball home.'

Nick took a sip of tea. He really couldn't face an argument. 'Take it or leave it,' he said simply.

'Let's hear what he has to say, darling,' suggested John. 'If we don't like it then we can let him go and we can still use my plan.'

'Oh, all right. But it'll be a waste of time.'

'Thanks for the vote of confidence. Now, do you want to hear it?'

'Go ahead,' said John.

Nick took a large gulp of tea and then put his mug down on the table. Ruth picked it up and put it on a coaster. Nick smiled and then stood up. Ruth and John sat together on the sofa. He was pleased to see that they were not holding hands. That would have been too much.

'Right, let me run through the whole thing, and then you can make comments if you need to.' He paused for them to agree but they said nothing. 'Is that OK?'

'Sorry,' said John. 'You asked us to save our comments until the end.'

Nick sighed. 'You've told Richard to have the money ready for today and await instructions right?'

John nodded.

'So today you will ring him and tell him to bring the money to Norgate Wastewater Treatment Works at five o'clock this evening. The lads at site will have gone home well before then. He is to come alone. He will then give you the money, and you will give him all of your evidence.'

'How do we know...?'

Nick glared at Ruth. 'You will also tell him, that if Ruth hasn't heard from you by five minutes past five, then she will ring the Police. And furthermore, if you are not back with her by five forty-five she will also ring the Police. This will stop Richard planning to kill you rather than giving you the money. I will also arrange for you to be accompanied by a couple of bodyguards as back up. They're a couple of thugs I've come across. Proper thugs they are, but they'll do as they're told if the money's right.'

It was John's turn to interrupt – as the concerned lover. 'But if I say that Ruth's providing this cover for me, what's to stop him getting someone to come here and stop her?' He was unable to say the words 'kill her'.

Nick glared at John this time. 'If you'd let me finish, I would have explained that Ruth won't be here.'

'Where will she be?'

'No need to tell you. Better if you don't know – just in case something does go wrong. I'll drop Ruth off when the time comes.'

'What do you think darling?' said John.

'I don't know. I'm not sure...'

'Well it sounds all right to me. I mean it's bound to be risky, but this way we have two levels of protection; the heavies that Nick can organise and the threat of you calling the Police.'

Ruth hesitated for a couple of moments, looked from Nick to John and back again, before saying, 'OK. I think it's better than our plan. It does have an extra level of protection.' Then she smiled like a little girl and added, 'It's so exciting!'

Nick rolled his eyes. 'One more thing, when you talk to Seaton he's bound to ask how he knows he can trust you. That you won't ring the Police after you've got the money. You say he can't be sure, but if you did ring the Police then they'd have you for blackmail. Anyway, what choice does he have?'

'I like it,' said John. Now if you'll excuse me I have to powder my nose. It must be all this excitement.'

As soon as he was out of the room, Ruth said in loud whisper, 'I thought you were going to arrange it for us to cut John out of it all.'

'I don't believe you!' retorted Nick. 'You clearly slept with the man last night. Although I don't suppose there was much sleeping going on; and here you are, still wanting to stitch him up.'

'I have needs. It's as simple as that. How many times has a man slept with a woman with the intention of dumping her the next day? I was simply having some fun while I could. Anyway, if I'd turned him down he might have suspected something. He knew how much I'd wanted him. Now answer my question. Do you have a plan to cut him out?'

'Of course I do. It's easy. The two heavies I supply will take the money off him on the way back here. That way Richard will think John has the money. My guys will threaten John's life and tell him to disappear.'

'They won't hurt him will they?'

'Just enough to make him believe them.'

'Oh, good,' smiled Ruth.

'Nice to see you two getting on,' said John as he re-entered the room. 'Now then, shall I make my phone call?'

Ruth almost rubbed her hands together in agreement, and John picked up his pay-as-you-go mobile phone and rang his victim's number.

The call went precisely as they hoped. Richard even asked the question about how he could trust John exactly as predicted.

'Right,' said Nick. 'I have a few things to arrange. You will meet your two bodyguards outside Norgate works at four o'clock. You want to make sure you're there before Richard. If the site guys haven't left by then it'll be a first I'm told. But if that's the case you'll just have to wait until they leave.'

'What are my minders' names?' asked John.

'You don't need to know their names. And don't ask them - they won't like it. I'll be with Ruth before five o'clock for when John is making his phone call check-ins. And one more thing.'

254

'What's that? Be careful out there?'

'No. My share.'

'Oh yeah, right. I was thinking ten percent. So that'll be two hundred thousand.'

'And I was thinking twenty-five percent, so that would make it *five* hundred thousand. But now I'm thinking six hundred thousand, and I'll pay your bodyguards.'

'What? You must be joking. All you've done is...'

'Oh, for goodness sake, John. Let him have the money. It's not as though we won't have enough.'

'*By which she means she'll have enough*' thought Nick.

'Oh, all right. Talk about easy money.'

'You're paying for my expertise,' replied Nick.

'I've said, "all right", haven't I?'

'Could I have a glass of water, Ruth?' Nick asked. 'I'm still feeling a bit rough.'

'Bloody hell! What did your last slave die of?' Ruth complained, never afraid of using cliché rather than wit.

As soon as she was out of the room Nick said, 'Right, give me your key to Maxine's house.'

'I don't know what you're talking about.'

'Don't give me any of that crap. You two must have been at it like rabbits – in her office for goodness sake - *and* you had this scam going. I'm sure you were able to come and go into each other's houses.'

John breathed out heavily and stuffed his hand into his jacket pocket and handed John a 'Yale' key. Ruth re-entered the room and gave Nick his glass of water. He took a sip and handed it back. Ruth tutted, 'Well that was a waste of time wasn't it?'

Nevertheless, Nick noticed that he was feeling a lot better now and he grinned broadly, as he took his leave. 'Right' I'll see you two later, when we'll all be a lot richer.'

As he walked down the drive to his car, he noticed that the sun was shining. It looked like it was going to be a glorious day. There were a few clouds scattered across the light blue sky. *'What were they called again? Oh, who cares? They're white and fluffy. That's all that matters.'*

He started up his car singing 'Good Day Sunshine,' as he looked forward to telling Jane the news. If anything could divert her from her infatuation for him, then it was the news that he'd found John and had set up a meeting between him and Richard. How she reacted to that was entirely up to her. The ball would be firmly in her court.

CHAPTER TWENTY-NINE

Nick made the necessary arrangements, as he'd promised John and Ruth, before he went to see Jane. He wanted everything to be in place before he met her. It was lunchtime by the time he arrived at her secretary's desk.

'You got the message then?' said the secretary.

'What message?'

'The message on your desk. I had to go around and stick it on your computer - when you didn't answer your mobile all morning.'

'Battery's dead,' lied Nick.

'Well I don't know what you've done but she's been on at me all morning to get hold of you. Still, you're here now so you might as well go straight in. Rather you than me!'

Nick opened the door confidently, ready for the congratulations that were about to come his way. However, he'd forgotten their last conversation.

Jane looked up from her desk and said, 'Close the door.'

Nick closed the door.

'Where the Hell have you been?' she demanded. 'I've been pulling my hair out all morning. Your phone's been switched off.'

'Battery dead; sorry.' *'Good lad. Keep the lies consistent.'*

'I thought you'd buggered off. I thought I'd scared you off with what I said on Friday... about how I feel.'

Jane was close to tears and Nick hadn't a clue what to do. Normally he'd have walked round her desk and put his arms round her, but who knows where that might have led? Well he did for one, and he didn't want to go there.

Unfortunately for him Jane got up and came round to him and hugged him close.

'Of course, I haven't done a runner. I wouldn't do that,' said Nick hoping that he sounded as though he wouldn't do that sort of thing to anyone – not just to her. But no time to analyze that now. He had news!

'I've had a very busy weekend and I have some fantastic news. I've cracked the case!'

He'd always wanted to say that; but instead of receiving the instant accolades he'd expected, all he got was a puzzled, 'What do you mean?'

'Go and sit down again,' he said, directing Jane back to behind her desk. He didn't want her sitting close to him on the comfy sofa – their knees touching. He sat down opposite her before explaining.

'As I said, I've cracked the case.' Already it sounded like a cliché, a line from a very dated movie, which of course it was, but he carried on. 'I've found John and found out what Richard is doing. Also that John is trying to blackmail Richard.'

Jane's jaw dropped. 'Oh my God! Are you serious?'

'It's not something I could make up. Believe me.'

'You'd better explain.'

'Richard is embezzling money from the Company via invoices for a company called Pearson and Toomey. He has been managing the contract entirely himself so it has been relatively easy. John and Maxine found out and tried to blackmail him. Maxine met Richard about it and hasn't been heard of since.'

'Are you saying he's....'

'Killed her? It certainly looks that way. I suppose he could have scared her off, or could even be keeping her somewhere, but that doesn't seem likely. That would be too messy, and given what happened to Martin Worsley and

Mike Shaw, Richard doesn't seem to have any compunction about killing anyone who gets in his way.'

'Now you're being ridiculous,' protested Jane. 'Martin's death was a terrible accident and Mike committed suicide.'

'Possibly. I don't have any proof. But I believe that Mike found out about what Richard was up to, and Richard had to get rid of him and faked his suicide. It was Richard who provided all the evidence. And from what Mike's widow told me it wasn't really questioned; it explained everything so neatly.

'I don't think that's very likely but what about Martin? Surely you don't have any proof about that?'

'None at all. But from what I've discovered it looks like Martin was in on it with Richard. Whether Martin lost his nerve after what happened to Mike, or Richard just got greedy, I don't know but....'

'My God, Nick! Are you on something? You seriously think that Richard has murdered two people? Have you lost your mind?'

'Well, I can't be a hundred percent certain about his being a murderer, but I *am* certain he's stealing from the Company and has been for years. Either that, or he's even madder than you think I am, because he's meeting John at five o'clock this afternoon at Norgate Treatment Works to hand over two million pounds.'

'He's what?'

'He's paying two million pounds to John to get the evidence that John has on him.'

'But if John believes that Richard killed Maxine, and Martin, and Mike, he'd have to be mad to risk meeting Richard on his own in some deserted place.... I presume he will be on his own.'

'Yes, but if he doesn't make contact with Ruth five minutes after he's due to meet Richard, then she will tell the

Police everything. Then he has to be back with her forty minutes later or the same thing happens.'

'Does Richard know this?'

'Yes. He has to.'

'So what's to stop him sending someone round to deal with Ruth? Or isn't she at home?'

'No, she'll be at Maxine's.'

'Maxine's? Well, I suppose Richard won't expect her to go there. But how come you're so involved?'

'I wanted to keep everything moving along until I had time to talk to you. I'm working for you so I thought it's up to you to decide what to do.'

'What do you mean?'

'Well, do you go to the Police or not?'

'I have to, don't I?'

'Not if you take the view that Ruth has taken.'

'What's that?'

'The money that Richard has stolen has already left the RWS and nobody knows. Ruth says therefore, that no one will miss it. The Company will be no worse off if *they* have it, than it is now. She simply believes that she and John may as well have the money - rather than Richard. You could decide the same. I mean that you could decide that the money has gone and there's no way of getting it back without the mother of all scandals breaking out. It would be the end of Richard's career obviously - and *yours* as well. The Company in its current form would not survive. God knows what would happen to the share price in the meantime. It would be a total disaster.'

'What's the alternative?'

'You could let the exchange take place and then simply sack Richard. That would be the end of it. John and Ruth would disappear with the money, but no one would be any the wiser. And you would be rid of Richard, so the stealing would stop.'

'What about Maxine and Martin and Mike? You said you think they were murdered. We can't just ignore that!'

'I only said I think that's what's happened to them. I couldn't prove it and I certainly wouldn't expect the Police to believe me.'

'Nick, I really don't know what to do.'

'Why don't you think about it?'

'But you said Richard's paying them the money today. Won't it be too late if I think about it?'

'Not necessarily. If you decided to go public with everything after the event then it'll be up to the Police to find John and Ruth. If you don't then as I said, no one's the wiser.'

'What about you? What's in all of this for you?'

'Keeping the customer satisfied. Of course a big end of contract bonus wouldn't go amiss. But that's up to you.'

'And what about us, Nick?'

'How about we put that on the backburner until everything is tidied up and you've decided what to do?'

'That doesn't sound like you're having difficulty holding in your passion.'

'Perhaps not, but it doesn't necessarily mean the end of us either. I do have an awful lot on my mind at the moment!' said Nick, hoping that was enough to keep Jane going for now.

She smiled. It was.

'So what do we do now?'

'You've got the rest of the day to decide if you want to call the Police and catch them in the act. Otherwise, you have as long as you like to "discover" what's been going on and go public... or not as the case may be.'

Jane looked at her watch. 'That's about four hours. What are you going to be doing?'

'I think I'll spend the afternoon writing up my report for you and tidying my desk. Whatever happens I think my second career at RWS has come to a natural end.'

'Then what? Are you going back to your place?'

'Yes. Nowhere else to go.'

'Perhaps we could celebrate tonight?'

'What's to celebrate? Have you decided what you're going to do?'

'No, but as you said you've done your job – that's worth celebrating. And I'll authorise that bonus!'

'OK. I'll give you a ring later.'

Jane couldn't resist, even in these circumstances, replying with a wink, 'I'll look forward to it.'

CHAPTER THIRTY

Nick didn't spend any time tidying his desk or writing a report. By two o'clock he was on his way. He drove straight to Ruth's house. He had decided that the sooner she was out of there the better. It was obvious when Ruth opened the door to him that she was very much on edge – teetering on the brink of falling off it. But she insisted she was fine and that they should just get over to Max's as soon as possible.

'I've changed my mind,' he said. 'I'm taking you to my place.'

'What on earth for?'

'Further insurance. John might try to come running to you once my two heavies have scared him off. You don't want him to find you do you?'

She had no argument with that and Nick watched as she picked up her coat and closed the door. Then he watched some more as she unlocked the door and went back in to pick up her handbag after he'd reminded her she would need her mobile phone. She reacted as though it were his fault that she'd forgotten it in the first place, but Nick let that go. He had too much on his mind, and not enough feeling left for Ruth, to be bothered to argue. He followed her as she drove, noticing that her driving was a little more erratic than normal – no indicating at junctions, breaking too sharply, kangaroo petrol evident when she changed gear.

Nick resisted the urge to comment on her driving when they arrived at his flat although Ruth could not do the same when she saw the state of the place. He had not cleared up after his night of whisky fuelled self loathing. He soon got her settled, having explained where the tea and cups were. It was still before three o'clock when he left Ruth, simply telling her he'd be back by four, and suggesting that if they spent any longer than an hour together they'd probably kill each other, well before John was due to ring at five past five.

Nick drove to a local supermarket and bought himself some milk; he'd probably get through quite a few cups of tea, while he was waiting for things to develop.

He was right. He was in the kitchen making his second cup when the doorbell rang. He looked at his watch. It was just before four o'clock. She was more or less dead on time.

He opened the door to find Jane standing in front of him. She looked very surprised.

Nick wasn't. 'Jane, you disappoint me; I *was* hoping you wouldn't turn up.'

'What are you doing here? I thought you were going to be at your flat.'

'More to the point what are you doing here?'

'You said you were disappointed to see me, so I presume you've already worked it out,' said Jane, as she reached into her handbag and drew out a small revolver. 'Let's go inside shall we?'

She waved the gun at him indicating that he should step back from the door, which he did very quickly after a moment or two to take in the fact that there was a gun in his face. In fact he almost fell over backwards in his haste to oblige. Jane stepped inside and closed the door behind her without taking her eyes off Nick. Then she made a similar wave to direct him to the lounge, whilst saying, 'In there,' just to avoid confusion.

She followed that with a final command, 'Sit down.'

She stood, pointing the gun at him for a few moments, as if considering whether to shoot him first and ask questions later. Nick for his part was beginning to sweat a little. No one had ever pointed a gun at him before. He knew that he should try to act cool, nonchalant - the hard-nosed detective. But that wasn't easy when he hadn't a clue how experienced the person holding the gun was in handling a deadly weapon. *And* he was scared shitless. He was frantically trying to think of something cool and witty to say, but he'd run out of ideas when Jane had pulled the gun out; or more precisely his brain had stopped working. This wasn't exactly going to plan. Jane saved him the trouble of starting the conversation by saying, 'You said you were hoping I wouldn't turn up. Explain.'

'Isn't it obvious?' He stalled trying to regain his composure. At least she'd stopped waving the gun around. That had been particularly alarming.

'Obvious that you had worked out that I was involved. I want to know how.'

'A couple of hunches really,' replied Nick beginning to feel a little more at ease. 'You said that you couldn't get me access to John's emails and that when you finally did get access, everything had been irretrievably wiped. I knew that IT can retrieve anything that has been deleted – they've done it for me before. So I rang the security manager myself to check about my getting access to John's emails. He said it wouldn't be a problem. You forgot, or perhaps never knew, that Eddie and I knew each other pretty well. And then you didn't want me to check through Richard's files. You got angry about it quite quickly. The icing on the cake was all that stuff about you realising that you'd fallen head over heels in love with me.'

'Not convincing?'

'Not after I thought about it. I'm not the sort of bloke women fall head over heels for. Ask Ruth. I presume it was just a smoke screen of some description. Trying to freak me out?'

'Very good, Nick. Exactly right.'

'Well that didn't work but you're doing a pretty good job now. Could you put that gun down or at least point it in another direction?'

'There wouldn't be much point in having it if I did that would there? I suppose it *must* be a bit disconcerting.'

'It is, but I'm trying not to worry about it.'

'Was that a joke?'

'Very nearly.'

'Well I'm not laughing. So you've worked out what's happened so far. What do you think happens next?'

There was no avoiding the answer. There was only one. He didn't want to bring things to a head yet so he said, 'Well presumably you came to take care of Ruth, to silence her and stop her ringing the Police, while Richard takes care of John. But before we get to what happens next why don't you tell me everything? You must be dying to tell someone.'

'That's true. There's only Richard left now who knows what we've done. And it's nice to share one's success with others - all those courses you think so little of say so. But from what you told me earlier, you know most of it already. Richard, Martin and I started milking the company years ago. Small amounts to begin with, but as we became more senior and took control of the budgets and procurement and finance systems it became easier to take bigger amounts.'

'You had fairly meteoric rises all of you.'

'Martin and I entirely on merit. Richard had a little help.'

'When Martin was in HR. I suppose he'd do anything for you. His mother said he was devoted to you.'

Jane laughed out loud. 'That's one thing you *have* got wrong. Martin was totally besotted with Richard. He was gay! He just never had the guts to come out. Something to do with not wanting to disappoint his father I think.'

'Do all the directors at RWS have issues with paternal approval?'

'What do you mean? Oh, you mean me and my constant attempts to impress my father?'

Nick nodded.

'I made that up ages ago. I use it every now and again when I want to appear human. Actually I really am just a hard bitch with no redeeming features. But as I was saying, before you so rudely interrupted me, unfortunately for Martin, Richard wasn't gay; although he kept playing Martin along for years – as though he had a chance, even after he'd married! Richard and I used to laugh about it all the time. Eventually Richard had had enough and began to treat Martin really badly. With utter contempt. But it didn't put Martin off. So when he started to lose his nerve, (after we'd had to get rid of Mike Shaw), Richard was quite happy to be the one who took care of him. He arranged a "morale raising" trip to our Middle East sites, and threw him off the top of some scaffolding. Then he dismantled a bit of the scaffolding and threw that down as well. It wasn't difficult to rig the investigation. Things like that come quite cheaply over there. I think Richard quite relished it.'

'Sick bastard.'

'Can't argue with you there. But he's cool under pressure, and that's what you need in this line of work.'

'Work? It's not work. It's a game! That's what it is for you isn't it? It's in the tone of your voice. And I said *Richard* was sick! And Mike, why did you have to kill him in such a horrific way?'

'Exactly as you said. He found out and we had to get rid of him. We had to make it look like an accident or suicide, so we made it look like he'd been stealing from the Company. Not in the same way that we were actually doing it of course, but with the three of us in the positions we were in, it wasn't difficult to provide the necessary evidence. The Police loved it. They were only too pleased to get an easy conclusion to the case. And the regulators loved our contrite apologies and reassurances that we would make sure it never happened again. We showed them that we'd put new, more stringent procedures in place under the direct control of Richard and myself. And they fell for it. Even so, there was a bit of a lull in our operations after that. What with Martin starting to lose his nerve, but then when I made Richard Finance as well as Audit director, it was too good an opportunity to miss. We had to continue. Richard must have got careless if you found evidence in his office so quickly. And then of course John and Maxine found out. Apparently John overheard Richard saying something on the telephone that made him suspect something. He and Maxine started the audits to try to get the evidence to confirm John's suspicions.'

'So what happened to Maxine?'

'She was stupid enough to go and see Richard on her own. For some reason she thought that keeping John in the background would give her some sort of insurance. It gave *him* some sort of protection - that was all. Of course she – they – had no idea what we were capable of. They met in Richard's office after everyone else had gone. He pretended to go along with her demands, said he was going to get out anyway, even suggested she might like to go with him. Said he'd always fancied her, that sort of thing. A little flattery will relax most people. They walked to her car together and then I popped up and we stuffed her into the boot of her own car and drove off to her place. She must have thought a lot of John; it took Richard quite a lot of effort to get his name out of her, if you know what I mean.'

'Like I said before, "sick bastard"'

'And like I said before, it's what you need in work like this.'

'Very useful for you that's for sure. He's done all the killing and only his and Martin's names appeared on the paperwork I found. Did he realise that he was *your* insurance? Your cover?'

'Probably never occurred to him. But it was never about providing me with cover in that way. It was more about trying to ensure that anyone who suspected Richard or Martin would report to me rather than feel that they should go to the police first. It worked with Mike Shaw. Obviously not so well with Maxine and Anderson; although at least they never realised I was involved, and that gave us an advantage in dealing with *her*. You know, we were planning to stop soon anyway, and leave the Company to "spend more time with our families". We just wanted to see the Company through the next external audit, to make sure nothing came to light then. But Maxine and John have brought our leaving forward. Once we've got through today, we'll be tendering our notices. Me first, and then Richard. Once we've done that we'll be gone quickly. Chairmen and CEOs don't like directors hanging about when they've tendered their notice. Tend to worry about them taking stuff to competitors. Not going to happen in our case. But they're not to know that. We'd have done it last week but John didn't react to the emails we sent him on Maxine's behalf for some reason.'

'They had special email accounts with code names, same with their phones. So when you used her normal email account and she answered her mobile phone with 'Hello darling,' he knew something was wrong and went into hiding.'

'I see. One thing you didn't tell me this morning; when did John turn up at Ruth's?

'On the Friday evening, after Maxine disappeared; the day before she hired me.'

'Then why did she hire you?'

'A similar reason to you I think – to make it look as though she was doing something. That *was* the same with you wasn't it? You didn't really expect me to find John. You were hoping he'd get in touch if he hadn't run for his life and left the country.'

'Half true. We *were* hoping that Ruth would tell you if John got in touch, and I thought that if I paid you enough then you'd tell me when that happened. We also wanted to know how John and Maxine had found out so that we could get rid of the evidence. That's why I had you looking at what John had been working on.'

'And all the sex?'

'Oh, that was just a bonus. A bit of fun. It was quite nice going to bed with someone who wasn't trying to be in control. That much was real. It *was* quite refreshing to be with someone who wasn't trying to impress by appearing to be super macho, capable of controlling me. I suppose that's because you knew you had no chance in doing that.'

'Never occurred to me to try. I was just going with the flow. One more thing. Did you pay Sally to tell Ruth she'd seen John and Max at it in her office?'

'Who?'

Nick's mood lifted slightly at the confirmation that Jane didn't even know who Sally was, let alone had paid her to lie.'

'Oh! The cleaner. No, but she had been to see me about it before she told you and Ruth.'

Nick's mood sank again.

'She saw me one night leaving the office as she was cleaning and said she had something to tell me, but didn't want to get anyone into trouble. That intrigued me of course, so I invited her into my office and put her at ease and got her to spill the "goss".'

'She really had seen Maxine and John at it in her office?'

270

'Yes! Isn't that amazing? I can tell you I nearly did the same with you just to see what it was like but I'm sure my secretary listens at the door sometimes. Anyway, I asked her not to tell anyone and that I would deal with it and thanked her of course for her discretion in telling me. Then I discussed it with Richard and we agreed that she should tell Ruth about it so that Ruth would be less likely to protect John if he did get in touch. So I got Sally, (is that her name?), back in, and said that I thought that it was only right that Ruth should know since she and John were supposed to be together. I said I knew that it would be very awkward for her but that I'd really appreciate it. And so would Ruth in the long run. And she did it. Bless her! I'm surprised that Ruth stuck with John though.'

'She didn't.'

'What do you mean? If I don't stop her she's going to ring the Police, when Richard has dealt with John.'

'John will be all right. Richard's not going to deal with him.'

'If you think that John can stop Rich....'

Nick held up his hand to stop Jane. His confidence had returned, things were back on track – apart from Jane's gun and he was hopeful that would be dealt with.

'It won't be John who stops Richard. It'll be the half-a-dozen policemen who are also there, who will look after him. Isn't that right Inspector?'

Nick looked beyond Jane towards the door.

Jane smiled, 'Nice try Nick, but if you think....'

Someone coughed behind her. She started to turn but then remembered Nick was still in front of her and turned back to him. Nick had rolled to his left as soon as she had started to look round. The movement he made caused Jane to react and she fired the gun at where he'd been sitting. It blew a hole in the back of the sofa in the still visible indentation made by his back. The gun went off again, this

271

time into the ceiling as the Inspector wrestled it from Jane's grasp.

A uniformed policeman appeared at the door and was instructed to cuff Jane.

'Jane,' said Nick from his half prone position on the floor. 'Can I introduce Inspector Lumsden and PC Benbow, from the local nick?

'Jane Edwards,' said Inspector Lumsden. 'I'm arresting you on suspicion of conspiracy to murder Martin Worsley, Michael Shaw and Maxine Hudson. You do not have to say anything. But it may harm your defence if you do not mention when questioned something which you later rely on in court. Anything you do say may be given in evidence. We'll get to the embezzlement charges later. Do you understand?'

'What about the attempted murder of Nick Howard?' protested Nick, having now recovered to a standing position.

'Never mind that for now. Do you understand Ms Edwards?'

'Yes. I mean no. What the bloody hell's going on Nick?'

'I would have thought that was obvious Jane. You're nicked! And so is Richard, or if he isn't yet he will be soon. As will John, for attempted blackmail I presume, Inspector?'

'Something along those lines, I would think.'

'It's quite simple really Jane. I suggested to John that he should have a couple of "heavies" with him in case Richard tried something despite the threat of Ruth ringing the Police. Then I went to the Inspector here, and explained the situation and he kindly supplied the heavies and a few more besides, as well as coming here himself with the young PC here to arrest you. I would imagine he has found your explanation of things most helpful. I told you that Ruth would be here because I knew you'd have to try to stop her acting as John's "insurance". I was surprised you

272

had a gun. I'd presumed you'd just hit her with something heavy when she wasn't looking. That gun threw me for a while, especially when the Inspector didn't pop out immediately.'

'We'd agreed that we'd let her talk first,' pointed out the Inspector.

'That was before we knew she had a gun.'

'You seemed to have everything under control,' smiled the Inspector.

Nick just shook his head. Jane had recovered some composure and had accepted her situation. 'Well Nick. I have to say I am impressed. I really did underestimate you. I didn't think you had this in you. You have hidden depths.'

'I've plumbed much deeper depths than you can imagine,' replied Nick. 'And by the way, you mentioned the Chairman and CEO earlier; how did you manage to get them to agree to your concentrating "Finance", "Procurement" *and* "Audit" into only two directorates run by your two closest friends? And *then* into just one when Martin died?'

Jane allowed herself a smug smile, 'It's amazing what you can achieve with a thigh-length slit in a tight skirt, Nick. You should know that.'

Nick feigned a shocked look and grabbed at his heart. 'You mean I wasn't your first? You have wounded me deeply.'

Another thought occurred. 'And you used those same charms to get the Regulator to let you off with Mike Shaw's supposed embezzlement?'

Jane's smile told him he was right. 'I think you'd better take her away, Inspector.'

'Constable, take Ms Edwards to the car.... I'll need a statement from you Nick.'

'Can I do that tomorrow Tom? There's somewhere I have to be now.'

'OK. Nine o'clock?'

'Fine, I've got used to getting up that early recently.'

Outside the house, Inspector Lumsden took a call on his mobile phone. When it had finished he turned to Nick and said, 'My men have arrested Anderson and Seaton. No problems.'

'Excellent,' replied Nick. 'I love it when a plan comes together.' (*'Something else I've always wanted to say.'*)

Then he watched Jane being driven away and gave her a wave and blew her a kiss. She returned neither.

He got into his car and turned the ignition. The radio came on automatically. Slade were shouting their goodbyes to Jane . Now even the radio was giving a commentary on his life.

Then he drove off quickly. He was going to be late!

CHAPTER THIRTY-ONE

It was after a quarter to six when he arrived back at his flat, and when he opened his door Ruth was at him immediately.

'Where the hell have you been? Why didn't you answer your phone? I've been ringing you non-stop!'

'Battery dead. Sorry. Is there something wrong? Where's John? Has he been held up?'

'That's just it. I don't know. He didn't ring at five past five, and he hasn't got back here yet. I've not heard anything!'

'Why didn't you ring the Police as agreed?'

'What? And say that I was part of a blackmail plot? I thought that was just for Seaton's sake. I never thought I'd have to do it. My God! Do you think Richard has killed John? Will he be looking for me now?'

'I shouldn't think so. I don't suppose he's given you a second thought.'

'But he knows that I'm involved! He knows I'll go to the Police if John doesn't come back.'

'I'm afraid that he knows something that you don't know.'

'What? For goodness sake Nick, tell me!'

'He knows that he and John have been arrested; him for murder and John for attempted blackmail.'

'What? How?'

Nick was enjoying Ruth struggling for words. He'd never seen it before.

'Simple. The two men John thought were his bodyguards were actually policemen. And they and a few others, who were hidden around the site for good measure, arrested Seaton and John when they got down to business.'

Ruth remained nonplussed, so Nick went on. 'You will be pleased to know that Jane Edwards has also been arrested.'

'Jane? You've lost me.'

'Yes, Jane. She was in it with Seaton. When I left you this morning I went to the Police and told them everything. And then I told Jane that you'd be at Maxine's house waiting for John to ring. I knew that she'd have to silence you. Then while the Police accompanied John to Norgate Treatment Works, an Inspector and a uniform waited with me at Maxine's for Jane to turn up. I must admit that it got a bit hairy - she had a bloody gun! But you'll be relieved to know that I escaped unharmed!'

'You mean you never meant to help me and John get the money? You set us up! You bastard!'

'Steady on there lady! I didn't set *you* up; only the other three. My statement to the Police will say that you were on my side. That you were part of the scheme to get John to meet up with Seaton, so that they could be caught together. You'll be all right!'

'All right? All right?' screamed Ruth. 'I thought I was getting my share of two million. Now I haven't got any of that and I haven't got John either!'

'I thought you didn't want John after you'd found out about him and Maxine!'

'I'd have had him if he had two million!'

'Oh, Ruth. When did you become so hard?'

'I'm not hard! You're soft that's all. You're as soft as sh...'

'Ruth! Shut the hell up. I don't think you know how lucky you've been. You were never going to get away with it. If it hadn't been for me, Jane and Richard would have killed you. Or if they hadn't got to you, then the Police

276

would have. If you can't get your head round that then you can piss off, you ungrateful bitch.'

Some of what Nick had said must have sunk in, because Ruth was again speechless.

Nick continued. 'I mean it, Ruth. Piss off!' said Nick pointing at the door. 'You can talk to me again when you're ready to apologise and admit that you owe me big time.'

Ruth snatched up her handbag and moved towards the door. As she opened it Nick added, 'And by the way you do owe me big time. Two hundred pounds a day we agreed if you remember....'

'Take it out of my share of the two million pounds!' shouted Ruth as she stormed out.

'Typical bloody Ruth. Can only ever see her side of things. Why did I expect anything else?' thought Nick.

But despite Ruth's reaction, or perhaps even in part because of it, Nick had the feeling of a job well done, and he broke out the single malt and sat down with a glass.

The job had ended up being a complete success. Jane had authorised payment for him before she was arrested – with a bonus – and she was in no position to rescind that now. He'd never get paid by Ruth, but what the hell? The mood she'd be in for the next few days was reward enough for him.

There was just one loose end.

He wasn't sure how he felt about Sally. He thought that they'd really had something and he'd been distraught when she'd thrown him out. Now he knew the truth. What difference did that make?

He picked up his mobile phone and dialled Sally's number.

'Hi Sally, it's me.'

'Stupid thing to say. I'm hardly likely to be somebody else,' he thought.

'I know,' replied Sally confirming his own thought. He noticed that her tone was hard; there was no sign of her being pleased to hear his voice.

'I just thought I'd let you know that I've cracked the case.' He regretted using the cliché immediately but he couldn't unsay it.

'Really?' Again there was no sign of interest.

'Yes.' He decided to say it matter-of-factly, rather than appear to be looking for her congratulations. 'Jane Edwards and Richard Seaton have been arrested for murder and John Anderson has been arrested for attempted blackmail.'

That hit home.

'Murder? Jane Edwards?'

'Yes, Jane Edwards, the woman you went to first about seeing John and Maxine in her office. The woman who told you to tell Ruth about John and Maxine.'

'You know about that then.'

'Yes.'

'So *now* you believe that I wasn't lying. I really did see them. And I wasn't paid to say anything!'

Sally obviously knew she should have told Nick about Jane - probably when he took *her* into his confidence about being a private detective, and told her what he was investigating. But she hadn't. In fact she'd lied to him and Ruth about being worried about getting into trouble for coming forward. Now she didn't seem to be about to admit she'd been wrong. There was nothing in her voice to suggest that she had forgiven him for suspecting she'd been paid.

'OK. Well I just thought you'd like to know....' said Nick.

'Well now I do. And I know what *you* did to Dave last night. He turned up at my door covered in blood. Taking it out on him were you?'

Clearly his warning to stay away from Sally hadn't worked. 'I was going to tell you about that. If you must know, I feel really terrible about what I did.'

'I don't care how you feel, Nick. I only know how I feel about what you did. I don't go around with thugs. I never want to see you or hear from you again. So you can piss off!'

So he did.

He put his phone down and took a sip of his whisky.

He was a real detective now. Never mind the cliché; he really had cracked his first major case. Exposed murder, embezzlement and blackmail. And had two lovers to boot! And lost them both! Nick Charles, Sam Spade and Philip Marlowe couldn't have done any better.

If clients and lovers really were like buses, then he might have to wait ages for another one, (or two), but at least he'd have some money in the bank, courtesy of Jane's generosity. He'd also get plenty of good publicity, *and* he'd made a useful contact in Inspector Lumsden, who had good reason to be grateful to Nick for handing him such a high profile case just about ready to take to court.

Yes, tonight he would relax and have another couple of drinks; he had no need to worry about the work now. He'd get enough to make a living. He could have the night off.

His phone rang.

'Nick? said an unrecognised voice.

'Yes.'

'It's Micky; Micky Smiff - from the hospital. I drove you there when you got mugged.'

'Oh yeah, Micky, right. How are you?'

'I'm OK ta. Listen, you're a Private Detective right? Like in the movies. It says so, on the card you gave me.'

'Not sure there's any like me in the movies.'

'But you do cases yeah? Like looking for missing peoples?'

'It has been known.' Nick couldn't resist gloating. 'Just finished a big case actually. It'll be in all the papers.'

'That's good 'cause I've got another one for you. Another big case I mean.'

'You have? What is it?

'It's my girl. She's gone missing. I want you to find her.'

'Is this the same girl – if you don't mind my asking – who dumped you at the Pub?'

'Yeah, that's right. Sophia. It's her.'

'What makes you think she's gone missing?'

''Cause I don't know where she is man.'

'But she dumped you Micky! You're not together anymore. Why *should* you know where she is?'

'It's not just me man. It's her Mum and Dad as well. They don't know neither. No one does. She's disappeared.'

Nick thought for a moment. If Micky wouldn't accept it was over between them, then he could have been pestering her. She might simply be staying with a friend to get away from him, and her parents might be lying about not knowing where she is. But Micky was pleading with him and he owed Micky *big* time. Micky had picked him up and taken him to hospital even though he was distraught at being dumped at the time. Not many people would have done that. Whatever was going on with Micky and his ex-girlfriend, Micky needed help.

There was only one thing he could do.

'OK, Micky, why don't you come over?'

It looked like clients came along more often than buses, (and lovers) after all.

THE END

280

Printed in Great Britain
by Amazon